urned his head away, but it was she'd already seen the effect her had on him.

H... get control of himself before he saw Ty... didn't want to make it any worse for him.

"T... sure. I'm racking my brain, trying to rem... if I told Ty about any of the skeletons in my closet or deep, dark secrets."

"Oh, don't worry. I wrote them all down in my diary and put them under lock and key."

He laughed, and it pulled his side and he grunted with the pain. She had him laughing through his tears. "Thanks. I needed that."

Piper nodded, and their gazes met and held. Suddenly he felt hot and it seemed as if the very air around them ignited.

* * *

Be sure to ...

To Protect an... ...ry
operatives and ...te...

D1005156

If you're on Twitter, tell us what you think of Harlequin Romantic Suspense! #harlequinromsuspense

Dear Reader,

We were just in the cold and snowy Rockies; now we're going someplace hot. Really hot and dangerous. Piper Jones is a senator and she's used to dealing with all the political intrigue on the Hill, but when it comes to being on the run in Afghanistan with a hot, sexy, wounded navy SEAL, she's so out of her element.

Lieutenant Dexter Kaczewski is recovering from an IED blast and the loss of men during his mission to rescue three marines. The last thing he expects to see is his buddy's sister standing by his hospital bed in the most dangerous place on earth. But she's there to make sure her brother gets the best care.

The Only Easy Day Was Yesterday is Dex's motto, and it's proven to be true when insurgents overrun the base and the hospital. Now they're on the run in a war-torn country. When Dex collapses, Piper is on her own. She's got a wounded, delirious man who saved her life bleeding out in the desert in a country where she doesn't know the language, doesn't know which direction to go.

They are running for their lives with no way of knowing whom to trust and each of them is trying not to fall for the other. Their biggest fear isn't surviving, but learning to trust in love again, which might be the riskiest move of all.

Karen Anders

A SEAL TO SAVE HER

Karen Anders

HARLEQUIN® ROMANTIC SUSPENSE

Recycling programs
for this product may
not exist in your area.

ISBN-13: 978-0-373-27993-7

A SEAL to Save Her

Printed in U.S.A.

Karen Anders writes a suspenseful and sexy mix of navy and civilians investigating murder, espionage and crime across a global landscape. Under the pen name Zoe Dawson, she's currently writing romantic comedy, new-adult contemporary romance, urban fantasy, syfy and erotic romance. When she's not busy writing, she's painting or killing virtual mmorpg monsters. She lives in North Carolina with her two daughters and one small, furry gray cat.

Visit the Author Profile page at Harlequin.com.

To all the Navy SEALs out there who have ever been cold, hot, exhausted, tested to the edge of their endurance and loving every minute of it. The only easy day was yesterday. Oo-rah!

Chapter 1

A hike into hell was a walk in the park for Lieutenant Junior Grade Dexter Kaczewski and his small team of SEALs. The rhythm, the heat and the years of working together made the first part of the trip rather surreal. Everything working perfectly. Dex checked to make sure all of his men were together. Nine ninja gunslingers, armed to the teeth, invisible. Without night vision, no one could see death approach.

After the UH-60M, a sleek, state-of-the-art Black Hawk, had set them down, the almost-silent blades vibrating the air with a faint *whop-whop*, Dex had crouched as they piled out of the opening, his heartbeat in his ears. When his feet were firmly on the ground, he'd waited for the dust to settle from the big UH-60M and the world to stabilize after the helos had lifted off. All the guys checked in through their radios, and Dex had signaled the "all go" for the jaunt.

They were going in looking for three marines abducted only twenty-four hours ago. They were part of the force currently training the Afghan Armed Forces.

This was a TST, or time-sensitive target, as SEALs categorized these missions. Which pretty much meant they'd play it by ear and make it up as they went, especially once they hit the dirt. The intel was solid and Dex's superiors figured that a small group of nine members of SEAL Team Three, Task Unit Trident, Bravo Platoon, were enough to do the job.

Hoo-rah!

"The village is completely dark. No movement in the target area," Wicked said through the com. Damian "Something Wicked This Way Comes" Merrick, or "Wicked" for short, was a lean, mean fighting machine, primary breacher, who handled all mechanical and explosive entries, and primary heavy gunner. He also had this uncanny ability to see things that weren't normally visible. He'd once saved a whole squad from an ambush just because he'd spotted one stone overturned.

"No enemy with guns who want to shoot us? That's a shame," DJ said with a short laugh. Jerry Sanders, the resident comedian and the best damn communication and air controller in the business, got his moniker legitimately. Back in the States, Jerry had been a radio DJ before his service.

Dex's vigilance, heightened by his night-vision goggles, showed every detail in the green environment before him. The village in the distance was their destination. They had been flown in by helicopter and dropped off, or "inserted," about eleven kilometers away and were currently tiptoeing their way to the medium-size village that was waiting for them in dark shadows with unknown assailants.

As Dex led them to the final delay point, they had

about five minutes to rest and reset for the final push and eventual assault. As he looked around, he realized they were in a cemetery. Several graves were fresh, and after counting over ten new digs, DJ stopped and leaned over to Dex. "LT, hopefully this isn't a zombie movie or we're toast," he deadpanned. On the team, "LT" was the universal nickname for all officers in charge and stood for *lieutenant*.

Dex laughed. "Don't worry, DJ. Your brain doesn't even make a meal."

"Not even a snack," Reindeer said, and all of them chuckled." Rudolf "Reindeer" Abt served more than just one role. He was their very gifted corpsman—a medic—but he was also a lethal sniper.

"Mmm, brains," DJ said in a deep, gravelly, zombie voice.

"Kennedy," Dex said softly. Kennedy was already up and moving toward the walls and getting eyes on the compound. Tyler Keighley was Dex's best friend on the team, his point man and lead sniper. He hailed from a political family, which was how he got his Kennedy nickname. They were in tune with each other. When Spaceman—Mike Carver, his current ridge boss and chief of his operations—retired after this op, Dex was considering Kennedy as his replacement. He was smart, resourceful and spoke his mind.

Speaking of minds, it seemed his men could read his. These guys were so well trained and worked so well together. Nolan "Minnesota" Quade was one of the nicest men he'd ever met until he was on a mission, then one of the meanest, a breacher and sniper. Roger "Green Bean" Deeds and Peter "Slim Jim" Camden rounded out the group. Kennedy gave Dex the all clear, and he motioned everyone onward. They moved like ghosts from the graveyard, right on schedule.

After Kennedy entered, Dex poked his head in to check the progress. The compound was empty and something started to itch, a combat itch that was giving Dex a momentary warning to get the hell out of there, but he felt that most of the time he was on a mission. It was most likely the feel of close and present danger. On cue, Wicked said, "Sir, I don't like this. It's too quiet."

"Anything concrete?"

"No, sir. Just a gut feeling."

"Your gut is outranked this time. One of those marine kids belongs to a one-star. We're going in, but keep your eyes open."

"Roger that, sir."

Normally, he would heed Wicked's call, but the one-star, General Seth MacDonald, had some pull and Dex knew how the military worked. The general would do everything in his power to rescue his son, even chew on some brass. Still, he'd never liked the sensation of having the grim reaper breathing down his neck. They entered single file, heading for the outlying buildings. After a quick search, Dex sent Kennedy, Minnesota and Slim up a ladder to snipe any baddies from the rooftop.

After ten minutes the compound was secured, but that only made Dex even more uneasy. There was no one here. No sleeping women or children, no old men. No one. He glanced at Spaceman and his look said he felt it, too.

"You want to abort?" he asked Spaceman. He and Spaceman had done extensive research on this village, situated just before the Pakistani border. The most likely place they were keeping his brothers in arms was a building in the middle of the village, forcing them to secure three large buildings on the east side to block any egress to Pakistan. If they ran, it would be across open ground.

He stood there for a moment, obviously torn between getting the marines out or leaving them to their fate. The pressure from the brass was as heavy as a fifty-caliber gun. Dex didn't give a damn about flak from the top. He was here in the field and the decision was his. That's why he got the big lieutenant bucks. Saving those marines was their mission, but he had to weigh the level of threat to his team. Leaving the marines to die didn't sit well with either of them. Spaceman had a kid the same age as one of the marines. Spaceman's eyes traveled around to make sure he had his finger on the pulse of this op.

"Let's get those boys and go home," Spaceman said. This would be his last deployment, and Dex guessed he wanted to go out with a win.

Dex motioned for Wicked, who was right behind him, meeting his dark, steady eyes. The man would go into hell if Dex ordered it, but he wasn't bashful about speaking up. It was clear the guy was getting the heebie-jeebies from this op.

"Sir…"

"Noted, Wicked. Get ready to breach the main building."

Wicked took a breath. "Wicked," Dex said, order in his voice. *"Breach."*

He delayed only a second. Reluctance in each word, he said, "Yes, sir."

Dex leaned in, listening for harsh language or suppressed shooting, and heard nothing. The walls were sixteen feet high and looked rather new—well, newer than two thousand years old, like the last operation's buildings. The gate was quite new—he thought maybe forty years old. How nice to see an upward trend in development in this war-torn country. He motioned to Wicked.

"Fire in the hole," Wicked said, and they moved a safe distance. The C-4 Wicked had attached to the door exploded when he set the charges off, and the door flew back and over their heads. As the smoke cleared, they started moving inside. Time always slowed for Dex when he was in combat, and everything seemed to pop out at him in Technicolor. Through the eerie green glow, he saw the bodies slumped in the corner.

The three marines.

Reindeer, the medic, was already moving, and Wicked said into the com, "This bites, sir."

Spaceman replied, "Ditto."

Dex knew the moment he saw them, and that itch intensified. Wicked swore low and vehemently.

"Dead…uh, LT…recently," Reindeer said, his voice full of the anger and frustration they all felt. "All of them head shots."

That's when all hell broke loose.

"LT! Bug out! Bug out! They're everywhere. Ambush!" Kennedy shouted through the com.

But his warning was a split second too late. Gunfire ripped into the room as Dex and the other SEALs hit the deck. Heated pieces of lead bounced and whizzed everywhere. Spaceman cried out in agony and another SEAL, Green Bean, was already there, slinging him onto his back. Without a word, the three of them—Dex, Wicked and Reindeer—each shouldered one of the dead marines into a fireman's carry. The remaining SEALs returned fire. No words were spoken, but they were all in agreement. *Never leave a man behind.*

DJ was shouting into the radio, calling in the current cluster and getting the helos there on the double for extraction. Kennedy's voice exploded on the com again. "RPGs! Freaking RPGs."

Dex could hear the rapid fire of their rifles in the open com. Damn, rocket-propelled grenades. Not good. "Haul ass!" he yelled.

They cleared the door as an explosion rocked the building, dust and debris flying around. More automatic gunfire as Dex turned with the marine still across his shoulders, pointed his weapon and opened fire, cutting down the bodies in pursuit.

Dex raced for the open compound gate and could see the helos landing a klick from his position. Running straight out, he deposited the marine into the waiting chopper along with the other two and the wounded Spaceman. But men were MIA. "Kennedy! DJ! Slim! Minnesota!" Dex yelled into the com, reacting from the adrenaline. But there was no answer.

Dex turned and ran back toward the compound and saw them pinned down. They were outgunned and outmanned, but he and his fellow SEALs never hesitated. Opening fire, Dex cut down the enemy to the left and Reindeer and Green Bean took care of the enemy to the right. Dex shouted, "Move it!"

Kennedy didn't budge until DJ, Minnesota and Slim reached Dex, laying down covering fire. "Kennedy!" Dex shouted, ten pounds of adrenaline drop-loading into his system.

Kennedy broke from cover and Dex and his men opened fire to cover his retreat. He reached Dex and they all turned for the big UH-60. Dex heard the whistle of the RPG, felt pressure and saw a flash as it exploded, the concussion knocking him off his feet, an excruciating pain slamming into his rib cage and waist. All of them were blown backward.

Dex hit the ground hard, dazed. Through the smoke and dust, he saw the others all lying so still. His head ringing, nausea twisting in his gut, he lurched to his feet, crying out at the sharp cut of agony in his side, his hand automatically going there, feeling the blood-soaked fabric. He stumbled over to them, falling to his knees. A second Black Hawk landed and marines poured from the open door. Dex slipped his hands under Kennedy's prone, unmoving form, his heart pumping hard, his body on autopilot. Ignoring the agony in his side, he lifted Kennedy—*ah, dammit, Tyler*—as men surrounded him. He lurched to his feet and started for the helo as the wet, warm blood of his friend and comrade coated his hands and soaked into his uniform.

He made it to the door; hands were reaching for Kennedy as Dex's knees buckled and he dropped. Someone caught him and hauled him into the chopper.

He grabbed at the medevac guy's uniform. "Don't you leave anyone behind," he shouted.

"Relax, sir. We got you covered," he shouted above the return gunfire from the advancing rescue team and the insurgents, growling engine and whirling blades.

He turned his head as someone ripped at his shredded body armor and clothing, exerting pressure to his side, making him cry out against the burning, rippling torment ripping through his body.

"*Don't* you die on me," he whispered. "Don't you *die*, Tyler." His jaw clenched as the agony of his wounds melded with his mental anguish. His vision started to narrow and dim as the slashing pain intensified until tears blinded him. He turned his head, kept his eyes on Kennedy's face—Tyler's face—as he felt the helo lift and watched as pooled blood ran in rivulets to the open door.

Watched until he was pulled down into a tormented darkness.

Chapter 2

Senator Piper Jones scowled. "It may be true there is plenty of resistance to this bill, Senator Mullins, but my late husband was in favor of this legislation, and I will be supporting it regardless of your opposition."

"Really, Senator Jones, you were appointed to your seat by the governor of California in an age-old practice of widow's succession and are merely a seat warmer. Everyone knows you don't have the stones to get anything passed, regardless of who your late husband was."

Piper felt a flush of anger rise up her neck and creep up her cheeks as the other senator glared at her from across the short expanse of her desk.

"Just concede defeat and we'll make this bill stronger and more viable…later."

Later in a pig's eye. Piper fingered the antique locket Brad gave her right before he died. Whenever she needed strength, it bolstered her. Senator Mullins and his minions would quash this legislation like a bug. "It's a minor change in corporate law, Senator, and is more holistic. Brad believed in the battle against corporate abuse strongly. He was a former securities attorney, and the provision—the one I'm pushing in his stead—provides for a company to change its mission from making money to corporate citizenship, which by its very definition is all about social responsibility. What do you have against protecting the common good?"

"It flies in the face of capitalism and corporate freedom! Everything this country stands for."

"Brad believed in being a responsible capitalist. His bill is the first step to reform that will save our country. He believed deeply in it and I believe it has a strong chance of passing."

She leaned back, decidedly holding her temper in check just as Brad and her formidable political family had ingrained in her over the years. She knew how to pussyfoot with the best of them.

Drawing in a slow, deep breath to steady herself, she tilted her chin and tried again. "I'm continuing on with what Brad wanted. That was my mission when I took his place." She leaned forward and showed Senator Mullins her backbone. "I will finish out the rest of Brad's term. I've been proud to serve the state of California and the US Senate as his steward to the best of my ability." She stared right back at him, refusing to be cowed.

He didn't like it, and for a split second something quite nasty filled his eyes, but was then gone. Her phone rang, but she ignored it. She wasn't going to show any sign of weakness or back down from that stare.

"Maybe you'd better find some stones if you're going to try to squash this. Brad had a very solid constituent and loyal backing. I am resolved on this course of action."

It was a dismissal, plain and simple. He pointed his finger at her. "I warned your husband not to make an enemy of me, Senator Jones. I'm giving you the same warning."

"Thank you for that. But I come from a long line of political pundits. I eat, breathe and live to debate."

"Fine," he said as he rose, tugged on his white cuffs and collected his jacket. He turned as her phone buzzed again, but she ignored it as he made his way to the door in his very expensive and impeccable blue pinstripe suit.

She picked up the phone.

"Is he gone yet?"

"Almost," she said.

"Was he blowing hard and issuing threats?"

She chuckled at her late husband's mentor and long-time good friend of the family, Stephen Montgomery, the powerful and wealthy CEO of the Montgomery Group, a technical company with numerous products utilized throughout the government and military. Like Bradley, Stephen was born and raised in California, but now made his home in Washington. Piper and Brad had spent time in both DC and San Diego in their gorgeous beach house. "Monty" was a staunch supporter of every bill Brad had written and gotten passed, which had happened mostly because of Stephen's help and backing. Her aide, Brock, opened the door as soon as Senator Mullins reached for the handle. The look on her aide's face made Piper's stomach knot. He came inside, brushing past the senator, and her anxiety climbed. Senator Mullins was tall and imposing, with very good but generic looks, like a news anchor. He looked innocuous, but Piper had seen the flashes of menace.

She shook her head as her aide opened his mouth, but he said, anyway, "Senator Jones..."

She held up her hand. "Monty, I have to go. My aide is here and quite agitated."

"Ah, he's a good man. Stop giving him a hard time. We'll talk later."

"We will," she said affectionately, and hung up. "Brock, what…?"

"Your brother, Edward, is on the other line. It's urgent."

Piper reached for the phone. "Edward…what?"

"Piper. Tyler…"

"Oh, God. What happened?"

His voice broke, then he recovered. "He's at Bagram Airfield, the hospital. They're stabilizing him now. It's bad. Really bad, Piper."

Her breathing was irregular as Brock came around the desk, standing at the ready. "No. Please, Edward."

"They don't know…"

"Don't say it!" she hissed into the phone, and Brock covered her hand. "I'm going. Clear it for me."

An incredulous huff burst out of her brother. "Piper, no! You can't go to Afghanistan. It's too dangerous."

Her spine stiffened. No one told her what she could and couldn't do when it came to her baby brother. "It's a fortified base. I'll be fine!"

"That country isn't stabilized! I don't want to lose my sister, too."

"We're not going to lose him!"

His voice got hard. "Piper, the only reason I know this information is because of Uncle Bill."

Her voice just got harder. Her uncle Bill worked for the assistant secretary of state for Diplomatic Security. "All the more reason to get me to Bagram. We have the pull."

"You can't go," he shouted.

"Watch me!"

He lowered his voice, his teeth clenched. "Dammit, Bulldozer, you can't…"

"Call Uncle Bill. You're a DS special agent, Edward. Nepotism has to be good for something! Tyler needs someone there!"

She heard Edward's frustration and the pain and terror in his voice. "All right. Be ready to go when I call."

She looked up at Brock, and he nodded to indicate he would move heaven and earth to make sure she was ready. "I will."

Bagram Airfield,
Parwan Province, Afghanistan

Fourteen and a half hours later, hot, hungry and achy, Piper walked off the military transport onto Bagram Airfield, the largest US military base in Afghanistan, named for an ancient city nearby. She was still dressed in her blue power suit and her kick-butt heels.

Her brother was at the Heathe N. Craig Joint Theater Hospital, a fifty-bed hospital. Flanked by her DS detail, she headed toward the main entrance. The two men in dark blue suits followed. After a call from the DS office to alert her the detail was there to pick her up and take her to the airport, they had boarded the military transport with her. She was assured both Agents Hatch and Markam had combat experience. Two agents she hadn't met before, but worked for Diplomatic Security, as evidenced by their badges. As soon as she got inside, a nurse was waiting to take her to her brother, who was in intensive care.

"How is he?" she asked as the dark-haired nurse indicated she should follow her.

"He's holding his own. There was significant internal bleeding, a fractured leg and arm, abrasions, contusions, concussion. You'll need to brace yourself for his condition, ma'am. He's scheduled to be shipped out to Germany in two hours. The doctor can give you more details."

As they walked into the room, Piper rushed over to the tan bed. Her brother was hooked up to both an IV and other health-monitoring machinery. His eyes were closed and his breathing was even. She gasped as she took in the cuts and abrasions on his face and the heavy bandages on his arm and leg. She'd been scared out of her mind that he would… A wall of emotion slammed into her and she was caught up in keeping her composure. After losing Brad and her unborn child, she'd never wanted to feel that kind of pain again…but to lose her brother—it would be unbearable, especially on the heels of her father's fatal heart attack a year ago. And her mother had died several years ago from pneumonia.

The nurse squeezed her arm. "He's doing very well, considering what trauma his body has been through. He's tough."

Piper swallowed her tears and pain and turned toward the nurse. "Thank you."

"I'm Christina Davis, if you need me." She nodded to a man with salt-and-pepper hair, who stood next to the bed reading a chart. He looked up as Piper reached out and touched Tyler's bare arm. He was warm and alive, and something cold and tight loosened up inside her.

"Senator Jones? Dr. Abraham."

"Yes, how is my brother?"

"He's made it through surgery. He's a fighter. Lost a lot of blood, but those medevac boys know their job.

If it wasn't for his team member Lieutenant Dexter Kaczewski's quick actions, he might not have made it."

"They're very close," she whispered, pulling up a chair and sitting down.

"Lieutenant Kaczewski is here, too. Injured, but not as severely."

"Thank God for that."

"It's been a tough day. Team Three lost three SEALs in that battle."

Tyler groaned and Piper's attention went to her brother's face. His eyes opened slowly, his pupils unfocused and dazed.

"He's heavily medicated," the doctor said.

"Tyler," she said, bending down.

He looked at her as if he was trying to assimilate the image of her with being in a combat zone, as if he might be dreaming.

"Yes, I'm here. You're going to be fine," she said, smoothing back his beautiful, caramel-brown hair.

He closed his whiskey-colored eyes and groaned. "LT. Find out about LT." His deep voice was filled with pain, his speech slurred. He started to get agitated and she soothed him.

"He's fine."

"Did you see him?" Tyler demanded, trying to push up, but collapsed down with a groan.

"No, but the doctor told me."

"Please, see him. Find out. Please, Piper." His expression was full of panic, as if he was sure Dexter was dead.

"I will," she said, rubbing at his arm. "Calm down. I'll find out." She'd never met Dex, but he was one of Tyler's favorite topics.

Piper leaned down and kissed him on his bristly cheek.

She left the room and tracked down the nurse who had brought her to her brother. "Nurse Davis, I'm looking for Lieutenant Kaczewski."

"He's in bed twelve, just one wing over. Why...?"

Piper touched the nurse's arm, her voice intense. "He's my brother's best friend and he wants me to check on him. I promise. I'll only stay for a few minutes."

Her face softened. "All right, but just a few minutes."

Piper nodded her agreement and headed down the hall. Her detail followed, but she had them wait outside the room. It was dim inside and she didn't want to disturb Dexter, but she wanted to quiet down her brother. He was so distressed.

The half-drawn curtain was a flimsy barrier and as she stepped closer she heard it. A choking sound, then another one on its heels. Then she was sure. He was crying...no—her heart contracted—sobbing. The kind of gut-deep sorrow she knew intimately. That car accident had taken everything from her and it had felt as if her whole world had ended.

He was brave, making noise, showing people his grief.

Piper's response had been different. The worst type of crying, the silent kind. The one when everyone was asleep. The one where she felt it in her throat, and her eyes were blurry from tears. The one where she just wanted to scream. The one where she had to hold her breath and grab her stomach to keep quiet. The one when she realized the person that meant the most to her was gone.

She knew how it felt. She knew exactly how it felt to cry in the shower so no one could hear her, and waiting for everyone to fall asleep so she could fall apart, for everything to hurt so bad she just wanted it all to end.

They must have told him about the three SEALs he'd lost from his platoon. He was hurting so badly, and part of that hurt had something to do with guilt...with Tyler. She was well aware of that, too, and how it could twist you up until it was hard to sleep at night.

She knew what it was like to lead, to be in charge of something so important it consumed her, but...*this*—leading men and being responsible for their lives, making life and death decisions, the weight of that... A rush of profound, heartfelt compassion made her whole chest ache.

Her throat tightened and all the fear for her brother and all the pain she had tried to dodge by working and numbing herself welled up in her. She should leave, and she even took a step back. She didn't want to let it loose, either. But the lost and broken sound of him reached out to her, touched her with the honesty of his emotion, the bravery of him to allow himself the grief, to feel the loss. She'd felt so alone, had shed the same kind of broken tears.

She changed her mind and stepped around the curtain. He was on his back, his eyes closed, his chest heaving, tears running down his cheeks, over dark stubble.

She must have made a sound because his eyes popped open. Caught off guard, his handsome face vulnerable and open, the agony of loss scored his cobalt blue eyes; pain contorted his striking features.

"Dexter," she said softly, as if she knew him. "I'm Tyler's sister." She'd never met him, but her brother had talked about him all the time whenever he was home on leave.

Tyler had said that his LT—Dexter—was the essence

of a navy SEAL, a guy who got into the mess with his men, led them with strength and courage, never let them down, hung with them through everything—whether they were up to their necks in a fight or wrecked over a breakup letter from their girl. He was sarcastic with a whiplike wit, made them work hard, learn about what made navy SEALs unbreakable so they'd be safe. It was Tyler who had introduced her to Lieutenant Dexter Kaczewski. Tyler had talked so much about Dex, Piper felt that she knew him already.

The introduction set him off again, and he covered his face and wept. It seemed the most natural thing to lean in and gather him against her. He buried his face in her neck and held on to her fiercely. And she held him, rocked him through that terrible storm. Her heart breaking for the heaviness of his burden, of leading men, coming to know them and love them, then losing them. Command had to be so very difficult.

"I'm sorry," she whispered over and over as he totally lost it, his tears wet against her neck. He made a soft sound of pain when he wrapped his arms around her waist as she pressed his head against her chest. His hair was soft, his scalp warm against her palm as she cradled him.

But what slammed into her and made her move forward and comfort him in this dark hour was that Dexter had saved Tyler, braved death to carry her baby brother to safety.

Dex held on to this beautiful blonde angel, whom he wasn't sure was real. She felt solid and her voice was sweet and calm, filled with the tears he'd seen clouding her eyes. He wasn't ashamed of breaking down. It was inevitable and his macho face would be back in place in only a few short hours, but now was the time to feel the loss of Spaceman, Slim Jim and DJ. Men he had nurtured, fought with and protected as best he could.

By way of Coronado, California, to Dover Air Force Base in Delaware, on to Germany, and finally they had dropped into the most dangerous place on earth. Hours after their team had been assembled for the mission, he was a world away from home. He knew he might not see his brother, Russell "Rock" Kaczewski, a former marine, or his dad, two-star navy SEAL Rear Admiral Matthew Kaczewski, stationed at the Pentagon in Washington, DC, or his sassy and beautiful mother, Thelma, again.

A SEAL's troubles were different from many kinds of civilian stress. He'd risked his life so many times in so many battles, but he'd never let it control his performance. He had only one regret, and that was how his deployments had really messed up his relationships. He wasn't sure why he was thinking about those now. But there were two to be exact. Melissa, who was a beautiful, soft, gorgeous soul. They had been heading for marriage. He had no doubt about it. But he'd wanted to be a SEAL, just after he finished the marine corps basic training. He had put in for a transfer to the navy and entered the Naval Special Warfare Preparatory School, then it was two and a half years of training before he became a SEAL. But when he made the decision to go into Basic Underwater Demolition/SEAL training, or BUD/S, they started to fight. He wasn't home enough. He was changing. He wasn't the same man. And her complaints only grew until there hadn't been anything left of what they once had.

Then there was Susan. Ah, Suzy. She had married him and he'd thought he had found a woman as strong as his mom. That unbreakable one he needed to match his spirit. To love him for what he loved to do. But she left him after a rather terrifying deployment when he'd gone MIA and out of touch for three weeks. That experience had been one of the toughest he'd ever endured. She'd told him tearfully that she thought she could handle it, but she couldn't.

He needed a woman like his mother, who had stuck by his father through every single one of his deployments. She had been strong, fearless and had instilled in her sons the very meaning of the word *brave*.

His dad—damn, he was so proud of that man—had been decorated and conducted his life both passionately and with a balance that had only rubbed off on his two boys. The four of them were a unit as strong as his team was to him. He loved them all deeply as he tried to absorb the knowledge that he'd lost three of his closest brothers.

He'd had a solid childhood, even with his dad's deployments. With the use of modern technology, his dad had always been there, even when he'd been working overseas.

He loved his job. Being a SEAL was it for him. Career. Battle always brought with it danger and the very real threat of death.

Death was unavoidable in war. It was a stone-cold fact. But the thought of losing Tyler, who was as close to him and as deeply entrenched in his heart as his brother, Rock, was unbearable. Hell, maybe deeper. Dex had fought with Tyler, watched Ty's back as much as he'd watched Dex's. There wasn't anything he wouldn't do for Tyler. And to lose him because Dex had somehow either miscalculated or screwed up would be even worse.

It tore him up that his sister was here. A family member he'd only heard great things about. Sad things, too.

He would take the comfort she offered because he needed it. He had to let all this go. Only an idiot would bottle up emotions and never give them free rein.

The ache in his throat intensified, and he swallowed, an agony of emotion clogging his chest.

After he was spent and the purge was over, he let her go. The loss of Spaceman—damn, his ridge boss, his friend, his tactical genius—it was too much. Slim Jim, who had just become a father, and—dammit, his eyes teared up again, his chest hurt—DJ. Man, he was going to miss him so damn much; him and his humor were often all that kept the platoon going when times got tough. Leaning back, his side protesting with each move, he wiped at his swollen eyes and met her gaze. "This is a hell of a way to meet Ty's sister," he said, his voice raw and raspy.

"Well, I would have preferred a family dinner or a barbecue, not a hospital in a war-torn country where people are trying to kill us."

Ah, thank God, the beauty had a sense of the ridiculous, which only helped to make this just a tad less awkward. He cracked a faint smile, nodding. "It's a pleasure to meet you, Piper." He reached over and turned on the bedside lamp. That's when he got a really good look at her. She resembled Tyler a lot. But his hair was darker, where she had a mane of tawny gold hair and heartbreaking whiskey-hued eyes with dark, thick lashes. But where Ty's features were masculine, hers were pretty in a quirky way, not elegant, but cute. Her eyebrows were darker than her hair; her chin was delicately angled, but definitely set with determination. At odds with her all-American looks, her mouth was lush, exotically full and covered with a smooth layer of plum-colored lipstick. Funny that the lipstick made him homesick.

Okay, one thing was for certain. That RPG hadn't rattled his brain too much. He was still thinking like a man.

About Tyler's *sister*!

Suddenly he had an insight into exactly why Rock resisted getting involved with Tristan Michaels's sister Neve. Maybe he would lighten up on his brother in that respect. Maybe.

"Once we're all home and I'm in DC, I think I will take you up on that."

She smiled and wiped at her own cheeks, reminding him that they had all been through two hours of hell.

"Tyler's pretty upset and heavily medicated. I'm not sure if he's thinking straight, but he was worried they weren't telling him the truth about you."

He got that damn lump in his throat again. "Then let's go prove it to him."

Alarmed and not yet sure about whether he was joking, she stared at him. "What? You're wounded. I promised the nurse I would only be here for a few minutes, not get you up and walking."

"Tyler is what's important here, not an injury that took some stitches to close." He gritted his teeth and pushed back the blankets. She looked horrified that he was actually going to stand.

"Dexter…maybe you should rethink this…"

He gave her a firm gaze with those intense blue eyes and his mouth tightened. "Nope. I want to see Ty before he's shipped off to Germany. I kinda need that myself. Could you indulge me here? Give a wounded warrior a hand?"

"A wounded warrior, huh?" she said, giving him a

hard, I'm-on-to-your-plan-mister stare. At his innocent
look, she sighed and huffed out a short laugh at his obvious manipulation, as if she was well aware he was just
like any other hardheaded man. He grinned at her and,
even though his side protested rather loudly, swung his
legs and set his feet on the floor.

She moved to his side and helped him stand. She
smelled really good, like some kind of floral fragrance
and the essential female scent that he'd missed since
being deployed two hundred and twenty days out of
the year. It eased some of the pain to have this strong
woman helping him.

She slipped her arm around his waist, covered in the
flimsy gown, and accidentally threaded right through
the opening in the back to his bare skin.

Hoo-rah, that surely made him realize that all his
parts were still working as nature intended. He was
well aware that her hand was only inches away from
his completely buck-naked ass.

He was going to chalk up his hard-on to adrenaline
overload, deployment and being male.

"Oh, the joy of hospital gowns."

Even raw, he chuckled, thinking that was the way
the world worked. The living kept on living, moving
forward and letting go. Not just yet, but with time, he
would. Damn if he wasn't liking her even more. "Robe's
over there," he said as she kept her arm around him and
stretched to reach the garment on the chair. She snagged
it and helped him into it, wisely leaving it unbelted.

"You're cool under fire, huh?"

They slowly headed for the door, dragging the IV
stand with them. "I'm a lawyer's daughter and come
from a long line of politicians. My two brothers, one
older and one younger gave me a run for my money,

too. So, I hold my own. I'll arm wrestle you once you're 100 percent. I would never take advantage of a *wounded warrior.*"

At the door, he huffed a laugh. "Ah, caught in the middle, were you? I have the distinct pleasure to be the baby. I have an older brother…"

"Russell—nickname Rock—former RECON marine, tough son of a bitch, owns Rockface, a sporting goods store. He and his best friend, Tristan Michaels, run it. He was also a former RECON marine. Engaged to an NCIS agent, Amber. Do you want me to go on?"

"Wow. You know a lot about me," he said as two agents fell into step behind them, keeping a discreet distance.

"You are Tyler's favorite subject."

He had to stop moving as the affection—brotherly love—he held for Tyler churned him up all over again. His chest expanded with the rush of ragged emotion blindsiding him.

"We can rest if you'd like," she said solemnly. "I didn't mean to make this harder, Dexter. It's just that Tyler loves you as much as our brother, Edward, and me, I think. You'll have to become an honorary Keighley, for sure."

He turned his head away and massaged his eyes, but it was clear she'd already seen the effect her words had on him. He had to get control of himself before he saw Tyler. He didn't want to make it any worse for him. He had listened to Ty talk about his sister and her strength throughout all the hardship their family had endured over the past three years, especially with her losing her husband and child. It was as if he knew this woman.

"That is for sure. I'm racking my brain, trying to

remember if I told Ty about any of the skeletons in my closet or deep dark secrets."

"Oh, don't worry. I wrote them all down in my diary and put them under lock and key."

He laughed; it pulled his side and he grunted with the pain. She had him laughing through his tears. "Thanks. I needed that."

She nodded and their gazes met and held. Suddenly he felt hot, and it seemed as if the very air around them ignited. She really had the most unusual colored eyes. For a few moments, they stared at each other until someone cleared her throat.

He turned to see Nurse Davis standing there with her hands on her hips. She was giving Piper what Dex considered a direct-order look.

"Uh-oh," he said under his breath.

"Lieutenant, I'm sure you're going to have a perfectly plausible reason to be gallivanting around the hospital after you've just been through a terrible explosion. If you rip out those stitches…"

"I do have an awesome reason for being out of bed. It's a fellow SEAL who needs some reassurance that I'm not lying in the morgue right now. Before he's shipped off to Germany, he needs to see me alive. Is that good enough?"

Her features softened and she sighed. "Yes, that's good enough. At least let me get you a wheelchair."

"No," he said through gritted teeth. "It'll have more impact if I'm walking, and to tell you the truth, it feels good to be moving around."

"Senator? You got him?" the nurse said, her concern obvious.

Piper looked up at him and he got another jolt through

his system at the way her eyes went over his face. "Yes, I've got him."

She sure had.

As they walked away, she said wryly under her breath, "I'll try not to keep you in stitches." She cut him a sly look.

He laughed again and she smiled. "Really, I'll be here all week. I must be punchy from that wonderful plane ride. Military transport is always so comfortable."

"Seriously, do you want to pull out all my stitches? Just think how much trouble we'll be in then."

She winced. "Sorry."

Had he made her nervous? Was she responding to that…whatever it was…that had passed between them? This was, again he reminded himself, Tyler's sister.

They hobbled the rest of the way to Tyler's room. As he entered, he moved away from her and walked the rest of the way on his own steam.

He swallowed when he saw the kind of shape Ty was in. His right eye was swollen shut and there were many scrapes and bruises on his face. His right leg and arm were heavily swathed in bandages. He had tubes and wires connected, but when Dex approached, he smiled a very relieved smile and his good eye, though dazed, brightened.

"Hey, buddy," Dex said, returning his smile.

"LT… Dex. It's good to see you. You okay?" Ty reached out with his good arm, and they clasped forearms, both grasping tight.

"Me?" He sat gingerly down next to the bed. "You're the one who spent most of our time here in surgery."

"They said you saved my life."

"Yeah, well, at the time it seemed like a good idea."

Tyler laughed, then winced. "Don't make me laugh,

man." His eyes darkened. "DJ...man, I can't believe it. Slim and Spaceman. What a loss."

"I know." Dex's chest got tight again.

Tyler said, "You don't think it's all your fault, do you, LT? Because that intel was good."

"Yeah, the intel was good, but something went wrong, Ty, and I have to take the responsibility for that."

"It wasn't your fault," Ty said again, looking mutinous.

"Don't get your shorts in a twist. I'm sure I'll hear from the brass soon enough."

Ty nodded. "They're shipping me off to Germany."

"I'll see you back in the States. I promise, Ty. Your job is to get well."

"Is that an order?"

"Yeah, it's a damn order."

Ty reached out again, but Dex simply leaned in and gave him a quick, hard hug.

Dex looked into Ty's eyes and Ty looked into Dex's; no words were uttered, but Dex had never before, and probably never would again, have a louder conversation.

He rose and gave Ty one last look, then he started walking out of the room. He heard Piper say that she'd be right back just as the room tilted a little. He made it out, but had to lean against the wall for support.

"Dexter?"

"I think I'll take that wheelchair now," he said. His buckling knees had her slipping her arm around his waist again as she instructed one of her detail to get a nurse.

As the guy ran off, Dex looked down into her sweet face. "Hey, thanks for the way you came to my rescue back there."

"You're welcome. I know something about loss. Not the same kind, but I've been there."

"Also, thanks for being a sport about getting me here." He closed his eyes. "It meant a lot to me and to Ty."

As Nurse Davis came briskly with the wheelchair, he had to let go of her to sit down. It would most likely be a while before he saw Tyler's delectable sister, so before he was wheeled away he looked his fill.

Back in his room, he settled against the mattress. "Do you need anything for the pain?" Nurse Davis said, her voice all of a sudden quiet and soft.

"Admit it," he said with a smile. "I'm growing on you."

She tucked him in and smoothed down his blanket. "As one of my most stubborn of patients. Oh, yes."

"One? I'd better work a little bit harder," he said, and this time, tough, no-nonsense Nurse Davis smiled.

He closed his eyes, his wound throbbing from just below his armpit all the way to his waist. The gash had been deep in spots, but especially over his ribs. He was hurting, but his commanding officer was supposed to be here shortly.

"Something mild," he said. "I need to be lucid for a debriefing."

"Really, Lieutenant…"

"Just until he leaves, Christina."

His firm tone and his use of her first name brought that stern look back. Then she shook her head. "All right. I'll be right back."

As she left, he heard her speaking with someone and her voice was soft and breathy. Then Captain Jeff Davis walked into his room and Dex's brain told him to jump to attention. He wasn't expecting the boss of the whole of Naval Special Warfare Group ONE.

"Sir," Dex said.

"I'm here on official business, and not to see my beautiful wife. You better be behaving for her."

"Your…wife."

"To the letter," Nurse Davis said, returning with his medication. She made goo-goo eyes at her husband and then left.

The captain pulled up a chair just as Commander Todd Hodges, the leader of SEAL Team Three, entered the room, and he pulled the curtain for privacy.

He'd brought his own chair, nodded to Dex and sat down.

"Sir?"

"I want your assessment of your previous op," Captain Davis said.

"I think those marines were nothing more than a smoke screen and they were killed just moments before we arrived. I think they were waiting for us, not because they knew we were coming for those men, but because they knew *when* we were coming. We were ambushed."

Jeff looked at Todd and he nodded.

He lowered his voice. "Lieutenant, we have a situation. After the smoke cleared on that cluster in the desert that robbed us of three of our best men and three damn fine marines, we found the body of a mercenary, or merc. An American by the name of Martin Carter, dressed exactly like an insurgent. After further investigation, we discovered he took on high-end types of jobs."

Dex swore through gritted teeth, the medication his nurse had given him not even touching his pain. His face contorted. After being in this war-torn country for almost a decade, he had met and killed some of the worst vermin alive—soldiers for hire. Men and even women who'd pull a trigger for money.

"We thought you should know. Think about it and report back to us if you have any information that can help. In the meantime, we're shipping you back to the States."

"Captain…"

"No, Dexter. You're going back to fully recover, and that's a damn order. I'm not losing another man. Oh, and we're awarding you…"

Dexter groaned; he didn't give a damn about another medal. He wanted to make sure that the men who'd died, men who'd trusted him, were avenged. Guilt washed over him.

"…the Navy Cross, so get used to it."

"Yes, sir."

The captain leaned in. "By all reports you saved lives out there and risked your own." He reached into his pocket. "I think it's time that junior grade was removed and we can make you a full lieutenant.

"Ten-hut," the captain said, and Hodges stood to attention. He opened the box and pulled out the lieutenant bars and pinned them to his gown. Then both Captain Davis and Commander Hodges saluted him.

He saluted them back, gritting his teeth against all the emotion welling up in him. Anger, frustration, pain and loss all got mixed into his being made a full lieutenant.

The captain offered his hand. "Thank you, Lieutenant Dexter Kaczewski, for your service."

He shook the captain's hand, then his commander's. "We'll make this official as soon as you're well enough to don that dress uniform."

"Yes, sir. About the op…"

"This isn't on you, Dexter. This op may have been compromised. We don't know for sure. I've asked the secretary of the navy for help and he's going to assign NCIS to look into it. There will be a thorough investigation. Petty Officer Carver…Mike served with me when I had my own team. I know this is a blow. He was an exemplary SEAL," the captain said, his eyes gleaming with memory.

"Yes, sir." Feeling ineffectual and helpless in the face of this information, Dex clenched his fists. SEALs were all about action, and he was out of the game. Nothing against NCIS, but he wanted to look into this himself.

He'd contact those NCIS agents assigned to find out the people responsible for this act of treason, and he'd ride them like new recruits until Dex had answers that would allow him to sleep at night.

He vowed that silently to Spaceman, Slim and DJ.

Piper was dog-tired one hour later as she said goodbye to her drowsing brother and they loaded him up and shipped him to Landstuhl Regional Medical Center in Germany. They had moved him out earlier than expected. She'd already talked to Edward, and she was going home as soon as the transport with a seat with her name on it landed in another two hours.

They had given her a bed to rest in, but she made them promise if it was needed she would be notified so she could vacate. She laid down and closed her eyes. She should have fallen asleep, but Dex's scent lingered on her and it smelled so good.

She closed her eyes against the unfamiliar surge of attraction. Here she thought she had been ruined, utterly ruined, by her deep love for Bradley Jones, the man of her dreams. He had swept her off her feet in college. The next steps of getting engaged and married so easy. Her father and mother had been ecstatic. Like royalty, they had merged their high-powered political families.

She bit her lip and opened her eyes. Reaching for her purse, she pulled out her wallet. There were times like right now when she couldn't remember his face and that caused her to feel a surge of panic. When she pulled out his picture, she breathed a sigh of relief. Ah, he had been so handsome.

But Dexter Kaczewski was lethally, dangerously handsome. And he was so alive. Virile in that wounded warrior's body, all those muscles. Brad had been lanky and nerdy, not like the lieutenant. She bit her lip, gazing at Brad's picture, the agony of losing him like a pile of rocks in her gut. This was the first time she'd ever thought about Brad in relation to another man, and the panic was just a result of feeling disloyal. He was gone, but did her attraction to Dex signal that she might be ready to move on? Especially ready for someone like Dex. She had never thought she'd be one of those women who would ever go for the muscled warrior type. She'd always loved the brainy men, but the lieutenant had that cutting wit and charisma to spare.

She'd touched his warm skin, felt the gauze where his bandage had been taped to the side of his body, reminding her that this man had a very dangerous job. A navy SEAL. Yeah, not the type of guy she wanted to even think about getting involved with. Not that it was possible. There was no time frame to moving on. The memory of loving him wouldn't fade. Was there room in her heart to love again? Her attraction to Dex was just that—a spark. She was heading home, so her meanderings were moot. He was stationed on the west coast in

Coronado and she was in DC. It was unlikely—unless
he made good on his promise for a family dinner—that
they would meet again.

Oh, God. The thought of him sent a flurry of weakness through her whole body, a body she thought had
been numb and unresponsive to any man's presence.
Her brothers had worried that she was acting in a very
unhealthy way, not letting go of Brad's memory, but it
was so difficult. Now, her head was filled with the scent
and sight of Dexter. She had to adjust to this involuntary reaction to him.

It had been eighteen months since she'd lost Brad.
She had only three months of his term left and she'd
fulfilled every one of his promises except passing the
bill Senator Mullins wanted to block.

Never mind. He couldn't intimidate her, impede her
or stop her. She wasn't interested in continuing in politics. It would be a daily reminder that her husband was
no longer on this earth doing the job he loved. That was
hard enough as it was.

It was political suicide to go up against a man like
Mullins. He was connected, rich as all get-out and powerful. It was rumored he had aspirations for the Oval
Office and that he would be a shoo-in if he ever decided to run.

Her mouth tightened. She had no doubt he intended to
run. And run over her. Well, he was going to be handed
his…defeat.

This bill was going to the floor. She bet that stuck
in his powerful craw.

She drifted after that thought. Dexter's gorgeous blue
eyes and striking features kept invading her thoughts
as she fell into sleep.

It seemed like only moments later when she jerked

awake. She lay still in the darkened room. Something was…different. She couldn't put her finger on it, but she heard nothing.

That was it. The hospital was eerily quiet. There was no sound, no voices, no…nothing. And in a busy hospital like Bagram, that was strange.

She rose and immediately slipped on her shoes and grabbed her purse, putting the shoulder strap over her head.

She moved toward the door, not understanding why everything in her screamed at her to remain quiet. She peeked out and her heart jumped into her throat.

Her detail was…gone. Both men were not at their posts. This was unprecedented, unless they had decided there was a threat to her welfare. It was their job to keep her safe. Take a bullet for her.

She slipped out of the room to the nurses' station, but there was no one there. She took a breath and a popping sound cracked just outside. She jumped and turned toward the door that led to the entrance and the airfield. She heard more popping noises.

Trying to rationalize that the sound must be backfiring vehicles, that it couldn't be…gunfire—could it?— trying to contain the quavering feeling in the pit of her stomach, she almost came out of her skin at the sound of an explosion so loud it shook the hospital.

Her gaze shot to the front door, her stomach now doing loop-de-loops before dropping to her feet.

The front door banged open and men in desert garb toting automatic weapons came through. They were not the Afghani forces she was used to seeing. She bolted behind the nurses' station before they could see her and tucked herself underneath the desk, going very, very still.

She could hear them fanning out and she peeked around the desk, seeing that they were looking into rooms, but the SEALs had been medevaced out. That only left—*oh, God*—Dexter.

Chapter 3

Dexter woke to the sound of gunfire, not sure it was a residual dream or reality. He lay very still, his hearing jacked up. Still groggy from sleep, he tried to clear his head. The base wasn't controlled by the US military anymore. It was a convenient way station, but not as secure as it had once been.

Then he heard it again and his thoughts went directly to Ty and Piper. That gunfire was close and another burst confirmed it. It was coming from *inside* the hospital.

He gritted his teeth and rolled out of the bed, crouching. Reaching down and ripping off a strip of tape and gauze from his side wound, he took a breath and pulled out the IV, setting the material against the puncture and taping it securely down. The drugs in his system were still numbing his side enough that he could function. It wouldn't have mattered. He'd learned and hadn't forgotten his SEAL training. If he had breath, he could fight. Pain was nothing but a state of mind. He'd worked through the pain and never, ever given up. It made him unbreakable.

Every bed in here was empty, except his. He listened and waited while he assessed the situation. He had nothing; his clothes and his weapons were shot and bombed to hell, all his ID sitting at home. He was completely unarmed and the first course of action was to get his hands on a weapon. Then he had to find Piper and Ty.

Hopefully they had already shipped out of here.

The sound of footsteps approaching had him readying himself. He heard them whisper in Pashto, "There's no one here."

"We better search, anyway."

He watched the progress of the two men, checking each bed, starting at the beginning of the room. His was about halfway down the row. Sliding under the bed, he waited until they made it past him.

Without even a whisper of sound, he ghosted out and came up behind them as they were checking the last bed. As the insurgent turned his head, Dex's quick jab caught him in the throat and he went down gurgling. The second guy reacted too late. Dex's arm went around his neck and he applied pressure until the man stopped struggling. It was hell with his wound, but he endured the pain. Without missing a beat, he reached down and grabbed one of the weapons, pulling the sidearm out of the man's holster. He checked the magazine and slammed it home. Full. Twelve rounds. Russian-made.

He stripped down, ignoring the feeling returning to his side and dressing himself in the pungent desert garb, including the head covering, which obscured his features. What the hell was going on?

The only easy day was yesterday. One of the SEAL mottos and very fitting right about now.

He strapped the assault rifle across his back, leaving

it dangling against his left hip and uninjured side. He was proficient in shooting with both hands.

He kept the pistol down as he made short work of silently moving along the empty corridors. When he reached the nurses' station, he was relieved there were no bodies. He could only hope that the captain's wife and the other medical personnel had made it to safety. Dressed as he was with command of their language, he took care of any threats with lethal force as he moved to this position. But one quick look into Tyler's room showed it empty. No bodies. Again, a sigh of relief. He passed the room, made it to the corner. An insurgent came out of a side door and Dex's gun came up, but the man saw him and ducked behind the desk. He heard a scream as he dragged Piper, kicking and fighting the man who held her, with him. His face was obscured by his head scarf, but the black automatic in his hand was in clear view.

He put the gun to her head. Dex watched as if in slow motion—the man's arms around her waist, her hair flying wildly and blocking her face as she struggled, kicking, throwing her head back into the man's chin and making his steps falter.

Dex stepped away from the wall, unable to get a shot off because Piper was still struggling and his aim was iffy with those drugs still in his system.

He tucked the weapon in the waistband of his pants and surged across the short space that separated them, slamming into the man at a dead run. Head down, Dex planted a shoulder in the man's chest, the rifle flipping from his grasp, hitting the floor and sliding a few feet away. The two of them landed on the floor, grappling as Piper, propelled by Dex's weight, spun away and hit the wall with a thud, groaning softly.

His total focus was on the guy who was swinging at him. Dex blocked, but it cost him a pulling, stinging agony in his side. The guy brought his other hand into play, but Dex blocked that, as well; he was in a fight for his life. This insurgent had some martial arts training and it flashed across his brain, lightning quick, that this guy was really dangerous.

The man fumbled at his waist for a pistol, but Dex got his hand on it. It bucked once, the explosion reduced to a soft thump by the silencer. The slug punched into the wall above Piper's head. Dex grabbed hold of the insurgent's arm and slammed it hard against the floor. But before he could shake the pistol loose, a white-hot pain sliced into his injury, momentarily shorting out all thought and all strength.

Howling in pain and rage, he punched the man in the face, the feel of liquid sliding over his hip. As Dex clutched his side, the man swung the gun up and slammed it into his temple.

Dex struggled to stay on top as his consciousness dimmed, but the world dipped and tilted beneath him. Then suddenly they were rolling, pain throbbing, muscles burning, hearts pumping.

He managed to get a hand on the man's throat and started to squeeze, but the insurgent was on top of him and pulling back, pulling away. Bringing the gun up, his attacker pulled the trigger and the sharp *thunk* of a bullet splintered the floor millimeters from Dex's head. Dex let go of the man's windpipe and knocked the gun hand to the side.

Dex surged up, twisting to reverse their positions. Pain sliced through his side, pounded in his head. He blocked it out and fought on adrenaline, groping, pushing, turning. The insurgent's back slammed into the nurses' counter and the gun came out of his hand and skidded across the floor, toward the wall.

He punched Dex in the ribs and the pain doubled him over; the insurgent shoved him away. Dex stumbled backward and fell to his back. The man set his foot into his side and grinded down on his wound, reaching for the assault rifle. Blinded by excruciating pain, Dex was barely aware when the man straightened and pointed the muzzle at his head.

His dazed brain sent a frantic message to his muscles to *move*! But before he could sluggishly do so, there was a muffled *pop* and the man stiffened. His eyes rolled up into the back of his head and he fell to the floor, blood spread out in an ever-expanding pool beneath him.

Piper stood there, her chest heaving, her eyes wild, blood on her lip, rolling off her chin. Her hands wrapped around the pistol's barrel in a white-knuckled grip.

She ran over to him and said, "Can you get up?"

"Yes," he said as she helped him to stand. He clutched his side, feeling the wetness of his blood. He took the gun out of her grip and put two into the guy's head. Then he went to turn away, but turned back, his eyes snapping to the hem of the guy's robe and the telltale view of the black trouser pant leg that was peeking out. His blood froze and he slowly bent down, supporting his side, and removed the head scarf referred to as a *keffiyeh* to expose his face. He reared back and Piper gasped as she looked over his shoulder. There was a reason the guy knew exactly where his wound was and how to hurt him.

"Omigod! That's Agent Hatch!"

He turned to look at her, her face stiff in horrible shock as if her world was crashing down around her. "One of the agents from your detail just tried to kill you? How is that possible? Aren't these guys vetted?"

She backed up, her eyes going to him, her breath hitching, rushing in and out. Oh, damn, she was hyperventilating. He rose and grabbed her by the back of the neck, pushing her head down. "Breathe, Piper. Breathe. Match me." He took deep breaths and then she was mimicking him.

As soon as she was calm, she raised her head. "I shot him. He was going to...kill you."

"I know. You did the right thing. You did good."

"Ty taught me to shoot. He said I should know how."

"*Hoo-rah*, Ty. You had no choice, Piper. It was him or us."

"I don't know why he was trying to kill me. I haven't a clue. He's supposed to protect me. It's his job."

"Diplomatic Security?"

"Yes. He was just assigned to me. I was told he was former military and would be more qualified to protect me on this trip to Afghanistan. I don't know him."

"Where is the other one...?"

"Markam. I don't know. When I woke up, they were both gone."

He went back and searched the body. He came up with the agent's badge, passport and wallet. Tucking everything away in his own pockets, he pushed up from the floor.

"We've got to get out of here. It's clear they were targeting you." He went to a small closet and pulled open the door.

He snagged a blue burka, a full body garment worn by many Muslim women, off a hook. There were spare ones for nurses who needed to go off base.

"Put this on and make sure to cover up your hair completely."

She pulled the robe over her head, donning the one-piece covering.

She reached out, her voice filled with concern. "Dexter, you're bleeding."

"Can't be helped. We need to move, double time. I'm getting my combat itch."

He took her arm and handed her Agent Hatch's gun. "Since you seem to know what you're doing with this, you take it. I want you to stay behind me at all times."

"Yes, sir," she said shakily. "Do I have to salute you, too?"

He chuckled and said, "No, ma'am. That's just for us military types."

"Oh, good. I'm not really good at taking orders, but I'll defer to you in this."

"Everything good with Ty?"

She looked at him blankly. "Yes, he was flown out over an hour ago. Do you think he's in danger, too?"

"I can't be certain about it. Do you have a cell phone on you?" he said, the wheels going in his head. The American merc, the ambush. He wasn't taking any chances.

She looked around and ran to the desk and snagged her purse. She reached inside. "Here. It's secure."

"Your brother's name…the DS agent?"

"Edward Keighley."

"Right." He dialed and the phone rang and rang, then went to voicemail. "Dammit…" He waited for the beep. Grabbing her arm and dragging her down the hall, he said, "Rock, it's Dex. I need you to get word anonymously to Edward Keighley that his brother, Ty, might be in danger. His sister Piper has been attacked, but she's safe with me." He moved down the hall until they got to the kitchen. "I'm okay. Don't tell anyone else I called. I'll be in touch." He found a backpack and went to the fridge and loaded up on water, taking whatever was portable and edible, as well. Too bad he didn't have his pack with his MREs, or ready-to-eat meals,

He dropped the phone and stamped on it with his boot heel. She looked up at him like he'd gone crazy. "I told you it was secure."

"It still has GPS. I'm not taking any chances." Ransacking the medical supplies, he grabbed some painkillers and downed a couple tablets. He shrugged into the backpack and frowned at her feet in the very nice heels. They made her legs look long and sexy. Slipping into a makeshift locker room, he spied a pair of sneakers near a locker. They looked a bit too big, but it was better than those heels. In those shoes, she'd for sure break an ankle. "Take those off and put these on."

They were going to have to hoof it and the terrain would not be easy to traverse.

She eyed the sneakers and said, "You can't be suggesting that we make a break for it?"

"I'm all that stands between you and death, ma'am. Now move your shapely ass before I forget I'm an officer and a gentleman."

She jumped, gave him a shaky but cheeky glance as she put on the sneakers and headed for the door into the hall. It was dark outside, which was to their advantage. In the distance, he could still hear automatic weapons' fire. Their best bet was to get off base and find a place to recon.

He reached back and took her hand. This was a very bad situation, and flying her out of Bagram wasn't an option at this point. He wasn't sure that going back to DC was a good idea, but it was a damn sight safer than staying here. But with the insurgents overrunning the base, their best bet was to get out and find another way to get her back. "This is going to get dicey. There is only one way to get off this base. The gates. They aren't just going to let us leave. But we can't stay here. For one, I have no idea what is going on with your detail, and we don't know if the Afghan forces can keep or maintain security on the base. It really wasn't a good idea for you to come here at all."

"I know it wasn't, but it was supposed to be quick. My brother is important to me and I wanted to…see him in case…" She trailed off.

"I get that, but this country is a powder keg and they don't need provocation to kill anyone." He took in her pale face, but her eyes were steady. He shook his head, sighing. "I'll do everything in my power to keep you alive and get you back to DC. We're going to be moving fast. Don't stop until I tell you to and, Piper, there will be shooting, so stay behind me and use your weapon without hesitation. Just, ah, don't shoot me. All right?"

"Is that supposed to be funny?" she said shakily.

"Ah, yeah."

"Ha, ha." Piper took a fortifying breath. When he looked back at her, several explosions lit up the night.

"They're blowing up aircraft," he said under his breath.

His mind worked furiously, but he could see no way out of this. They had to get off the base. A loose and desperate plan formed in his mind. He dragged her down the hall and went out one of the side exits that gave them some cover from the open area where the road was. He stepped outside and paused. It was pitch-black except for the ambient light from the yellow and orange glow of the fires. What he wouldn't give for his night-vision goggles.

He ducked to the side, bringing her with him, looking right and left for any threat. He moved again, threading through the maze of buildings and heading for one of the gates, avoiding the main one.

Much of Afghanistan consisted of mountains cut by deep and narrow valleys, few and poor roads and thousands and thousands of small villages. Where the land flattened, the summer heat was even more intolerable. He knew it from experience. Even though it was the middle of the night, Dex was already sweating from the ninety-degree temperature.

As he stopped and took a few quick looks around the side of the building, they ran into trouble. Up a long alley of concrete barriers, the gate was blocked by at least eight insurgents. He could see the bodies of the dead guards lying in the road.

There was no way to sneak past them. They would have to try another gate. Just then someone started yelling, and most of the men there took off in that direction, which only left two. That was more manageable.

"Give me the pistol." He traded the assault rifle for her weapon. "Stay here," he whispered, close to her ear, trying not to breathe in any more of her scent than he had to; the woman was distracting and he had to keep himself grounded in pure warrior mode to get her out of this danger zone.

Crouching, he ran to the side of the building where one of the men was standing. An eight-mile perimeter road circled the base, and just beyond the road were wire fences separating the base from the treeless fields of the local villages. Rectangles of metal, printed with skulls and crossbones, dangled from the fences, dancing in the wind against the wire, providing a metallic warning of minefields. Both men had their backs to Dex, but they were a little too far apart for a quick, unarmed double takedown. *Good thing the gun had a silencer.* He hated to waste even two bullets, but it couldn't be helped. If they were caught, it was over. He aimed, bracing the barrel of the gun on his forearm as he lined up his shot. He took three deep breaths and then pulled the trigger. The closest guy dropped, and he moved just a few inches and neutralized the second one without a sound.

He quickly motioned her forward and they ran full out toward the gate, kicking up dust and displacing gravel, and didn't stop running until they were clear of the outside walls and heading into vegetation on the side of the road.

He immediately hit the deck and a fiery blaze of pain flashed across his side, burning like a freaking hot poker from one edge of the wound to the other—and it didn't stop. The pain just sat on him and burned. Gritting his teeth, he pulled her down with him. Poking his head up, he watched and waited to make sure they weren't followed. The locust trees were in bloom with their stubby trunks of thick interlocking ropes of blackened bark and their white blossoms that filled the air with a sweet aroma that mixed with jet fuel, diesel and the always-constant, unrelenting rising dust. The combination of pollen, fuel and dust produced a light paste that covered everything on base. An odd perfume of summer, accented by the smells of war.

Any minute movement set that agony off now that the drugs were wearing off. Right now it would be easier to just pass out, seek dark oblivion.

The only easy day was yesterday. That was quite fitting here.

Right. He was about to get comfortable with being uncomfortable.

As soon as he was sure they hadn't been followed, one hand cupping his side, he took her hand and started following the road, alert for any kind of danger. Now that they were away from the base, the constant aching of his side throbbed harder with every beat of his heart.

Damn, that hurt. Every single part of him hurt like a son of a bitch. He swiped his sleeve across his brow and tried not to feel so freaking awful—he was in trouble. He didn't have to look down at his wound. He knew what he felt.

He was still bleeding, but he wasn't going to tell her and he wasn't going to stop. They had no choice but to move. He would patch himself up once they got clear of the baddies he was certain were after them. As soon as they reached a mile away from the base, he led her to a small outcropping of rock and hunkered down. The sweat was pouring off him now, and he was worried that he was going to lose whatever food was still in his stomach.

A wave of dizziness washed across the back of his skull—not the first of the night, and sure as hell not the last. He carefully lowered his head, fighting it, focusing on his breathing, making it deep, making it count, and he held on. Losing blood and hyperventilating were a bad combo. Passing out meant they would be toast.

"Dexter?"

He took one more fortifying breath. His hand was wet against his side. That bastard had done a number on his wound. It took Dex a moment to find his breath, another couple of moments to work through the pain and find his voice, but when he did, he laid it out for her. "We're going to head to Charikar, which is about twelve klicks from here."

"Klicks?"

"That's military speak for kilometers. So, that's a little less than twelve miles."

"You think you can make it that far?"

"Once there, we can hire a cab to take us to Kabul and the airport. I speak the language, so let me do all the talking."

When his eyes met hers through the mesh of the burka, he could see her concern, her fear.

"You really need medical attention."

She was as perceptive as she was beautiful. "Not… going to…happen. We can't stop and we can't go back. There's only moving forward. Are you with me?"

"What about you checking in with your superiors? Won't you be considered AWOL?"

"That's the least of my worries right now. There is an unknown threat against you and I'm not leaving you until I know that it's neutralized. I'm still uncertain if Markam, your other agent, is involved or dead. In fact, I don't trust anyone at all, except you and my family."

"What? There must be some mistake. Why would anyone want to kill me?"

"I don't know? This could be someone with pull and could lead right back to Washington. You must have pissed someone off."

She ripped off the top of her burka, her face moist, her blond hair in damp clumps against her sweaty neck. "I'm a lame-duck senator. I'm almost at the end of my term—my husband…late husband's term. I will admit that I've been pretty fearless because there's little fear of consequences."

* * *

"You're not staying in politics?"

"No. I'm…it's not for me. I did this for Brad." Piper closed her eyes, the reality of what he had said sweeping through her with a decimating force, shaking so badly she almost felt faint, definitely sick. She drew up her legs and locked her arms around them as she pressed her face into her knees. "Oh, God," she whispered. "I almost got you killed. And the people at the base."

The awfulness of what had happened, what she might have unwittingly caused, unfolded in her mind—grim, wrenching. On top of that, Ty might be in more danger. She didn't know how or why, but she trusted Dex. Dex, this amazing, wounded warrior, was now risking his life for her.

She was cold, even as the sweat ran down her back in the stifling heat, dreading donning the burka again, a garment she was beginning to actively hate with a passion—a reactive kind of rage and, worst of all, a devastating sense of betrayal filling her.

If Ty died… If Dex gave up his life for hers… She didn't think she could bear it. The fresh grief overwhelmed her when she thought about the work she had been doing for Brad. How much she missed him. How big of a hole his death had left in her life. It all got mixed up with her emotions for her brother and these new, as-yet-uncategorized, strange, warm feelings for Lieutenant Dexter Kaczewski.

A ragged sob tore loose, the pain from all the collective eighteen months and the last few hours colliding into a wrenching, devastating, all-consuming agony. The numbness she'd built over the months, painstakingly every day, broke beneath the pressure, and grief, sharp and rending, overwhelmed her.

"Oh, damn, Piper…don't. For Christ's sake." There was the sound of movement, then the warmth of Dex's hand around her wrist, and Piper locked her jaw, an awful pressure expanding in her chest.

He tugged at her hand and she dropped them from her face. "No, this isn't on you! This is on whoever is trying to kill you. I'm not leaving your side until I know you're safe and the person responsible is either captured or, preferably, killed."

She met his gaze and he stared at her, then closed his eyes and gathered her up in a tight, enveloping embrace, cradling her head against his shoulder. "It's going to be all right," he murmured. She sagged helplessly as he gathered her closer with his good arm and stroked her back, his hand cupped around the back of her neck.

His warmth finally broke through, and Piper huddled against him, pressing her face along his jaw, feeling as if it was the most natural thing in the world. Her breath catching on a sob, she wound her arms around his neck, despair slicing through her as she finally let go of the shock that had paralyzed her. "Dex…"

She hung on to him, the port in the perfect storm of her emotions. He tightened his hold and rocked her as desolate sobs shuddered through her body, one desperate emotion after another ripping at her. Bottled up for long months, it all came pouring out—how Brad and she had been driving home from a fund-raiser. She had been seven months pregnant and he would joke that he had only two more months to go before he could hold the child that was doing cartwheels in her tummy. How they'd been forced off the road and had tumbled down an embankment on the GW Parkway. How she had lost him while she was trapped and saw the light go out of his eyes and the rush of amniotic fluid. The loss of her baby cramping deep inside her.

He stroked her hair back and framed her face with his big hands. "Ty said you've lost a lot recently. I'm sorry for that. I truly am," he whispered roughly, an agony of feeling in his softly spoken words. "But I need you to pull yourself together now because we have to get out of this so that whoever caused this can pay. Live for that. Can you do that, Piper? I need you to find the unbreakable in you." Damn him for being so understanding and for asking her for courage and strength when she was running on empty right now.

The sound of his voice and his long, soothing caresses brought her back from the depths of desperation, and she was finally able to ease her hold on him.

Taking a deep, cleansing breath, Piper shifted in his hold. He didn't say anything, just continued to rub her back.

She sniffed and brushed at her tears. "I'm sorry."

"It's okay," he said softly, his own thumb swiping at her tears, and she got this rush of emotion, so strong for this man, for his compassion and his caring. "Are you with me?"

"Thank you," she said, leaning forward and pressing a kiss to his jaw. She didn't mean to linger, but she couldn't seem to help it.

He let out a controlled breath when she finally moved away. "What now?"

"That's the stuff," he said with a brief smile. He pointed off into the distance. "Change of plans. There's a family I know in a village not far from here. We stop there and rest, fix my wound, wait until nightfall. It's almost dawn." He rubbed at his temple and she met his eyes. They looked a bit unfocused. He was hurting. It was clear in the pinched quality of his handsome face. He looked worse for wear.

She got immediately alarmed. "Dex, maybe…"

"I'm fine. It's just so damn hot."

She nodded. Reaching down, she donned the hated burka and settled it in place. He rose slowly, painfully clutching his side. Then he doubled over and lost whatever little he had in his stomach. She immediately pulled the pack off his shoulder and pulled out a bottle of water. He leaned heavily against the rock, breathing hard. When he straightened, he took the bottle, rinsed his mouth and drank heavily, draining the bottle. He went to take the pack back, but she pushed his hand away.

He gave her a look that made her tremble, it was so complimentary.

They started walking, but after about an hour Dex stumbled, then righted himself quickly. But a few more steps and he stumbled again, then he went to his knees. She'd been trudging along behind him, thoroughly drenched beneath the burka, but quickly covered the few feet separating him from her. She reached him barely in time as he started to collapse. His eyes completely glazed over as she caught him against her, his weight bearing her to the ground.

"Dex?" she said, and he didn't respond. "Dex!" she said, her voice strident.

Then she saw his bloody shirt and bit her lip, panic slicing her insides. But before she spiraled out of control, she thought of his calm voice. *Are you with me?*

She was in one of the most dangerous countries in the world; she didn't speak the language and had no idea where to go.

His eyes fluttered open. "Get Afsana…" he mumbled, his head lolling to the side. She reached for his face to bring it back to her and gasped. He was burning up. Oh, God, he was feverish, delirious and losing blood.

Chapter 4

"Dex!"

He opened his eyes and the sky seemed too blurred and gray. The face above his was a woman's face. A stunningly beautiful face. He frowned. He knew her from somewhere. He reached for the elusive thought, but it tumbled around in his fuzzy brain.

Her delicate features were concerned, her whiskey eyes wide and…frantic, her skin glistening. He tensed, automatically bracing for danger he couldn't see. In the back of his mind, he realized he was always ready for danger.

Something told him she was the dangerous one.

He was so hot. So thirsty.

Where the hell was he?

He tried to sit up and his side sent white-hot agony through his body. He winced, falling back, moaning and clutching his side. It was wet with blood and everything rushed back at him. Piper. The insurgents. Saving her life. *Her DS agent tried to kill her!* The desert. Afsana and help.

"Help me up," he said, and she leaned into him, her

body soft and strong at the same time. She smelled good, musky and female. He hadn't been with one or close to one in a long time, and she pushed his buttons. Every single one—even those that hadn't been pushed in a very long time.

Cupping his back and using her forearm, she helped him to sit. He was breathing hard, and waves of dizziness and disorientation crashed through his brain.

But his brain was his best and truest weapon, even fuzzy. He didn't think he could move. He was delirious, probably had an infection and ripped stitches, but his wound was manageable and their lives depended on getting out of the sun and to the safety of that village three miles away.

Would he make it because he was a cocky son of a bitch? Hell, yeah. But would he make it because he intended to survive and he intended for Piper to survive? Hell, yeah, times two! His edicts were simple. Protect the weak. Defend the innocent. Stand up to tyranny and unjust behavior.

It didn't hurt that he was attracted to her on a huge freaking scale. The only drawback, and it was a big one, she was Tyler's big sister.

That sucked big-time.

She helped him to stand and he liked that she kept her hands on him, mostly out of concern that he would fall on his ass again.

"Can you make it, Dex? It's so far away."

"I can and will make it. We're in this together and there is no failing." His brain, even feverish, latched on to three things: *shade, water, shelter.* That's what it took to survive in the desert.

"I'm glad you're so sure about this."

"I am, sweetheart." He reached for the head scarf

that was currently around his neck and with slow, pain-ful movements wrapped it expertly around his head, making sure the back was flopping over his neck. "It will take some work, but everything worthwhile does. Staying alive is the goal."

She looked up at him and what he saw bolstered him. He smiled. "Those are warrior eyes, Senator. Are you thinking about rushing that hill?"

"You're not in any shape exactly for rushing, but a good, solid shuffle sounds great to me." This was de-livered with a wry tone and a wicked sidelong glance. "I'm thinking about getting you where we need to go."

He chuckled. The woman had backbone and humor in a dire situation. Two weapons that would work for them. He thought immediately of DJ and his chest tight-ened. He could almost hear the man's voice.

Yeah, I know what you're thinking, LT. I'll cut you some slack for the fever. But get your head out of your pants. Shade, water, shelter. Then, if you're lucky, sex.

"I think our first priority would be to find shelter and then proceed at night, but we don't have that luxury. We have assholes after us who want to kill us. Thank God we have enough water."

He laughed again. She was a riot. She helped him over to a rock and lowered him down. Pulling the pack off her back, she pulled out three water bottles and handed him two. "Drink all of that."

"Yes, ma'am."

She unscrewed the cap off hers, brought the bottle to her lips and chugged the whole thing. He got caught up in watching her.

"Drink, Dex," she prodded, taking one of the bottles and opening it. He could smell the water, groaning at the sudden damp feel of it on his lips and tongue, craving the hydration for his overheated body. He didn't need any prodding to down the second one.

She shouldered the pack again and reached for the burka. She settled it over her head and turned to look at him. "I'm not going to let you die because I held you back. I'm never the weakest link. That's a promise."

She bent down enough to get her shoulder under the arm of his uninjured side and helped him to his feet. "Well, I'll hold you to that campaign promise, ma'am. If I fall, do whatever you need to do to get me up. I also don't want to hold us back."

"That's good, Dex. Because I really need you." She nodded. "I'll owe you dinner when we get back to the States," she said. With a set look on her face she took the first step and he stumbled, his mind still reeling. She was there, steadying him.

He loved that she was already projecting into the future. This was a woman after his own warrior heart. Think ahead. Strategize. She was a gem. "Deal. I know this great place in DC."

"All right. Less jawing and more walking," she said.

He chuckled, then gasped as fire laced his side. It wasn't that she wasn't scared. That was evident. But courage could easily be described as doing what needed to be done in the face of that fear.

"Keep talking to me," he said. "That will help me to focus."

"How long have you been a navy SEAL?"

"I think I was born in combat gear."

"That must have been hell on your mom."

He laughed, lost his thread of the conversation as he was suddenly in a field of dead men, everywhere. He shook his head to clear his vision and Piper looked up at him.

"What's wrong?"

"Are there dead bodies here?" he mumbled, swinging his head around, the faces of the dead grotesque.

"What?" She looked around and said, "No, just brush, rocks and dirt." Her voice was hushed.

"Damn, I must be hallucinating. Don't let me go running off if I lose it."

"Don't lose it, Dex. I'm only cracking jokes because I'm scared as hell."

He closed his eyes, trying to clear his mind. Focus. "Keep talking."

"Why do you say you were born in combat gear?"

"I come from a long line of military heroes. My dad is an admiral who served as a SEAL, working out of the Pentagon, and I have two retired uncles that also served as SEALs. War is in my blood." She was so close to him, supporting his body, and he turned his head. His eyes focused on her mouth and even in the midst of running for their lives, the heat, the danger, the need for speed, he wanted to kiss her.

Yeah, his brain had checked out.

Except the thought kept rattling around. *I want to kiss her lips. Drop on her like a battalion of marines and hold her down and kiss her.*

"Right, and I already know about your sniper brother, Rock. He was the black sheep of the family, huh?" She looked up at him, her eyes behind the mesh hard to read, but he caught the glimpse of amber. He didn't have to see her to know the delicate bone structure of her face.

"Yeah, he chose the marines over the Navy. He's a pain in the butt. But I wouldn't trade him for anyone." He tried not to let the horrific landscape of dead men distract him, but he closed his eyes, trying to think around his dancing brain. *Kiss me.*

His eyes popped open and he tried to clear his head. Had he said that out loud? He studied her for a moment and realized that it had all been in his hot, horny head. "What about you? Ty hasn't really talked much about his family."

"Well, if war is in your blood, politics are in mine. I was born into a political family."

"Right, that's why we call Ty 'Kennedy.' Your family on that level?"

"Yes, my father, uncle and husband were all senators. My uncle, William Keighley, works for the assistant secretary of state for Diplomatic Security. He was former CIA, but he'd never admit to that. You already know my brother Edward is a DS special agent."

"I'm surprised Edward didn't come to Afghanistan instead of you. He's a badass, I hear. A bit of a rogue who has to be reined in from time to time."

"He has less flexibility than I do, and all that's true."

Dex squinted his eyes. Was that a…a snowstorm in the middle of the Afghan desert in July? He shivered, getting colder. Sweat was running down his face, down his body, and it was all he could do to keep from keeling over.

"He's…unconventional and overprotective, often circumvents protocol while he's negotiating domestically and globally, and he's so damn shrewd." She tightened her hold on him, feeling his shivering, no doubt.

"A regular smarty pants."

The bodies were starting to pile around his feet. Every time he took a step, he'd trip over one and that would jar his side, sending more pain lashing at him. He gritted his teeth. In the distance he could see the tan, sandblasted walls of the village of Safid Darreh. Afsana and rest were there.

How could he be so cold? Now the bodies were covered in snow and frozen. It was like trying to walk through boulders.

"Through my uncle, Edward's the one who pulled the strings to get me here."

He stumbled badly, but Piper caught him and held on to him. "You should have stayed in DC," he growled.

"But you couldn't have saved me in DC," she said, stopping as Dex drooped, his legs buckling.

"Dex!"

He fell to his knees. Damn, he couldn't remember ever hurting like this. That wasn't so good, but the blood…yeah, the blood was a problem. He'd lost too much. The quick patch he'd done was soaked through. He hadn't dared stop long enough to really bind himself up, not with unknown armed men on their asses. He wanted to get up, but there were just so many bodies in his way.

"Get up. If I have to haul your ass the rest of the way, this could get ugly. You'd have to explain to your buddies why you got carried by a girl."

He went to all fours, and even as he felt as if he was being swallowed whole, still shivering, aching like a son of a bitch, he burst into laughter.

Breathing hard, his brain ping-ponging around in his head, he turned to look at her.

She looked like a commando, even through the mesh.

"That's the best you got? Trash talk."

"It's not trash talk if I say I carried you. Who's to say I didn't? You're delirious and there are no witnesses… I see a book out of this, and with my political clout I'm sure I could get six figures. I can see the title now. *How a Girl Saved a Navy SEAL*—you do the math."

That made him laugh again. "I bet you're dynamite on the Hill, lady."

"Can I sweet talk with the best of them? Damn straight I can. Now on your feet, sailor, before I start to babble in terror. I might be a senator, but I'm leaving no man behind."

"Give me a minute," he rasped between groaning in pain and laughter. He was going to have to dig deep here. Deeper than he'd ever gone, deeper than that exhausting hell week during training. The week that had prepared him for this. He was past empty, past the fumes. He was running on sheer mental energy and guts. And he *still* wanted to kiss her, even more now.

"Let me at least put another bandage on your wound."

"We can't spare the time," he said, not sure he wouldn't pass out, and unlike the snow and the dead bodies, that was real. As real as dying here. If that happened, Piper might survive, but her odds were better with him than without him. And just for the record, he wasn't ready to check out anytime soon. He was directing this shindig. Putting distance between them and their pursuers actually put them in charge of distance and with that came the next rule of combat. Their pursuers were reacting to them and their choices. Everything in Dex wanted to go on the offense, take these mothers down, but he wasn't in any shape to do that, so it was lay low, heal up, fight another day.

Another one of his edicts: stand tall in the face of adversity.

He stood only with her help, but it cost him some more energy and the fever addling his brain made it difficult to think, to reason. "If I pass out, the name of the woman you're looking for is Afsana Jamal. Her house is located in the courtyard beyond the side gate where we're headed."

"We can trust her?"

"With our lives. We're halfway there," he said. "You're doing great." That was a lie. She looked shell-shocked. He could imagine what was running through her mind, and none of it was good.

She held his gaze, and right before his eyes he watched her pull herself together. She nodded and with a monumental effort, a lot of grunting and pain, he got to his feet. Piper was right there to support him every agonizing step of the way. They started off again, the village now in view and closer with each step. As they approached the wall, the bodies were getting waist-high in his vision and dragging at his energy, and finally when they reached the closed side door, he felt his edges get a little blurry and start to turn black. Bodies began to pile up on him and even though he fought he couldn't push them all off. He tried to remember to keep breathing…and forgot as the suffocating darkness engulfed him.

When Dex went down, he pulled her with him and she landed on the hard earth.

"Dex?" she whispered in his ear.

No movement.

She shook him.

Still nothing.

"Oh, God," she huffed out.

She rolled him off her and put two fingers to his carotid artery on his neck. For a split second, she didn't feel anything, then the steady beat of his heart.

Her breath rushed out of her. She'd been holding it and she deflated like a balloon. The relief was so intense tears clouded her eyes, but that was as far as they got. She didn't have time for losing her cool. She rose and looked around. There was absolutely no one to help them. She would have to leave him here and go on alone. *Afsana Jamal.*

That was all she had to go by. Through the door, into the courtyard—her house was supposed to be just beyond the gate. She took a breath and reached for the door handle, her hand shaking.

Turning the knob, which squeaked loud in the still of the late afternoon, she pushed it open a crack and scanned the immediate area, her eyes darting, her body vibrating with tension. Other than a few goats milling around, she saw no movement. Again there was no one there. She could hear normal village sounds coming from beyond Afsana's proposed house. She took one more look at Dex. His closed eyes, his dark lashes thick against his skin, pale beneath the tan. She'd supported him because she had to.

She wasn't supposed to note the thick muscles of his back or the height of him, the sexy way his voice rasped, the stubble on his cheeks. Her heart did a little spin; her body seemed so alive around him. They'd connected so fast, so deeply, it scared her. In life and death, there was only the moment as it ticked by. She felt every roll of sweat, every beat of her heart.

Even when he was unconscious and helpless, he still felt dangerous to her heart.

She couldn't let him die.

Sweat pooled at the base of her spine, at her temples, running down her cheeks. God, she hated this damn burka. The clamminess of her skin reeked of fear.

This was all about being on the run, and the fact that he *had* risked everything for her. She could do no less.

She might have talked a good game, but she was right on the verge of hysteria. Taking several deep cleansing breaths, she cautiously approached the house, hoping to God she got the right place.

She knocked lightly and heard footsteps from within the house. The door slowly opened to reveal…a man.

Bagram Airfield,
Parwan Province, Afghanistan

A black stealth chopper with Outcast stenciled on the side touched down without so much as a peep onto the pitted and ragged runway of Bagram. Raoul Markam, solidly built, with broad shoulders and an elegant, aristocratic face, formerly Senator Piper Jones's DS agent, walked up to Carl Kruger, CEO of Outcast, a joint South African–British private security company registered in the British Virgin Islands.

Carl was thin and ascetic, his clothes all black, his eyes ice blue. It was suddenly winter in July. "What the hell happened here? All this carnage to kill one unarmed woman and blow up a SEAL?" His thick British accent got thicker when he was angry.

"Two SEALs."

"What?" The one word cracked between them like a gunshot.

"That unarmed woman was saved by a wounded SEAL." Raoul handed him the medical file. "Lieutenant Dexter Kaczewski." Carl scowled down at the service photo. "I'm going to need some more men. We've already cleared this area and taken care of the insurgents. But Jones and this SEAL disappeared."

"Unbelievable! You said this was a cakewalk!" The shadowy man in the US who had hired them through

Markam couldn't be pleased, either. He hated screw-ups and he really hated wild cards like Kaczewski. Carl had built his company up from nothing after he'd gotten out of the military. A year after his birth, there was a shift in apartheid, but a man of mixed birth didn't fit into either world. With that stigma, he was going to make everything he did all about him. The more money and power he accumulated, the more he could punch his own ticket. Now all that was being jeopardized by Kaczewski.

"It *was* a cakewalk! Tyler Keighley was flown out ahead of schedule to Landstuhl. I heard they nabbed a body from the SEAL ambush. That's not good."

"I'll spin that and anyone who investigates that Mr. Carter left my service and went rogue. There's going to be backlash and they'll probably have boots on the ground within twenty-four hours. I'll search from the air. You need to find that damn woman and whoever is helping her and put them down. Understood?"

"Yes, got it."

"And Raoul…you screw up this time and I'll freaking kill you myself."

Headquarters, Naval Criminal Investigative Service, San Diego, California

NCIS special agent Austin Beck said, "Lavender," and tossed the Nerf basketball toward the small hoop attached by suction cups to the wall. It missed, went wide and Austin cursed softly, then chuckled as it hit fellow special agent Derrick Gunn in the head.

Derrick grunted from his desk and threw a sidelong glance at Special Agent Amber Dalton, rolling his eyes. "Boring, surfer boy."

She laughed and eyed the two men. "You guys are no help at all."

"What do we know about colors for a wedding? Derrick's color blind."

"I am not," he said, snatching up the ball. He threw the spongy orange orb back at Austin, who caught it, exploded from his desk chair and did a layup, as if these points would be the win for the last few seconds of a crucial NBA game.

"Score and game!" he said, walking around with his hands in the air. "The surfer boy is all about the pastels."

Amber's brows rose. "Pastels. Wow, good color vocab, Gunn."

"Yeah, he'll make someone a good little wife one day." Amber's eyes shot daggers and Derrick just shot that death stare at him. "Okay, I'm getting serious," Austin said when he saw Amber's long-suffering look. "How about a creamy yellow the same color as warm butter?" He stuck out his chin and spoke with an upper-crust British accent. "Since it's an evening wedding, it would go with black."

"Not bad actually, Austin."

"What? The color or the accent?"

"Both," Amber said.

"I'm sure your bridesmaids will look smashing in yellow." Supervisory Special Agent in Charge Kai Talbot, Austin's boss, breezed into the room and they all stiffened. "Gunn, Beck. SECNAV is waiting for you upstairs."

SECNAV—better known as the secretary of the navy—only got involved for the big stuff. Austin got excited. Big cases meant he'd get into the thick of it, do what he was trained to do. He was well aware that Derrick thought he was lacking in abilities because he projected a laid-back surfer look, but there wasn't anything laid-back about him when it came to carrying out his duty as an NCIS agent. They looked at her blankly for a moment. "Go."

"You putting us in, coach?"

She grabbed a file off her desk and started for the stairs, giving Austin an indulgent but stern look. Okay, so something big was definitely up. He dashed after her, with Derrick bringing up the rear, shooting Amber a sorry-you're-not-included look of sympathy.

As they entered the ready room, SECNAV Stewart Olsen was at his desk. When Kai, Derrick and Austin walked in and stood before the big screen, he got right to the point.

"There's been an incident at Bagram Airfield in Afghanistan. Senator Piper Jones is missing. She went to Bagram to see her brother Tyler Keighley, a navy SEAL who was just in an ambush not more than eighteen hours ago. He's safe at Landstuhl. Another US Navy SEAL, Lieutenant Dexter Kaczewski, is also missing." Austin recognized that name. He thought immediately of Amber. Her husband-to-be, Tristan, was in business with a Russell Kaczewski. Could these guys be related? He refocused on the SECNAV. "He was leading that team and he lost three men. After the dust settled, one of the dead men was identified as a member of a security force—" he looked down "—Outcast, a joint British and South African outfit out of the Virgin Islands, run by Carl Kruger. The dead mercenary's name is Martin Carter and is so far our best clue there was something off with the SEALs' op. Start there."

"Sir, you think the SEALs were lured there?"

"They were extracting three marines who were all killed execution-style, then we have the senator's missing security agent. After talking to the surviving SEALs, they all felt the op was compromised. Said it was as if the insurgents were waiting for them. The brass wants answers. That was a top-secret op."

This just got real. Three of his brothers had been executed to lure a SEAL team into an ambush. Yeah, this surfer boy was locked and loaded.

"I'm sending you both in. Agent Gunn, your expertise is invaluable, and Agent Beck, you're a pit bull when it comes to sussing out information. Find them and get me any information you can on this ambush. If there's a leak, I want to know about it."

"Sir, why aren't we liaising with State?"

"Because, Agent Beck, her detail may be involved."

Holy crap!

"We're inserting you into Kabul until the base is secured and an investigation can get under way. Track down Kruger and interview him. I'm sending you all that we've gathered on him and his company so far. Bring Senator Jones and Lieutenant Kaczewski home."

Chapter 5

Piper stood frozen to the spot. This wasn't a woman, and now she had no idea what she was supposed to do. If she made a mistake here, they would both be dead.

The man waited and when she didn't speak, he said something unintelligible. She started to back up when the man peered at her face, then his eyes widened and his voice got agitated. Before Piper could back up, he grabbed her arm.

She fought him, her breathing ragged, adrenaline kicking her system into overdrive. She was so exhausted when she'd knocked; now it felt like she was infused with jet fuel.

"You are safe, American," a soft voice said, and someone touched her arm. "Enough, Raffi. She is terrified."

Breathing around her hysteria, she backed against the wall, her heart hammering. "We mean you no harm," the man, Raffi, said.

"Dexter," she managed, breathing hard. "Please help him."

The woman's eyes widened and she shot forward. "Dexter! Where is he?"

"Outside the gate. He's wounded. Please."

"Raffi, come. You stay."

Ripping off the burka, Piper sank down to the floor and leaned her head back, her breathing quieting.

Moments later, Raffi came back with Dex slung across his shoulders, just as the sound of a helicopter flew overhead. Could that be their enemies? Did they have that kind of sophisticated equipment at their disposal?

The woman snatched up Piper's burka and hustled her behind them into a small room. She ran and closed the shutters as Raffi carefully set Dex down.

He was so quiet and still, the blood bright against his clothes, and her stomach protested. She wanted to go to him, but the woman drew her aside.

"What has happened? Who are you?"

She glanced at Dex, but he was still out. He trusted this woman enough to bring her here. He'd saved her life and now she had to put her trust in him.

"My name is Piper Jones. I was visiting my brother, a SEAL at Bagram. One of my own security people tried to kill me. Dexter saved my life."

"Jones? Tyler Keighley? Kennedy?"

"Yes, that's my brother."

"Yes, he spoke of you. We are honored to have you in our home. Come with me. I am Afsana Jamal. Raffi is my husband." She had long, black hair that was plaited into a braid down her back. Her eyes were a crystal blue, a striking contrast to her dark hair. Her cheekbones were high and her lips full and pouty. Afsana was gorgeous.

"Dexter."

"My husband will tend to him."

She brought Piper to another room with a basin of water. "Please wash up, and you may use anything in my closet." She reached under the small basin that was placed on a table and, as she passed, took Piper's wrist, setting soap in her palm, then closed it. "We are here to help you. Please, be at ease."

"Thank you so much."

Piper made quick work of stripping down to her soaked and soggy underwear, dropping everything into the corner. She scrubbed herself with the tepid water and only wished it was cold. Getting out of that heavy and hot burka was heaven.

After looking and finding underthings, but no bra, she went without it. She donned a simple cotton blue dress, drying her hair with a towel beside the basin.

She went back through the house until she came to the sleeping area where Dexter was laid out. As she came in the door, she gasped. They had taken off his shirt and exposed his raw, torn and bleeding flesh. As they cleaned the wound, Piper could see it was red and swollen.

Afsana, her beautiful eyes concerned, came over. "He is very bad. His stitches have torn and will need to be mended. I'm also afraid he has the fever. He must receive antibiotic. Soon."

"Do you have any?"

Her face went grave and she glanced at her husband, whose lips thinned. He was distraught, to say the least.

"We are sworn to an ages-old Pashtun tradition known as Pashtunwali. We will help and protect anyone in need, friend or enemy."

"We're not your enemy."

"This we know. Dexter is our friend and that is a true fact."

"How can I get him antibiotic?"

"This is very distressing. My cousin, who is not sympathetic to Americans, is due to arrive at any moment. If we are not present, it would be very bad. It would be dishonoring to him. Therefore, to protect Dexter, we must stay here. My husband can go with my cousin to get the crop to market and I will conceal Dexter."

"What are you saying?"

"You must do this for him."

"Oh, God. But how?"

"There is a town not three miles from here."

"Charikar."

"Yes, that is it. There is a woman, Dr. Blessing Contee, who runs a World Health Organization clinic. She knows Dexter and will help. She will come here and tend to him. But you must make the trip."

Piper's knees went watery and she groped for a chair to sit down. She stared at Dexter, who was now tossing and turning, totally lost in the fever. His handsome face was taut with pain. If he didn't get the medical attention he needed, in his weakened state... "I'll go." Groaning, she said, "More of the burka. Sorry, but I know it's your custom. I don't know how you handle wearing it."

She smiled and said, "I'm not overly fond of it myself, but we can't dress you as a woman. They usually travel in groups and a woman alone would be suspect."

"Then what...?"

"One moment." Afsana disappeared for a few minutes and came back with...men's clothes.

"You want me to dress like a man?"

"Yes, but keep the head scarf wrapped around your hair and most of your face. This is very risky, but a lone man will not cause much alarm. These belong to my son." She took Piper's wrist and dropped two metal pieces in her hand. "I took these off the ruined clothes Dexter was wearing."

Piper looked down at the lieutenant bars. Back in Afsana's room she put on the clothes—a pair of loose-fitting cotton pants, a long overtunic, a dark vest and leather sandals. She pinned the bars inside the fabric and just the thought of having them there bolstered her.

Afsana handed her a bottle of water from their stash and what looked like small dumplings. "Walk straight out of the village. Do not talk to anyone. If someone talks to you, touch your throat and then your mouth and shake your head to indicate you are mute. Most people will leave you alone. Be very careful on the road. There are still some rebel convoys. They shouldn't bother you. Once you get to the city, do not take a cab. I will draw you a map and you should be able to navigate. It usually is crowded and you shouldn't be noticed. Never look anyone in the eye. It's very difficult to see from a distance and most people will not get that close to you. You should be safe."

"Could I have a moment alone with him, please?"

"Of course. Raffi, come."

They left the room and Piper went to kneel beside Dex. His handsome face was ashen, but he groaned and his eyes fluttered open. For a moment he looked up at her. "Beautiful angel," he said softly.

"I wish I was an angel and I could come up with a miracle."

"You're safe with me," he said. "I'm a SEAL. We don't wish for miracles, we make them."

"Then that would make you the beautiful angel."

He smiled in his delirium. "I've thought about nothing but kissing you. Okay, maybe I did think about surviving and killing anything that threatened you, but kissing was definitely in the top three."

She should have been shocked by that, but she wasn't. Everything in her world was topsy-turvy and she was losing her perspective. They had supported each other and were in survival mode. Somehow DC and Brad seemed so far away.

"So kissing was up there with killing and protecting?" Before she even realized what she was going to do, she touched the side of his face, thrilling at the rough stubble on his cheek. Ah, the way *this* man felt beneath her fingers, it was like she was coming out of some kind of delirium herself. The minute their gazes met, something inside her collapsed. His eyes were so blue, so deep with concern, and she tried to be practical and cool, but she realized that she might not make it back here, and if she didn't, that would mean she was dead. Because nothing short of death was going to stop her.

His face softened, his full lips parting, but even as a wave of pain shuddered through him, he didn't take his eyes off her. The thought of not kissing him ever was too much for her. Her attraction to him might have been adrenaline-induced, but this felt…real.

He reached up, his hand tangling in her hair. He closed his eyes, drawing her down, the rush of sensation so intense she had to grit her teeth against it. He tightened his hold on her; her heart was hammering, her breath constricted. He pressed her face against his in such a tender move that she clutched his head, her hands curling around his scalp. She made a low, desperate sound and twisted her head, his mouth suddenly hot and urgent against hers. The bolt of pure, raw sensation knocked the wind out of her.

She widened her mouth against his, feeding on the desperation that poured back and forth between them. She made a soft sound and clutched at him.

"I'll be back," she whispered against his lips.

She rose away from him, and in his confusion, he said, "Back? Where are you going? Don't you do something stupid, Piper." The warning in his voice was filled with anger, but it wasn't directed at her.

"Everything is okay," she said in a soothing voice. "Afsana?" she called, and they both came back into the room.

Every muscle in her body protested moving, and her nerve endings felt as if they were stripped raw, but she tried to ignore the feelings pounding through her. She had no idea what she was doing or what he'd done to her.

"Piper," he said weakly. "Don't you dare…" He trailed off, rolling to his good side and pushing up, gritting and gasping in pain. She ran back over and supported him against her, his glassy eyes pleading. "I can get up. We have to keep moving."

"No. You can't. Stop being a macho idiot. I've got this covered."

He writhed in pain, his head rolling. "The bodies… stop pulling…stop dropping… I can't breathe…" He passed out again. There wasn't anything he could say that would stop her. She gently laid him down.

They walked to the door and Afsana wrapped the head scarf tightly, pulling the material up over Piper's face, tucking the ends in securely. "Good luck, Piper. I'm sorry I couldn't go with you."

"No, I understand and we can't wait. I'm sure it will be fine, but if I don't come back…"

"You will, but we will take care of him. I promise."

The door closed behind her and she found herself on

a dirt road, where several children were playing and an old man was working an outside kiln. Some shopkeepers had small carts and were selling food, the aroma hitting her hard.

She started walking, not looking right or left. Walking briskly, already feeling the effects of the heat, no one paid her any heed except for a wave from the guy with the kiln. She waved back and kept moving. She reached back as she walked for a bottle of water and the food Afsana had packed. Slipping her hands to her mouth, she ate and drank as she hit the outskirts of town. Her stomach tightened, but she kept walking, rounding a bend in the road, and the trees crowded closer, forming a scrubby wall on the side of the road as it dipped to a small, narrow bridge with plank decking. She crossed the bridge and followed the curve, soon hitting the paved road that stretched out into the distance, mountain ranges up ahead. After thirty minutes, she couldn't see the town anymore.

Suddenly there was a rumble from behind her and she bowed her head and kept walking. She heard someone speak in the Pashto language, but she kept walking. She stopped when the voice got insistent.

Turning her body so she could see better, she froze. Her heart stalled, then dropped in a sickening rush. There was a convoy of soldiers alongside her.

There was a man who was motioning out of the side window of the lead truck, the back full of men carrying guns and what looked like grenade launchers. She stared at him, a wild, tense flutter taking off in her middle. She had no idea what he was saying; her brain froze.

Gripping her hands together, she tucked them into the wide sleeves to hide her light skin and to help stop the trembling, she swallowed hard, her mouth dry, fighting against the knot of fear in her gut.

She bowed her head, touching her throat and then her mouth. The man yammered at her again and pointed to the back of the truck. She felt as if every ounce of warmth had drained out of her, leaving her cold and clammy, while he stared at her, looking angry and grim. She would bluff her way through this... Dex's life hung in the balance. She had to get that antibiotic.

Feeling completely unsure, she took a breath, trying to remain outwardly calm, her heart pounding even harder.

She finally got it, a shock of realization through the paralysis. He wanted her to catch a ride with them into the city. She shook her head, bowing and moving off. He said something else and then the convoy started moving again.

She kept walking, her breathing erratic and her heart hammering inside her chest. The ache in her throat so intense that she was afraid she was going to cry. Putting one foot in front of the other, she kept heading toward town. She watched as the trucks kept moving, and finally relief washed through her.

Consciously resisting the pull of old memories, Piper watched the changing sky, listening to the rustle of the leaves and the stirrings in the bushes.

That kiss had really rocked her, her attraction to Dex overwhelming even with her grief over the loss of her husband. With guilt heavy on her, she had to admit she hadn't felt like this, ever. That also shook her quite a bit. Brad had been the love of her life, but with Dex...it was different. Hotter, more intense, totally consuming. But it had been eighteen months since Brad had died and her world had collapsed. Losing their unborn child and the complications, making it unlikely she would ever carry another, were also devastating losses.

Even if she could get past all that, Dex was a SEAL, a man who lived his life in constant danger, gone on deployment most of the year. She wasn't sure she wanted that in her life. When she committed, it was 100 percent. She was the kind of woman who worked closely with her man, stuck by him when times got tough, even though the political trail was an exhausting one. She'd been fearless back then, before the accident. But loss had a way of changing someone and the pain of losing somebody she loved again would be too hard.

She tried not to think anymore, downing the last of the water just as two men appeared, each riding a small donkey and leading two camels laden with what looked like wheat cropped at the bottom of the stalk and tied onto the tall beasts. She could almost believe she was in Utah, the landscape was so familiar, but seeing the camels drove home to her that she wasn't in the United States and she was far from safe.

The memories of Brad dredged up her longing for a family of her own—a solid, close-knit one. Brad had been like Dex—fearless, strong, his principles and convictions driving him. Such a good man.

Well, this wasn't doing her any good, thinking about Brad and guilt and Dexter's very hot, very real kiss. She closed her eyes briefly, battling with the lingering feel of his lips against hers. She was trying to deny she was thinking about Dex, wanting more with him, using fear and adrenaline as excuses, but deep down she knew neither of those biological reactions had anything to do with the very feminine reaction she'd had to that gorgeous mouth. Tears stung her eyes as she recognized that maybe she was ready to take that step.

Her gut twisted with her real need to get beyond feeling disloyal. Brad would want her to move on. Wouldn't he? But that uneasy feeling persisted as the city materialized in front of her in the haze of the heat. Her heart did a little spin, remembering the way his lips had tasted, the deep, melting blue of his eyes and the immediate response she had of craving more. They had connected so fast, so deeply, it scared her. More than being alone with nothing. She was used to nothing.

She had to concentrate on getting out of this mess and saving the SEAL who had saved her, not spinning fantasies that would easily dissolve in the harsh reality of running from unknown assailants who wanted her dead for God knew what reason.

She breathed a sigh of relief when she saw the convoy drive off the road and head into the distance in a cloud of dust. They were bypassing Charikar. That was a good thing.

She noticed with a start that there were two armed guards, part of the Parwan security forces, manning the entrance into the city. People were moving easily around a cylinder, a long, green-and-white striped pole similar to a parking garage barrier gate. The gate stretched across a turquoise blue-and-white stylized arch as it was lifted for entrance and lowered to stop vehicles for searches. She lifted her chin, relaxing her muscles to look more natural. She didn't want to draw any attention. The two guards at the gate were busy searching a vehicle and she sauntered through without any problems. Once inside the bustling city, she pulled the map out of her pocket and studied it.

The WHO office was downtown and that was still a trek. With a city of ninety-six thousand people, it was as crowded as many places in the States, only the cars were older and rougher-sounding. People moved briskly along and Piper didn't slow, but waded into the crowd. She was jostled and had to sidestep often.

Taking a left, according to the map, put her in a residential section with the same sandy-colored houses that she'd seen in the village, only a little less worn. She found fewer people here, but continued her pace.

Turning right this time, she went down a long street and came out to a main thoroughfare. She'd reached the center of town. As she traversed deeper into downtown, Charikar hummed with commerce. She encountered more and more people. Passing the bazaar that was marked on her map, she breathed a sigh of relief.

She was almost there. Feeling the effects of too much adrenaline, dehydration, shock and terror, she reached the clinic's doors and pushed through them. She stumbled down the corridor and came out into a waiting area.

There was a woman behind the counter and she looked up, her dark skin glistening with sweat. She said something in Pashto, but Piper couldn't catch her breath, she was so hot.

Piper swayed, feeling dizzy. For a moment, she couldn't speak, then she rasped, "Help me."

The woman's eyes widened and she rushed around the desk as Piper started to fall. She caught her and bodily dragged her to a chair, pulling off the *keffiyeh*. Her eyes widened when she saw her blond hair.

"You are American?" the woman said.

Piper nodded. "Water, please," Piper rasped.

Just then two Afghan soldiers walked in and Piper stiffened. It wouldn't do for anyone to know she was an American and draw attention. Piper switched to French and said, "Please help me."

Immediately the woman responded. "Of course. Tell

me what is wrong." Piper relaxed as they lost interest in her.

The woman called to the back in rapid French and a dark-haired man emerged and started to speak to the soldiers. He nodded and went to the back. When he came out he handed them something and they left.

"What are you doing here? This is no place for an American woman alone."

"I'm here for Lieutenant Dexter Kaczewski. He's wounded and has a bad fever."

The woman's face went from professionally detached to concerned, then she yelled, "Pierre!"

The dark-haired man came rushing out and spoke more of the rapid French as he went into the back and brought a bottle of water. Piper drank.

"Are you Dr. Contee?"

"Yes, but please call me Blessing," she said with a thick French accent. "Anyone who is a friend of that fine man is a friend to me. This is my husband, Pierre. Let's get you cooled off."

"There's no time. Dex."

"All right, then." She turned to her husband, a large, imposing man. "Keep giving her water." She walked over to two white cabinets and opened the door to the first one. "What happened to him?"

Between sips of water, Piper explained everything from his RPG wounding all the way to when he collapsed at Afsana's.

"He was bleeding?"

"Yes, a lot."

"Still when you left?"

"Yes. When he got into that fight with the insurgent, I think that guy pulled his stitches. Really, it's only been a day…"

Her voice hitched, but Pierre set his hand on her shoulder and squeezed and it helped. She looked up into his kind brown eyes. He smiled. "You have done well to get here, little one. The heart of a lion, yes, wife?"

"I would say that's true." Blessing smiled at her husband.

"A day since he was injured. He was amazing and he saved my life."

"Ah, there's no doubt that is true. He is a warrior and a protector. But he is in good hands. Afsana and her husband are very liberal, but must hide it, I'm afraid. They are good people. Dex is safe with them." After grabbing several ampules, syringes, gloves, gauze, antiseptic and bandages, she stuffed everything into a black bag.

"I must go with this woman to help Dexter. You stay here and I will come back as soon as I can." She cupped his face and kissed him on both cheeks, then the mouth. *"Sois prudent, mon amour."*

He nodded and repeated it as if it was their ritual. *Stay safe, my love.* How sweet. She immediately thought of Dex, and although he wasn't her love, she got a little discombobulated thinking about that kiss, as if the sentiments were the same.

They exited the clinic through the back door to an alley, where a tan Jeep was parked. Piper was so thankful that she didn't have to walk any more in this heat and they were going to get back to Dex swiftly.

Blessing slipped into the driver's seat and started up the car. Putting it in gear, she edged out of the narrow driveway into the street as people passed by. No one paid them much attention. When she reached the gate, she spoke fluently to the guard, who, after a cursory search, let them pass.

They were flying along when Blessing said, "What are you doing in Afghanistan?"

Piper explained the situation and Blessing's brows rose. "A US senator attacked by her own people. Sounds like there is trouble for you at home. This is why you haven't contacted the authorities?"

"Yes, Dex insisted we couldn't take the chance."

"Then I would heed his warning. He is the best judge."

It wasn't long before they were entering the small village, and even though some people glanced in their direction, no one came over. Piper had already recovered her head with the *keffiyeh* and they knocked.

Afsana answered the door all smiles. "Come in. You are welcome." As soon as the door closed, she embraced Piper, then Blessing. "Thank you for coming. I knew you were going to be okay."

"How is he?" Blessing asked before Piper could answer, a lump in her throat.

Piper spied two small boys, one about eight and the other not more than six. They eyed her shyly, the little one smiling at her.

"This is Israr and Emad, my sons."

"They're beautiful," Piper said. Especially the oldest one with his dark shock of hair and gorgeous blue eyes.

"Raffi is going to take them to my cousin's for a visit."

Just then her husband came out with the boys' traveling cases, greeted her and hustled them out of the house.

They all made their way to the small sleeping chamber. Dex was shirtless with a white bandage from just below his left armpit to his waist, bathed in sweat, and Blessing knelt down next to him. She rolled up her sleeves. "Afsana, *s'il vous plaît*, hot water, and keep it coming."

Piper swayed; the relief was almost overwhelming. Afsana steadied her and she clasped the woman's hand. "He is going to be fine. I have seen him worse. He is a fighter."

Piper nodded and went to kneel beside his head. She took up the cloth, still in a basin of water, and started to smooth it across his forehead. He turned his head toward her and his eyes fluttered open. "Ah, the angel is back."

"Hello, Dex. I got you a doctor."

He sighed and his gaze flicked toward the WHO worker. "Hello, Blessing."

"I see you've gotten yourself into another pickle, handsome."

"Yeah, just a flesh wound," he said.

Blessing rolled up her sleeves, chuckling as she donned the gloves. "SEALs like to understate things, I think." When she removed the bandages, he groaned and rolled his head; her eyes went grave. "Yes, indeed." She glanced at Piper and said, "I'll need your help."

Chapter 6

Piper couldn't seem to keep her hands off him. It wasn't just the fact that he was in pain. She needed to touch him. Could it be because, even in this state, he made her feel so safe? Was it reassurance?

Shaking two pills into her palm, Blessing grabbed a water bottle and handed it to Piper. "Get him to swallow these."

Donning a pair of rubber gloves, Blessing pulled out a vial and a syringe.

He turned his face away. "I'm allergic to…"

"Morphine. I remember. Those pills are a pain reliever and a fever reducer."

He took the pills and dry swallowed them, following up with a sip of water.

"Dex, I would really like to stop meeting like this," she said, starting to work on the wounds with the needle, applying anesthetic.

"I have to agree. But you're good for my health."

She flashed a wide, white smile, pulling a small pair of scissors and tweezers out of her bag, swabbing both his wounds and her instruments thoroughly and eliciting a quick indrawn breath from him. "I don't want sewing you up to become a habit." She started to cut the stitches and pull the threads, along with any stray pieces of stitching caught in his skin or the ragged wound, shaking her head. "Someone did a number on him. I've never seen stitches pulled out of the skin like this," she said.

Feeling a little queasy at the sight of his torn and ripped flesh, Piper said, "The man who tried to kill me stomped on his wound on purpose, but it only slowed Dex down."

"I hope he kicked the bastard's ass."

"I did, and then Piper plugged him right through the heart," he said, and he sounded proud of her. She looked down into his pain-filled, glazed eyes.

"Then he shot him again. Twice."

He closed his eyes, his hand grasping for hers in blind agony, crying out, the sound cutting through her. She threaded her fingers through his as he squeezed, his jaw flexing under her hand. "Insurance," he said raggedly, the word slurred.

"That still hurts, huh?"

A small, pain-filled laugh huffed out of him. "Your bedside manner needs work, Doc."

Blessing stopped what she was doing and picked up another syringe and injected more anesthetic until Dex seemed to relax some. Then she went back to work.

His eyes were so dark, so deep, falling into them would be way too easy. But avoiding his eyes only centered hers on the long, lean line of his body, the heavy, glistening muscles and the tantalizing hair that started at his navel and dipped under that precarious sheet. Blessing seemed immune to the glorious view, but Piper hadn't seen a man like this…since Brad…okay, never. Brad never looked like this…this warrior. Her throat immediately ached. This seemed like a betrayal, that she was lusting after all those hard-packed muscles.

"It's a wonder he made it this far. Some of these wounds are deep."

"They were ambushed, from what I could gather. My brother Ty was also involved. He's more gravely wounded, but is receiving care at Landstuhl."

"That is a very fine facility. I'm sure he's in good hands."

The only sound in the room was Dex's labored breathing. He had his eyes squeezed tight, but as Blessing got to the end of the wound, she sat up to relieve the strain on her back by stretching.

She irrigated the wound again, then threaded a curved needle. Dex's head lolled and his breathing was heavy and even, his hand now loosely clasped with hers. She touched his face. It felt as if his skin wasn't as hot.

"It's easy to care about him, *oui*?"

"Yes. He's pretty dynamic."

"And stubborn and brave, and downright annoying." She chuckled as she made neat, small stitches. "And—" she sighed "—quite handsome. If it wasn't for my Pierre…"

Piper instantly got a pang of jealousy. There was no denying that Blessing was lovely and Dex had affection for her, but Piper was quite suddenly glad she did have her Pierre.

She really had no claim on the man. She'd just met him only a day ago. It was shocking to her how much had changed in just hours. Someone tried to kill her in a way that would make it look like she'd been a victim of insurgents in a freak hospital takeover in Afghanistan. Nothing but a lead in a news story. Instead, Dex had saved her. She reached for the cloth in the basin and smoothed it over his forehead, cheeks and neck.

"I see there is no ring on your finger. You aren't married?"

"No. I was. He died in a car accident eighteen months ago."

"Ah, I am sorry for your loss, Piper. That must have been very difficult."

"It was. Brad was a very good man. It's his seat that I took over to help fulfill some of the promises he made his constituents."

"Bah, politics. I am not a fan."

Piper smiled and said, "A necessary evil."

"No children for you and your Brad?"

"No, I lost my unborn child in the same accident."

Blessing eyes softened in sympathy. "You have known heartache."

"What about you? Children?"

"No, not yet. I think that Pierre and I will plan to have children, but not in this war-torn country. Perhaps once I have left this post and we settle somewhere more stable and safe."

"How do you know Dex?" Piper asked.

"When the conflict was intense here, it was very difficult to keep medical supplies stocked and available. I was handling a lot of casualties—my little clinic was overrun." She wiped away some blood with a gauze pad. "When we lost a large shipment of medical supplies, Dex and his team went after them, got them back and, with them, my husband. They had taken him to administer to some gravely wounded guerrillas. I will always be grateful for Dex stepping up and trying to make a difference in these people's lives. That's the thing with him. He never judges anyone, not by race or religion. He treats everyone on an even level. It's not to say he isn't vigilant and very competent, for the record, but he's just got a way about him that a lot of people respond to. He seems to know what to say and doesn't hesitate to do what is right."

Piper set the cloth in the basin and reached for another gauze pad, blotting the sweat from Blessing's brow. Blessing said, "I would do anything for him. Even keep my mouth shut about a US senator hiding out in a small Afghan village and sewing him up in a place that isn't as sanitary as my clinic."

Piper returned that bright, flashing smile. "I appreciate that."

"What are you going to do?"

"We're going to try to get back to the States."

"I believe I could help you with that. I want Dex to rest at least three days. Then I will come back and take you both to Kabul. You should be able to charter a plane home."

"Yes, we have a company on retainer, so that will be a piece of cake. Thank you very much. That would be such a big help."

Blessing finished up his stitches and swabbed his wounds with more antiseptic. She packed up her bag and rose. "I want him to rest for three days solid. That will give him time to heal and to recover from the fever. Not enough time, but it will have to do for now. Here are his antibiotics and more pain meds." She put the bottles and a package of syringes in her hands, explaining the dosage of each. "Make sure that he takes plenty of water and broth. Afsana makes excellent broth. Oh, and the antibiotic needs to be injected into his butt."

Afsana nodded from the doorway, carrying a plate of food and a bowl.

Piper's face heated at the instruction, but she would have to follow the doctor's orders to the letter. She wanted Dex well and able to travel. The faster they got out of here, the safer they would be. The only threat would be from the unknown, not people in a hostile country interested in kidnapping or killing Americans, especially a high-ranking official and a navy SEAL.

"If his fever doesn't lift or he gets worse, come and get me in Charikar and I will come back, but I don't expect that will happen. He really belongs in a hospital, but such is the life of a navy SEAL. You also, eat and get some rest. Becoming exhausted will not serve either you or Dex. *Êtes-vous d'accord?*"

"Agreed," Piper said as Blessing embraced her.

"You are a very brave and strong woman," Blessing said.

"Thank you," Piper said with a soft smile.

Piper folded down next to Dex as Afsana placed a plate in her hands and some broth for Dex. She left to walk Blessing out. A few minutes later, she heard her Jeep start up. Piper sent her hands through her hair and pulled off the neck wrap and vest. She shook Dex slightly and his eyes opened slowly.

"Time for more medication and some broth."

"I missed Blessing? Damn."

Piper smiled at him. "You actually had a conversation with her. You were out of it. She just left, but she's coming back in three days."

"We need to get moving."

"No. We're safe here, Dex, and you need to recover. We're not going anywhere for three days."

"What?"

"Doctor's orders."

He sighed. "Looks like I'm outnumbered."

"How are you feeling?"

"Like hell."

"Hungry?"

"A little."

She settled close to him and picked up the bowl and spoon, then realized he couldn't eat prone. She set everything down and moved around him. "Let me get behind you so that I can feed you."

"You don't think I'm capable of feeding myself." He sounded completely exhausted, his words still slurring together, but they had a lilt to them as if he enjoyed challenging her.

She raised a brow. "Are you?"

"No."

"Then be quiet." She slipped her hands under his shoulders, splaying her legs and scooting her butt forward until his torso was cradled in her lap, the back of his head resting just below her chin.

"Yes, ma'am," he said softly. His hair was soft alongside her neck; the weight of him seemed so right against her, and a weird, protective sensation rolled over her, clutching her heart. She was powerless to stop these feelings even as the guilt churned within her. There wasn't a man she met since she'd lost Brad who was able to get past these barriers. But in one short day, Dex had stripped away a defense system that had been in place since she'd woken up alone and empty in a hospital bed in DC.

Everything tingled, as if her body had been asleep and was now waking up, the pins and needles a reminder that blood flowed through her veins.

He made her feel so alive.

She picked up the broth and brought the spoon to his mouth. Clearly agitated, but still a bit out of it, he didn't respond. "Don't make me do the choo-choo train noises," she threatened.

"I'm not five," he said, the muscle in his jaw twitching.

She gave him a narrow, chastising look. "Then don't act like it." She nudged him and he opened up so she could pop in the spoon. Dex was the kind of man who was used to being in charge, and it obviously rankled him that he couldn't even feed himself.

His little hum of satisfaction went through her like a knife, the vibration from his chest through his back only making her more aware of him.

"See. It's good."

He tilted his head to look up at her. "It's damn good." He studied her face and said, "How are you doing?"

She barely knew with all that had happened in the past twenty-four hours. That fact that she was running for her life with a navy SEAL who was making her feel more than she had in months, the fear and danger they were in, not to mention that she'd killed a man, it was all so overwhelming.

"I've had better days. I really don't know how you do all this."

"It's my office," he said, accepting and swallowing another bite. "I would go stark raving mad having to yammer at people all day and not have them heed a single thing I said."

"You like giving out orders and having them followed."

"War is easy, Piper. There are enemies and you kill them while trying to stay alive. It doesn't hurt that I'm in charge of a bunch of great knuckleheads." His eyes glinting, he shook his head, watching her with those piercing blue eyes. "In politics, you never know who will be stabbing you in the back. Five minutes with

a double-talker and one of us would be leaving in a
body bag."

The way he said it made her laugh—really laugh.
"I'm guessing it wouldn't be you."

He chuckled. "No. Probably not."

"Not a really good way to get a bill made into a law.
We might have to go over diplomacy and conflict reso-
lutions that have nothing to do with 'move your shapely
ass' or the business end of a handgun."

He grinned at her, meeting her gaze directly, and they
exchanged a long, silent look—a shared joke, a compan-
ionable closeness, a kind of unspoken honesty.

"You have a gift of negotiation," he said.

"Gift?"

"Yes, the most dangerous or useless gift is one that
isn't earned. You've earned yours. It took guts to do
something that would remind you every day of what
you lost. Fight for something that your husband passionately believed in and was dedicated to doing with
his life. It's admirable."

Feeling unexpectedly close to tears, she whispered,
"I couldn't do anything else."

"You're actively pursuing your passion. Wildly committed to doing this because your husband can't. I call
that an unbreakable spirit. Most of what I do is ninety-
nine-point-nine percent mental. I only use my physical-
ity to carry out what my mind dictates. Getting through
combat is all mental—failing and getting up, again,
all mental. Everything I do comes from up here." He
tapped his temple. "It's the engine that runs me. I regret that what I've chosen to do with my life has taken
a toll on the people I loved and who loved me, but not
enough to stick by me when the going got tough. I've
had two relationships and lost them both. So, being a

SEAL is my passion, something I'm wildly committed to and what I tell myself every day is worthwhile. It makes me unbreakable."

His words touched something inside her that no one had ever touched and made her feel so much closer and intimately attached to him. She was carrying out Brad's wishes, but after she vacated his seat, she had no idea what she really wanted to pursue. She'd been supporting Brad for so long, she'd lost any sight of her own goals. Dex really gave her something to think about. She forced him to finish the broth, even though he grumbled. She could tell he was getting fatigued and the pain was creeping back. She gave him his meds and then came the part she had blushed red at—the antibiotic shot.

"Why are you looking like you have a job to do and it's not going to be your favorite?" he asked, his sleepy blue eyes roving over her face.

"I need to give you a shot of antibiotic."

"O-kay…"

"In the biggest muscle on your body."

"Oh, right." He smirked. "Trouble with the location, Senator?"

"I'd say the second-biggest muscle since your brain is obviously the largest."

He chuckled. "I'm buck-ass naked, lady, so have at it."

He was clearly laughing at her discomfort. Okay, maybe not out loud, but his laugh lines were all crinkled, and there was a wicked, wicked sparkle in his eyes.

She cast him an annoyed and embarrassed look. "It's not funny, Dex."

The glint intensified. "Oh, *butt* it is."

She made an exasperated sound. "Need I remind you that I'm the one with the sharp instrument and I've never stuck a needle in anyone before?" It didn't help that Piper was so aware of Dex; it was as if her body had a million little sensors in it.

He rolled gingerly to his side and she reached out a trembling hand and moved the cotton covering just enough to expose the top of one of his cheeks. The man was a study in thick, ropey muscle as the big muscles of his back tapered down into the smooth definition of his rump. My God, the man was so beautiful.

He looked at her over his shoulder. She met his gaze and her heart rolled over, a strange, fluttery feeling unfolding in her middle. His expression was wry and wickedly teasing. "Piper, are you going to stick me, or are you just staring at my ass?"

Oh, God. She *had* been staring at his fine butt. He pulled the blanket, revealing the full view of his posterior, and her mouth went dry. That knocked her out of her reverie and she stuck in the needle and pushed the plunger.

"Ouch!" he said, and reached down to rub the area, narrowing his eyes.

She raised her chin. "Serves you right for *needling* me." She reached out and flicked up the blanket to cover all that gorgeous muscle.

Then she bit her lip. "Did I really hurt you?"

He laughed softly. "No. A gnat could have done more damage. But you can kiss it and make it better if you want," he breathed.

She sucked in a breath at the thought of putting her lips anywhere on his body.

He carefully transitioned to his back, his eyelids drooping, the medication she'd given him kicking

in. But he met her singed look with something direct
and heavy enough to set off so many alarms in her,
all amusement gone. He watched her with an intent,
steady look, as if he was thinking something wholly
sinful and definitely wild. His voice was quiet and low
when he spoke. "You look tired. You should sleep." His
eyes closed and he took a deep breath and opened them.
"Beside me, Senator. That's an order. Stick close to me."

Piper could handle that kind of concern. Barely. But
she could handle that. Then Dex blew it. As if not even
realizing he was doing it, he reached out and ever so
carefully tucked her hair behind her ear. Then he ran
the backs of his fingers along her jaw. "Close, Piper,"
he said, his voice husky. "Real close."

It was too much. Piper's knees went immediately
weak and her breath jammed up in her chest. It was all
she could do to keep from folding into his arms. And
all those feelings she'd tried to hold at bay came rushing
through her, sending a fountain of need surging up. As
if trapped by his gaze, she stared back at him, unable
to break away—not really wanting to. She was so lost
in his eyes, in the pulse-racing weakness…

He tried to keep his eyes on hers, but the medication proved too strong and he was battling pain and
fever. His blinking got longer and longer until those lids
stayed closed and his breaths became even.

With her lungs seizing up and her heart pounding,
she watched him sleep, things happening inside her that
made her heart pound even harder.

"You haven't even touched your meal," Afsana said,
coming into the room and picking up Dex's bowl. "You
must eat, Piper, to keep up your strength."

"I will," she promised. "How do you know Dex?"

Afsana's dark eyes filled with affection. She glanced

at Dex and crouched down. "My husband wanted a better life for us. Better than the Taliban could give. He didn't like the way I was treated or the pressure they put on me. So, he has been working with the Americans since they came here. Dex was wounded in a battle not far from here, before Bagram was reclaimed and built into that big base it is now. We found him and your brother and helped them. Nursed them back to health and smuggled them to safety. When my husband was accused of being part of the Taliban, a case of mistaken identity, I was so worried and scared. I went to Dex and he got my husband released and back to me. We would do anything for him." She reached out and snagged the plate, setting it into Piper's hands, then she squeezed her arm. "During war, where brutality reigns and justice seems lost, sometimes bonds are forged in turmoil and blood and are some of the strongest ones there are. Because of the unselfish acts of people you don't understand and are so foreign to you, you have a hard time trusting them. Dex proved he was here to help us. He is a man of his word—so very, very brave and always does the right thing. No matter the cost. That's how I know him. Now eat."

Piper picked up her fork as Afsana left the room. From the moment she'd met Dex, she saw something in him that was clearly unbreakable, wild and massively appealing. It was no surprise he'd stepped in for Afsana and Raffi, and she melted inside at his compassion and the way he was always true to himself. Unable to help it, she moved closer to Dex, the chaos inside getting worse. As she took the first bite, she thought this situation was crazy. So insane. She wanted him to touch her all over. She wanted to lie in his arms like she had the right to do so and she wanted to hang on to him and never, ever let go.

Chastising herself for thinking that way, she finished her meal. She lay down next to him, trying to disconnect from the unsatisfied ache lying thick and heavy in her. But she couldn't disconnect, no matter how hard she tried. Feeling shaky and out of control, she moved closer until she could feel his skin inches from her. It was clear that Dex was the kind of man she would seek out. Strong, true, honest and dedicated. But he was also someone who put his life on the line every day he went to work. That was…just too much; hit too close to her fears. There was no future in thinking about him as long term, and the short term was so full of danger. She might not even get out of this alive.

He was so warm, safe and solid. Easing in a deep, uneven breath as his presence physically enveloped her, she planned on taking care of him through the night. Whatever he needed.

Her eyes fixed on his handsome face. The beard stubble added to his dangerous appeal. Her tears flowed, unloaded from all the fear, shock and experiences she'd endured in the past twenty-four hours; some of those tears she cried were because she was afraid she was incapable of letting go, of finding something new, of taking a chance.

She recognized that he could be the man that made her whole again, if she had the courage to let go. But fear was a powerful barrier, and that settled inside her like a beast she had to fight.

He shredded her, too, with the way he looked at her and his character and his beauty.

He was wrong. She didn't have that kind of courage

or fortitude. She'd already been shattered into pieces that she was still picking up.

She wasn't unbreakable.

Chapter 7

Splintered silvery pieces of awareness and a heavy warmth pressed to him filtered through Dex's consciousness. Pain radiated, just enough to be felt. The meds must be wearing off. He was reaching for his weapon even before he was fully awake, but all he could feel was soft, warm skin. *Nice*, he thought, sighing, then drifted a bit until pieces of reality filtered through: the jumble of bedding beneath him, the smooth texture of the cotton against his bare skin, the light that spilled into the room from between the shutters.

He took stock of his situation as the edge of pain pulsated a little harder. The whole side of his body was raw and sore and, from the feel of it, padded with thick bandages. One of the wounds from the shrapnel of the mortar had cut deep, but the others were shallower. It was that deep gash that was causing most of the throbbing pain.

Then his hand ran over his hip. What the hell? He was buck-ass naked, the cotton blanket pushed all the way down to his groin. Who had stripped him? He just couldn't remember anything except the hallucinated bodies pulling him under. Then bits and pieces…warm lips. Responsive warm lips. Had he kissed her? *Ah, you freaking moron.* Had he or had that been part of a great, fever-induced dream?

Wait a second. More memories flooded his brain. Had she really been here and had she stuck him with a needle…*needled*? Oh, damn, Piper had given him a shot in his butt and he'd said something wholly inappropriate, or had he dreamed all of this?

Nope, he didn't think he had when the memories came back to him.

Damn, that had freakin' hurt, and even trying not to react, the low groan was something he couldn't stop. He'd been out of it for most of the day. How had Blessing gotten here? He tried to search his memory banks, but nothing registered.

He remembered, groaning again, when Blessing had stuck him with a needle and soft hands had cradled his head. He'd moved his legs restlessly. It had stung like hell, but then blessed relief. Must have been the pain meds he'd taken and then the numbing from the anesthetic she'd no doubt injected him with as a lethargy had mercifully spread over him and his mind swam.

Something had happened to him, but that was blurry, too.

"Will he be okay?" Piper's soft, husky voice had asked, filled with concern and worry. He liked that she cared about him. But then, why wouldn't she? He'd saved her life. Tyler's sister. Right, Ty. He hoped he was doing okay. Her hand had smoothed across his forehead again and threaded through his hair. He couldn't think straight. He was floating, the pain now dull, and he was so damn tired.

His eyes popped open then and he completely lost

his train of thought as he realized Piper was there, her face close, her nose almost touching him. She was the weight he'd felt when he woke up, and sweet Jesus, she was snuggled up to his uninjured side, her fragrant body draped over his chest and her cotton-clad leg running the length of his. Her arm resting on his pecs, elbow bent, she had her hand on his face as if she'd fallen asleep checking for fever.

Wow, how long had it been since he'd woken up to a woman he'd known for more than a half an hour? One who obviously cared? Seemed like a long time, maybe a year. Between his deployments and his reluctance to do the bar scene now, female companionship had mostly consisted of his mom and acquaintances, both personal and job related.

But nothing had changed about his reaction to waking up. Morning wood was typical. Even wounded, he knew what he wanted. With her so close to him, stimulating him, it jumped and he wanted to groan at the throbbing ache that started at the base and moved up.

His body hungered and stirred up a sexual restlessness in him. He closed his eyes, wanting her. Wanting to drag her across his body, have her straddle his hips as he slipped inside all that slick heat.

The pleasant feelings were suddenly dominated by a feeling of enormous responsibility. He wasn't going to let anything detract from getting her to safety, not even his dumb-ass urges.

And there was his brother Rock's voice in his head. *You don't do a brother's sister or think about his woman.*

Ah, damn, Tyler was his best friend, and here he was having luscious thoughts about his sister. *Get tough, man, buck up.* Yeah, that was part of the problem. He was *up.*

She was limp, draped over him like an exhausted kitten, her delectable mouth partly open, smudges below the thick, blond lashes. The complete package was so exquisite it broke his heart.

She was taking care of him, the big, bad SEAL—yeah, that felt good.

Incredibly good.

Except, right now he didn't feel big or bad, just humbled by the courage of this five-foot-four woman wrapped around him.

Taking care of him wasn't all she'd done. It didn't take too much brain power to see that, because his was fried right now as he realized that she'd gone after Doc Blessing.

Goddammit!

All the way to Charikar on her own and, judging by the way she was dressed, she'd done it disguised as a man.

Son of a bitch!

His estimation of her went up a whole freaking notch, maybe two. That took some major guts and he was pissed that he couldn't have minimized the need for that, but his wound was infected. He was feeling more lucid, but the vestiges of the fever took their toll. He knew that much and regardless of whether he liked it or not, the mission was necessary.

But knowing that didn't stop his gut from clenching, thinking about the danger she had been in.

She mumbled something unintelligible, burrowing even deeper into him. Damn, this was not only a nice way to wake up, but he could so easily get used to this.

No, you moron. She's not for you. This was about danger, adrenaline and fear. It wasn't conducive to forging any kind of romantic or soft feelings, for that matter. He had to get healed up. Stay tough and move her out of here. Three days, his ass.

He groaned softly. Had she injected him or had that been Blessing? Had he actually told her to kiss it and make it better?

He felt her stir and waited. There it was. She stiffened, but didn't move, and he couldn't help feeling good about that. She liked where she was…maybe? She opened her eyes and he didn't even blink. "Good morning, sunshine."

She met his gaze and blinked, then held him transfixed, the rising sun making the flecks in her amber eyes look like pure gold. "You still feel warm, but I think your fever broke," she murmured, moving her hand on his face, down to his neck. He had to clamp his teeth together, forcing a breath out of him, a new rush of heat sizzling through him.

She was wrong. He wasn't warm, he was hot.

"I think I have you to thank for that." He'd already kissed her once. He was sure of that, that he'd kissed a US senator while his brain was swamped with fever, and he couldn't even use the excuse that it was the illness. It only allowed him to follow through on something he'd wanted to do since he'd laid eyes on her.

Startled, Piper looked up at him.

"You went all the way there to get her, didn't you?" For the first time in his life, Dex was breathless. The anticipation of kissing her riddled his blood like a burning fuse on its way to detonation, along with anger that was just as explosive.

"You're pissed."

"By yourself. You went alone."

"I knew you'd be upset."

"Lady, you haven't seen me upset," he growled.

"I have caused you nothing but problems," she murmured. "It was the least I could do for all that you've risked for me." He never wanted to give her one single reason to think what he had done for her was against his will. He would do it all again in a heartbeat.

He meant to open his mouth and tell her, but she already knew. He saw the knowledge mirrored in the deep, tawny depths of her eyes that pulled at him like a vortex. She twisted him the hell up, and his anger only got worse; it was because, for the first time in his life, he felt bone-deep fear that ate him up. Hell, he was a commanding officer, and he'd just been promoted to full lieutenant. He led men into battle, engaged the enemy in hand-to-hand combat, killed without an ounce of remorse, and this woman, this freaking brave-heart woman, was breaking him down. He meant to talk, but instead he hauled her up against him.

"You are a freaking piece of work." He pressed his forehead to hers, trying to overcome his emotions, his system overloading, his pulse heavy, his heart laboring against it. She stared at him, her eyes wide, with a sheen that made him want to put his fist through a wall.

"I was so scared." Her voice was softer, huskier, more seductive. Seductive because she wasn't telling him that she was afraid for herself. She'd gone into danger for him and his heart felt suddenly too big for his chest. Closing his eyes, he swallowed hard and tightened his hold, the rigidly suppressed feelings boiling up inside him. Getting close to her was the worst mistake he'd ever made.

His throat tight and his eyes burning, he took a pain-filled breath, his own voice low and rough when he said, "If something had happened to you…"

His mouth brushed hers and she made a wholly feminine yet utterly involuntary and soft sound.

"I wasn't going to let you die or suffer needlessly," she whispered against his lips.

He made a raw, aching sound and grasped her jaw, covering her mouth in a wet, deep, blistering kiss. Gathering her against him, working his mouth hungrily over hers, Dex couldn't breathe, couldn't think. She made another helpless sound against his mouth and he tightened his arm around her and dragged his lips away, his breath labored.

"This isn't a good idea. There's too much fever and my mind is screwed up with these drugs. I'm crazy pissed at you, but dammit, you're one ballsy woman."

It took everything he had to let her go, but they were in a house full of people and he was jacked up in more ways than one. Dex didn't do well when his head wasn't screwed on right. His judgment was definitely skewed right now. Shot to damn hell.

She brushed at her cheeks and the sight of that tore him up inside, but he was suddenly exhausted, the pain in his side breaking through. He felt like raw hamburger meat.

His throat tight and his jaw clenched, he took the tablets she handed out and made no comments when she shot him in the butt with antibiotic. Then Afsana was there with more broth, and he gritted his teeth between sips until he refused to take any more.

Guilt punched him hard. He was the navy SEAL. He was supposed to protect her. Probably sensing the tension between them, eyeing both Dex and Piper, Afsana left.

He closed his eyes and stewed and fumed, but with the meds and the fever he was still fighting, he fell asleep.

When he woke up, Afsana was there with his broth and water. She raised a brow. "How are you feeling?"

He shifted and growled, his voice sleep-roughened. "Where's Piper? Out saving the freaking world?"

"No. That's your job," she said wryly. "She's outside milking our goats and weeding our garden."

His grunted, and amusement at Piper milking a goat almost overrode his grumpiness.

"I think you're being unfair and you're angrier at yourself than you are at her."

"I'm hungry," he said to try to get her to stop talking about Piper. He had one more thing to be mad about. He'd stepped over the buddy line, big-time. He felt the reprimand from his brother more than seven thousand miles away. How could he have forgotten that Piper was Ty's sister? *Yeah, right, you were thinking with the wrong head.*

He'd put his heart on the line two times before when he'd thought the woman in his arms was his match, but he'd been disappointed twice. How could he trust that Piper wouldn't get sick of him being gone, sick of his deployments and the danger, and leave him? He didn't think he could handle that again.

Experiencing an acid rush in his belly, he shifted his arm and stared at the ceiling, his head fuzzy, feeling disconnected and hating it. He wasn't going to get sucked into old crap—not now when he needed every brain cell to get them out of this.

Before he realized it, he was waking up again and it was dark in the room. He shifted and swore softly as pain rushed at him. A soft light flooded the room and then Piper's gentle hand took his wrist and put the tablets in them. She handed him a bottle of water. He closed his fist over the pain meds and her mouth tightened.

Aware he was heading back onto dangerous ground, he made himself disconnect from those thoughts.

He somehow had to get them both out of this without doing any more damage. Taking a minute to get a grip, he didn't say anything.

"I can get Afsana…"

"No," he said, his voice gravelly. He caught her wrist and stopped her. Feeling burned, he immediately let her go. "Don't. I need to talk to you and I want to be lucid when I do."

She went still, then her eyes widened, and there was an instant when he saw incomprehension on her face. Then he saw the flash of uncertainty, of apprehension, and it hit him that she wasn't sure what kind of reception to expect from him.

Despite all the reservations he had, despite knowing this had been one big mistake as far as he was concerned, he couldn't let her think this was meaningless. If nothing else, she had saved his life, and he owed her for that. Experiencing a sharp, clenching pain in his chest, he said, "I'm sorry. It was a knee-jerk reaction to you being in danger. I wasn't really pissed at you. I was more pissed because I couldn't handle the situation. Typical alpha behavior."

"I'd say," she responded, and seemed to relax some. "I'm sure a navy SEAL hates it when he's not in control."

"Bingo. But that's not all."

"No? What more is there?"

"Ty is my best friend, and I don't want to jeopardize my friendship with him by romancing his sister, especially in the kind of situation we're in."

She huffed out a laugh. "Yeah, this isn't the most romantic setting."

There was another long pause before Dex released a heavy sigh and spoke. "I don't want you to think I'm not taking this seriously. I am. There is attraction here, I can't deny that. I think you're beautiful, strong and competent. We should keep our eyes on the ball. Getting back to DC and figuring out who's threatening you needs to be our priority."

Her face was so open and vulnerable his heart pulsed hard. "I have my own reservations, Dex. I know that it's not a betrayal because my husband is dead, but I'm just not ready for anything like this. I can't handle it."

Her honesty made his heart roll over and his chest clog up. Feeling as if he might turn inside out at any minute, he hadn't expected this attraction; that, he was honest about. "I think you can handle anything," he said huskily, feeling like a first-class bastard. Inhaling heavily, he said, "But we'll figure this out together. Deal?"

She nodded and met his gaze with so much gratitude in her eyes it nearly broke his heart. "I'd rather work with you than have you pissed at me. It's not a good look on you."

"I thought I explained that. I wasn't pissed at you."

"Felt that way, but I get it. I understand."

"Let's move on. We can agree on that?"

"Yes. We can."

"*Hoo-rah*, that's something. Now why don't you tell me who could be behind the attempt on your life? Who would go to these lengths to try to kill you?"

"I can't imagine I'm that important enough to send a hit squad after me."

"Are you sure there's nothing that comes to mind? Anything, even if it's small."

"Other than my terrible car accident, I am trying to get a bill passed. It could be damaging to corporations… Wait, I had a break-in after Brad died. A window was broken."

"Was anything missing?"

"No, not that I could find?"

"You have opposition on this bill?"

"Yes, Senator Robert Mullins from New York and he's been pushing me, then threatening me, not to go through with the legislation. It's the only business I have to complete for Brad. My term ends in three months. It takes a lot of effort to get a bill through the Senate and then through Congress, especially one like this, but I'm close to victory."

"New York, huh?" Dex rubbed his hand over his stubble. "That means Wall Street. Could he be simply protecting his constituents, or does he have a shady deal going?"

"I have no clue. I don't really know that much about him and his business or his dealings. Really, like I said, I'm a lame-duck senator with no pull. I think most people just feel sorry for me because I lost Brad and my baby."

"He's going to the top of our list. We need to figure out how to get back to DC."

"I think I have a plan for that."

"Okay, shoot." He was starting to feel uncomfortable, but resisted taking the meds until they were finished talking about these important issues.

"I still have my purse and all my IDs, including my credit cards and passport. Blessing is going to be here tomorrow to take us to Kabul and I can charter us a jet home. You have Agent Hatch's ID, but you shouldn't need it. All my personnel have already been cleared. It should be just a matter of getting on the plane and flying back."

"That will work."

"Don't you think you should contact your commanding officer at least? Let him know you're safe and you're helping me?"

Afsana came into the room carrying two dishes, interrupting them. "Let's try some solid food, Dex, if you think you're up to it."

He realized he was starving and took the plate. She was serving them *mantu*—dumplings filled with onion and lamb—steamed and topped with a tomato-based sauce, and *qoroot*, a dip that was a mixture of yogurt, garlic and split chickpeas. It smelled heavenly. He forked up a dumpling and savored the bite, rolling his eyes. "Delicious, Afsana. You are an excellent cook."

"I agree. Could I get the recipe for these and for the kebab you made the other day and that…qor?"

"Qorma Lawand?"

"Yes, that's it. It was to die for, Dex."

"I've had it. Onion-based with yogurt, turmeric and cilantro and chicken."

"I'll let you get back to your discussion. I'll be back for the plates. I'm so glad to see you looking better than when you arrived, Dexter."

"Thank you for your hospitality again, Afsana. You and Raffi are our saviors."

"It is our pleasure. Raffi wouldn't even be here if it wasn't for you, Dex. He and I must go to our cousin's tonight like we planned, for the celebration of the birth of his second child, so we will say our goodbyes before we leave. I am so glad that you are both all right. If there is any way you could get word to us that you are safe in DC, we would be so grateful. Enjoy."

Dexter picked up on the thread of the conversation. "No. I'm not risking a call to my commanding officer."

"You don't trust him?"

"It's better to keep him and anyone out of the loop

until we're sure you're safe. That means finding out who's behind this. Do you know anything about Agent Hatch?"

"No. I don't even know his first name. Hatch and Markam were assigned to me by DS and took me to the airport. I was told they had military training and could better protect me in Afghanistan. I didn't think anything of it. I've always trusted the DS."

"Why wouldn't you? They're sworn to take a bullet for you, not to put one in you."

"This is all so distressing. Edward must be going out of his mind with worry."

"Speaking of that. Do you trust him? He knew you were going to Afghanistan."

"Edward? Why would he want me dead?"

"Any family fortune issues, disagreements over property…anything like that?"

"No, nothing. We all got a fair share of the estate. Edward inherited the house, but I didn't want it and neither did Ty. He was more interested in becoming a SEAL and really didn't want the responsibility. It's a big mansion and it's drafty and costs a fortune to up-keep. I already have the home I bought with Brad, so no interest in that."

"All right, so we eliminate Edward, and we have Senator Mullins and your potentially damaging legislation. Babe, people have killed for less."

"It's hard to believe that he would jeopardize his standing that way and the fact that he's making a bid on the White House. He actually had the nerve to ask me for an introduction to one of Brad's hugest campaign contributors, Stephen Montgomery."

"Montgomery? Not the billion-dollar tech mogul, CEO of the Montgomery Group?"

"That's him. I know he's famous, but I've known him since I was a child. He's an old family friend."

"You do run in some rich circles."

"Oh, Dex. I am rich, filthy rich. Brad had a fortune he left to me. I have more money than I know what to do with. Someday I'm going to figure out how I can use it to help people."

This woman had a way of blindsiding him. She rattled off that she was rich and no way would he have ever guessed from the way she handled herself that she was a blue blood. But it was clear from the way Ty had described his family that they were wealthy.

"So, Blessing said she'd be back tomorrow. We should get some sleep and be ready to travel."

"How is your wound and your fever?" Instead of waiting for him to answer, she pressed her palm against his forehead, displacing his hair, then slid all that softness down his temple over his rough cheek. "Oh, that is much better."

He was doing everything in his power to keep his hands off her and here she was touching him. Unable to move, feeling as if someone had dropped a boulder on his chest, he tipped his head back and swallowed hard. He knew he would relive all these moments with her thousands of times in his mind. If he lived to be a hundred, he would never forget her.

His jaw locked and she stiffened, realizing what she had done. She went to pull away and he grabbed her wrist.

"I know what we agreed. But you are still sleeping right here with me."

Hell, that would cost him. He'd really need those pain pills tonight.

Chapter 8

Austin woke up when the military plane touched down on Kabul's runway. Derrick was already awake, and Austin wondered if the guy ever slept. Normally, Derrick looked like a shrewd, elegant spy, an American 007—the kind of guy you didn't want to piss off. But in combat gear he looked different…dangerous and deadly. For the hundredth time, Austin wondered what Derrick had done before he'd become an agent.

Austin sent his hands through his messy blond locks and stretched. Derrick looked pensive, like he was rolling something over in his head.

"What's going on over there?"

"Follow me on this. According to Kaczewski's brother, Russell—"

"Wait. When did you talk to him?"

"Just now, when you were visiting the back of your eyelids."

"Ah. Continue."

"Russell tells me that Jones's brother Tyler is tight with Dexter."

"Yeah, so."

"So, I figure Senator Jones and the SEAL had to have met at Heathe. Probable?"

"I'd say."

"According to his record, Kaczewski is a Boy Scout. Odds are he headed right for Jones the minute something went down. Hatch was killed dressed as an insurgent. Could be he dressed that way to throw them off and protect the senator?"

"What's the alternative?"

"I don't know at this point, but no one's come forward with any type of ransom or claiming responsibility, yet the SEAL and the senator are gone."

"You think they're still alive? On the run?"

"If that's the case, what are they running from and why haven't they checked in?"

"Good question."

"If you were a wounded navy SEAL and your best friend's sister was in danger, what would you do?"

"Take out anyone threatening her, haul ass and lay low. Try to find out who's trying to kill her."

"Exactly. Markam is in the wind."

"That's my guess. No body. He could be with them. Let's get settled and get your computer up and running and do a little digging. We find Markam, we get answers."

Hours later, Austin was propped on the hotel room bed and Derrick was on the other one, both busily clicking on their computers. Austin had been digging up information on Markam since they hit the hotel room. "These guys are clean as a whistle. Who assigned them to Jones?" Austin growled.

"I talked to the duty guy. He said Jones's brother Edward made the request," Derrick said.

"I talked to Edward and he said he requested his uncle pull strings to get Piper to Afghanistan to see their wounded brother, but doesn't know anything about a request for a special detail for his sister," Austin said.

"It makes sense they would want agents with military background. What branch of the service were they in and what did they do?"

Austin brought up both files. "Markam was a marine, and he was stationed at the International Security Assistance Force headquarters out of Kabul, working as a liaison to…security forces."

"Fancy that. What security forces?"

"Just a general statement in his record."

"How about that security company, Outcast?"

Austin brought up a list of security contractors working with the government during the time Markam was a marine. "It's on the list."

"We have a dead Outcast member involved in that SEAL ambush. That's a connection. I say we go have a word with Outcast."

"Sounds like a plan."

They caught a cab outside the hotel and were soon at the Outcast offices. Once inside the lobby, they stopped at the desk.

"Can I help you?" the receptionist, a brunette with black-rimmed glasses, said.

"Special Agents Beck and Gunn, NCIS. We're looking to talk to Carl Kruger about a marine that might have worked with you guys about six years ago. Name's Raoul Markam."

"Just a moment." She got on the phone and within ten

minutes someone showed up. "Hello, I'm Ted White, here to escort you. I'm the co-owner."

They followed the guy up the elevator and into a hallway filled with offices and people busy working. He took them to a door at the end. Ted opened the door and ushered them inside, closing the door behind them.

A man sat behind the desk with salt-and-pepper hair; cold, wintery blue eyes regarded them. He rose. "Special Agents Beck and Gunn. Welcome to Outcast, gentlemen. Have a seat."

They strode forward and settled in the two chairs in front of the desk. "What can I do for you?"

"We're working a case that involves Raoul Markam." Derrick pulled a picture up on his phone and showed Carl. "Do you know him?"

Carl shook his head. "No, I'm sorry. What's this about?"

"We're not at liberty to say, sir, but we have reason to believe that he may be involved in a kidnapping and murder."

Carl looked surprised and shocked. "How is he tied to Outcast?"

"He was a marine six years ago and worked as liaison to security."

"I see. We worked with a lot of people back when the war was in full swing, but I don't know him."

"How about Timothy Hatch?" Derrick showed him his picture.

"No."

"How about Martin Carter?" Derrick held the phone up with the picture of the dead man.

Carl's lips thinned and he blinked several times. "Yes, I do know him."

"He's employed by you?"

His voice and face were perfectly neutral, but Austin saw his eyes dart. He was lying. "No, not anymore. I terminated him about three weeks ago. I understand he was killed by SEALs during an attack."

"That's correct. A top-secret SEAL mission, as a matter of fact. We would like his employment records." It was clear Derrick was not asking.

Carl nodded. "Of course, I'll get those for you."

With Carter's records on a flash drive, Austin and Derrick left the Outcast offices and hailed a cab.

"What do you think?" Austin asked.

"Just what you think."

"Yeah, the guy's lying. I think he knows Markam."

Derrick tapped his nose. "Exactly, and if he's not involved with him, why did he lie?"

"Bingo. Carter is involved with the SEAL team ambush, which tells me that Tyler Keighley might have been the initial target."

"I think you got that part right," Derrick said.

Austin's phone rang as the cab pulled up. "Beck."

"Austin, Bagram is secure. You and Gunn can catch a helo there now," Kai said.

"Yes, ma'am." Austin told her where they were on the case. She told them to keep digging and to keep her posted. He hung up and told Derrick.

He had a gut feeling that he would have something for his boss very soon. They had pieces and all they had to do was fit them together.

And Austin was very good at puzzles.

Outcast Headquarters, Kabul,
Parwan Province, Afghanistan

Carl picked up the phone, fuming as it rang.

"Hello." Ted had left after the NCIS agents did. He had a mission. "Ted?"

"Yeah, it's me," he growled.

"You with Markam?"

"Yes, Carl. I found him."

"Good. When you find that SEAL and the senator and kill them, dig a hole and bury them deep, and anyone helping them. Make sure those bodies are never found. And, Ted?"

"Yes."

"Make sure Markam's body goes in before you cover them up."

"What about the money?"

"We've gotten half, and this is heating up." His voice was flat. "NCIS has already connected us to Carter and now Markam. If they nab him, he'll rat us out to save his own hide." Carl enjoyed his cushy life way too much and he wanted to protect what he'd built. "His plan is to pretend that he got kidnapped by insurgents and escaped. I don't think the story that insurgents killed the senator and the SEAL will fly now that they've connected him to us. We're cutting our losses."

"Yes, sir. You got it."

Bagram Airfield,
Parwan Province, Afghanistan

Austin and Derrick climbed out of the helo once it set down on the runway at Bagram. Colonel Aazar Aziz, the Afghan commander, met them and turned them over to a guy who escorted them to Heathe. The place was in shambles with bodies laid out on the side and covered with sheets. Hatch's body had been flown out two days ago and was already being autopsied. NCIS tech Lara Comstock was busy analyzing the blood and the ballistics on the bullets that had killed Hatch.

"Special Agent Beck?" a female voice said, and he turned to find a dark-haired woman standing behind him. She reached out her hand. "Hello, I'm Christina Davis, and I was here when the insurgents attacked. I understand you need to talk to me."

"Yes, thank you. Is there somewhere we can go that's private?"

"Sure, the nurses' break room."

Once they were situated, Austin said, "Can you tell me what happened the night you were attacked?"

"I was just coming back from the runway after loading Petty Officer Keighley onto his flight for Landstuhl. The flight was early and I had to hustle to get him there. When I was walking back to Heathe, I saw them overrun the gate."

"What did you do?"

"I tried to make it back to warn people, but I was too late. They were already coming through the front door. I managed to alert most of the nursing staff and we all barricaded ourselves into the supply room."

"Did you see Agents Markam or Hatch?"

"No. I didn't."

"How about Senator Jones and Lieutenant Kaczewski?"

"No. Senator Jones was sleeping in a room just off the front doors. She was waiting for a military transport back to the States. Lieutenant Kaczewski was in the wing over from this one. He was the last of our patients and was flying to Walter Reed in the morning."

"Did Senator Jones and Lieutenant Kaczewski speak?"

"They did more than that. He got out of bed and went to Petty Officer Keighley's room with her help."

"So they had contact?"

"Yes, sir."

Austin smiled. "Thank you for your time, Lieutenant Davis. We're glad you're okay."

"They didn't seem to be interested in us. We were quite safe in the supply room. No one even came near the door."

Austin's phone rang as soon as Christina left. "Beck, it's Lara."

"What do you have for me, O-forensic-goddess?"

She chuckled. "The blood they found on the floor at Bagram. It's Lieutenant Kaczewski's and Agent Hatch's. Looks like they went at it." She paused and he heard tapping. "I also did ballistics on the recovered gun and the bullets that killed Agent Hatch."

"And?"

"The guy was killed with his own gun. One right through the heart. The two bullets in his head don't match anything on record."

"That all you got?"

"Agent Beck, aren't I a goddess?" she said with pique.

"I thought I detected a smug tone to your voice. What is it?"

"I got prints off the grip and the barrel."

"Who do they belong to?"

"That would be two whos."

"Really?"

"Yup. Senator Piper Jones and Lieutenant Dexter Kaczewski."

"No way?"

"Way. But Kaczewski's is only on the barrel of the gun. Senator Piper Jones is the one who pulled the trigger."

After Austin related all this information to Derrick, he got back on his computer and started digging some more. As night transitioned to day, he and Derrick had a chance to look around outside. Just past the main gate and across the road, Derrick found some prints. Some small enough to be those of a woman. He also found dried blood.

"Looks like they hightailed it into the valley."

"What's close to here?"

"Charikar is twelve miles from here, and there's a number of small villages all over this area."

"All right, let me do more research on Lieutenant Kaczewski and see if I can unearth any clues while you start cataloging the villages. We can get an interpreter."

"No need. I speak the language fluently."

"Do you?"

Derrick looked across the expanse of wilderness and Austin knew they were working against the clock. It seemed to him that Senator Jones's protection detail had been compromised and she had not only killed one of the men who was supposed to be protecting her, but she was also supporting a wounded navy SEAL. They were running for their lives. Which begged the question: Who wanted Piper Jones dead enough to go through all these hoops to make it look like an insurgents' attack and why? Also, that SEAL ambush was all about Tyler Keighley. He was the bait to lure her here. Those marines didn't die in battle. They were casualties of a damn conspiracy to take out a US senator. Outcast was most likely involved, but who hired them? How far did this conspiracy go? All the way to the White House?

Safid Darreh,
Parwan Province, Afghanistan

Dex woke, his heart racing, as if something heavy was sitting on his chest. Like the walls were closing in on him. He was glad that Blessing would be here today to get them out. Once in Kabul, they could fly out of Afghanistan and back to DC to get to the bottom of this mess. The sooner he figured out who was trying to kill Piper, the sooner he could get the hell away from his best friend's sister.

It was still dark and he drifted off again, only to jerk out of a sound sleep. His fever was gone, but not the fever of wanting her. His heart was still pounding and his breathing heavy, as if he'd been running with the dream still fresh in his mind. It might have been created from the meds in his system, the wild kiss they shared yesterday and the fact that he was hot for her. But it had seemed so real; his whole body throbbed with a heavy, pulsating ache—one that left him with a hard-on and a fierce emptiness when he woke up.

It was bad enough that Piper infiltrated his waking thoughts, but now she had also infiltrated his dreams. Sweet, sensual dreams, hot, erotic dreams, that left him so shaken, so achy, he was twisted the hell up inside.

Except that last dream, the one he was having before he woke up, had been more intense. More explicit. More real.

Damn, he had to make them stop. But that was hard when she was again snuggled up to him as if she, too, couldn't keep away from him in sleep.

He heard a small sound, like a catch in her breath, and she started to shift against him. He looked down at her. "Piper?" he said.

There was a soft, muffled sound, and his heart jammed up in his chest, then started to pound in a different rhythm. She didn't wake up. Instead, she cried out in her sleep. "Brad! No. No. Please, God. Please. I'll do anything. No!"

She was sobbing now and the sound was of the deepest agony; he realized how much she had loved her husband and she was once again reliving that nightmare. And he knew how real it could all seem.

Dex knew he couldn't let her continue. He shook her hard. "Piper. Wake up!"

She came out of the nightmare sobbing, as if she didn't quite realize she was awake. He rose into a sitting position; his wound was aching, but it was bearable. Bracing himself against the wall, he brought her up with him.

"It's all right, sweetheart," he murmured gruffly. "It was a nightmare."

She resisted for a moment, then relented, her arms sliding around him, drawing a deep, shuddering breath as she cried, her tears running down his chest. "It was so real."

"I know," he whispered. Pressing her head to his shoulder, he gathered her up in a tight embrace and his hand tangled in her hair. Shifting so she was flat against him, he shut his eyes, the rush of tactile sensation so intense that he had to grit his teeth against it. He tightened his hold on her, his heart hammering, his breathing constricted. She moved, sending a shock wave of heat through him, and he clutched her head, the feel of her almost too much to handle.

His fingers snagging in her hair, he tucked his head against hers, forcing himself to remain immobile. Every muscle in his body demanded that he move, and his nerve endings tingled as if they were stripped raw, but he tried to ignore the feelings pounding through him. She had no idea what she was doing to him, but he was all too aware of what was happening.

It took him a while, but he finally got himself under control, and he could finally breathe without it nearly killing him. He adjusted his hold on her, drawing her deeper into his embrace, his lungs constricting. Seeing such a strong, brave woman come apart like this humbled him; there was so much pain inside her that she finally had to get it all out. The thought of her going through something like this a second time made him completely understand all her fears. It sobered him like little else had, and he pressed her head against him, a dozen regrets settling in his chest. If only... If only...

Knowing nothing good could come from going there, he tightened his arms around her and simply held her, the fullness in his chest expanding. She was so torn up. And vulnerable. And he wasn't sure how he was going to get them both out of this without getting in a wreck.

He was so close to the edge that it wouldn't take a whole hell of a lot to push him over. And she felt so good and smelled so good and, damn, he wanted to feel her flush against him.

Unable to control the urge, he pulled her across his lap, turning his face against her neck and clenching his teeth. He hoped she was so far out of it that she wouldn't notice the state he was in.

But she wasn't that far out of it. She went still in his arms, then made a low, desperate sound and twisted her head, her mouth suddenly hot and urgent against his. The bolt of pure, raw sensation knocked the wind right out of him. Dex shuddered, and he widened his mouth against hers, feeding on the desperation that poured back and forth between them. She made another wild sound and clutched at him, the movement welding their bodies together like two halves of a whole, and he nearly lost it right then. But the taste of tears cut through his senses, and he dragged his mouth away from hers, his heart pounding like a locomotive in his chest.

Wrong. God, this was wrong. She was an emotional

wreck and she didn't know what she was doing—she was just reacting, reaching for comfort. And it was dangerous. There was too much going on here, between them, to them, too much need, and it would be too easy—God, so easy—to just let it happen.

Trying to regain some control, he held her with every ounce of strength he had, fighting for every breath. Somehow he had to put the brakes on. Somehow.

Inhaling jaggedly, he pulled her head closer, turning his face against hers. "Easy," he whispered against her hair. "Easy, sweetheart. It's all okay."

An anguished sob was wrenched from her, and she clutched him tighter, as if she were trying to climb right inside him. There was so much desperation in that one small sound, so much fire, it was like a knife in his chest. Her arms locked around him and she choked out his name; then she moved against him, silently pleading with him, pleading with her body—and any connection he had with reason shattered into a thousand pieces.

The feel of her heat against him was too much, and he clenched his jaw, turning his head restlessly against her soft hair. His face contorting from the surge of desire, he caught her around the hips, welding her roughly against him. God, he needed this—the heat of her, the weight of her. Her. He needed her.

Piper made another low sound, then she inhaled raggedly and pulled herself up against his erection, her voice breaking on a low sob of relief. "Dex. Please, I need to feel alive again." She moved against him again, and Dex tightened his hold even more, unable to stop as he involuntarily responded. Body to body, heat to heat, and suddenly there was no turning back.

When he'd woken up, she'd been so close to him, her hand on his face as if in the night she'd needed to check for fever. He was toast. He took a deep breath and got all of her deep into his lungs. She slowly opened her eyes as he exhaled. For long moments she just stared right into his soul. Then he smiled because he saw her soul, and this...*this* was an unbreakable woman. Tears gathered in those goddamn beautiful eyes. Silently they tracked down her cheeks. She cupped his face, her palm traveling over three days' growth of beard, her thumb caressing his cheek, and then she swiped right over his mouth. He closed his eyes to better absorb the sensation. He felt her tremble and he opened his eyes, reaching up to brush away the tears.

"I was so, so scared."

"I know, but you were so damned brave, baby, so brave. You saved my life."

She closed her eyes and buried her face into his neck. Her mouth connected with his skin with an electrifying sensation like nothing he'd ever felt before. He grabbed her chin and dragged her face up, settling his mouth over hers with a soft groan of need.

Shifting her head, he covered her mouth in a hot, deep kiss, and she opened to him, moving against him with an urgent hunger. It was too much and not nearly enough, and Dex hauled her across his lap, grunting at the pain of using his torso muscles under the wounds, but not letting it deter him. With one twisting motion, his hard heat was flush against hers. Grasping her buttocks, he thrust against her again and again, a low groan wrenched from him as she moved with him, riding him, riding the hard, thick ridge jammed against her. But that wasn't enough, either. Dex nearly went ballistic, certain he would explode if he didn't get inside her.

"Piper...babe. I need to get...free."

Making incoherent sounds against his mouth, Piper

twisted free, and a violent shudder coursed through Dex when he felt her hands fumble with the cotton covering him. The instant she touched his hard, throbbing erection, he groaned out her name and let go of her, desperate to rid them both of any barriers.

Somehow he got her pants off and pulled the tunic over her head, but the instant he felt her hand close around him, he lost it completely. Jerking her hand away, he lifted her up against him. On the verge of release, he clenched his eyes shut and thrust into her, unable to hold back one second longer. The feel of her, tight and wet, closing around him drove the air right out of him, the sensation so intense he couldn't move.

"Dex, please," Piper sobbed, and locked her knees against his thighs, her movements urging him on, and Dex crushed her against him, white-hot desire rolling over him. Angling his arm across her back, he drove up into her again and again, the pressure building and building. A low, guttural sound was torn from him, and his release came in a blinding rush that went on and on, so powerful he felt as if he were being turned inside out. He wanted to let it roll over him, to take him under, but he forced himself to keep moving in her, knowing she was on the very edge. She cried out and he clutched at her back, then went rigid in his arms, and she finally convulsed around him, the gripping spasms wringing him dry.

His heart hammering, his breathing so labored he felt almost dizzy, he weakly rested his head against hers, his whole body quivering. He felt as if he had been wrenched in two.

"You pack one hell of a punch, lady," he rasped.

It wasn't until he shifted his hold and tucked his face against hers that he realized her cheek was wet with tears. Hauling in an unstable breath, he turned his head and kissed her on the neck, a feeling of overwhelming protectiveness rising up his chest. There was no way he could let her go. Not yet. God, not yet. He waited a moment for the knot of emotion to ease, then he smoothed his hand up her back.

"Are you all right?"

She nodded once and tightened her arms around him. "You are such a beautiful man," she whispered. "You feel so good inside me. So good." Sharply aware of her full breasts pressed against his chest, he tightened his hold as he twisted and settled her beneath him. With her still straddling him, he drew her head into the curve of his neck and released an unsteady sigh. She tightened her hold on him, and when he settled his weight on her, she shuddered as she took him deeper inside her.

Hit with a rush of emotion, Dex nestled her tighter against him and closed his eyes, slipping his hand up her rib cage over the swell of her breast, thumbing the nipple, needing the feel of her skin against him. He kissed her on the neck as she shivered again and melted around him, and his heart rolled over.

Struggling with guilt and desire, he needed her, feelings he didn't want to acknowledge crowding in on him. She swallowed and swallowed again, and he realized she was struggling with some very raw emotions, as well. His own throat closed up a little. In spite of what they had said, he didn't want her thinking this was just sex. Sex could never be meaningless with her.

"It feels good to be inside you, kissing you. I love kissing you."

Feeling a little raw himself, he grasped her jaw between his fingers and covered her mouth with a soft, searching kiss, trying to give her some comfort. He tightened his hold on her jaw, then kissed her harder.

He trailed his mouth down her throat and covered her nipple, sucking hard, then used his tongue with a slow, lazy thoroughness. Her breath caught again and she moaned softly. She tasted so good, felt so good, better than anything had in his life.

Her fingernails scraped against his abdomen and he let his breath go in a rush, an electrifying weakness radiating through him. She did it again, and he tightened his hold on her breast, biting her nipple, his shaft growing hard inside her again.

"Dex," she breathed. "Don't stop."

Her breathing grew ragged and uneven, and he shifted his hand lower, rubbing her. A sob was wrenched from her, and she clasped his hand, running her palm over the back, urging him on.

He raised his head and captured her mouth again with a thoroughness that made his own heart stammer. This time he was going to make it so good for her that there would be no doubt in her mind what was happening. This time he was going to show her that, in spite of everything that had happened in the past, she was alive. They were alive.

He flexed his hips, and she rose up to meet him, tightening her muscles around him, and his mind was filled with only her. He couldn't ever get enough of her.

Chapter 9

Carl was drifting in his chair when his cell rang. "Yes," he croaked into the receiver.

"I've got something," Ted said.

"What?"

"Kaczewski saved some villager's life and there's a piece in the *Navy Times*. His name is Raffi Jamal."

"What village?"

"Safid Darreh. It's not far from here."

"It's early yet. Get your asses there and find that villager. If the SEAL and senator are there, you know what to do."

"Yes, sir. Consider it done. I'll call you when it's over."

Safid Darreh,
Parwan Province, Afghanistan

Piper's rise out of the soft drift of sleep was a lan-guid affair, a lazy meandering of her mind from one pleasant thought to another, the limp relaxation of her body, the comforting sensation of overall well-being. It had been a long, long time since she'd awakened with a sense of such rightness with the world.

Maybe she would get up and go get a double-chocolate mocha latte. She could get triple whipped cream and work those calories off at the gym later. Yeah, work out…

Her eyes popped open on a flash of sudden and total awareness, every cell coming fully awake, the full extent of her current situation hitting her all at once with startling clarity. It wasn't whipped cream she'd worked off and it wasn't the gym she'd used.

Nope, the equipment belonged to Lieutenant Dexter Kaczewski, navy SEAL. The man who had risked his life for her, had pulled stitches and gotten an infection, dragged his wounded body ten miles in blistering heat and had made blazing love to her, explosive sex right here in a village home in the most dangerous country on the planet.

Unprotected sex—because she'd been lost in her misery and her pain and she hadn't been thinking.

Oh, my God, what had she done?

Thank God she couldn't get pregnant.

Very carefully, holding her breath, she slanted her gaze to the right.

What had she done indeed?

Damn, but that was a boneheaded question. What she'd done was as irrefutable as the six feet and two inches of purely nude, achingly male, gorgeous SEAL lying next to her. So obvious as the heat coming off him and the power that so clearly oozed from his body, as she remembered the feel of the dormant energy in the muscles of his arms as he'd held her.

Easily the most beautiful man she'd ever known. The harsh angles of his face were softened by sleep and the morning's pale light. His hair was thick and silky and the color of midnight. Beard stubble darkened his jaw. He looked like a dangerous and disreputable rogue, so removed from her blue-blood world as to be almost unreal.

The covering, pushed down from their tussling, was bunched at their feet. He was completely naked except for the white bandage, and she…she didn't even have a bandage or any decency to call her own right now.

This had been an unexpected situation almost from the beginning when she'd found him devastated over the loss of his men and comforted him. She'd never felt raw and exposed and vulnerable in any man's presence before, not even her husband; but there was something about Dex that reached deep inside her and twisted.

He was the first man since she was twenty-two and had fallen for Brad to make her feel like this…like a total and utter mess. But, oh, God, he was so good at being who he was and she had to admit that she loved that about him.

His honesty was just as true to his nature as his courage.

But this wasn't a normal situation. They were fighting for their lives with death breathing down their necks. Dex wasn't a normal guy; he was an elite navy SEAL, trained in this battleground that until now she'd only seen from afar and in the safety of her own home. Her brother was a SEAL and she was quite aware of how often he got deployed and how little she saw him.

That just wasn't the kind of life she wanted to handle.

Dex had made her think, though. Think hard.

Maybe it was time she took stock of how she'd been

living and giving up every shred of her personal life to chase Brad's dream, to live in despair of his loss and the loss of their child. If she kept to this path, she would die inside.

Slowly, a painful, unfulfilled and bitter path.

That's why she'd pushed him. She needed to feel alive. Desired. Wanted.

Dex made her feel more alive than she'd ever thought possible.

"You're thinking pretty hard over there."

The sound of his deep, husky voice made her look at him. His eyes were caressing her face with that look that made her knees weak. She had no barrier to those eyes and what he held for her in them.

"I'm sorry," he rasped out, and that was suddenly there, too, in his eyes, his big body turning toward hers, a flinch on his face when he moved.

"No." She covered his mouth with the tips of two fingers. "Please, don't regret this. I don't. I wanted you. I needed you and you didn't let me down, again."

He swallowed and pushed her hair off her face. "You are a piece of work, lady. If it's any consolation, I was blindsided by you, your beauty, and I've wanted you almost from the moment I saw you."

She had to smile at that because he looked so contrite. "I don't need consolation, Dex. Not with you."

He took a deep breath. "This was about us only being able to rely on each other. Adrenaline, attraction…it's the danger, Piper. Right? We just lost control."

He was giving her a way out and she took it, because even though she realized that she'd been hiding and running for the last eighteen months, she still didn't have the courage to let go. Her fear of loss was much too embedded.

"Of course. You're right. But I don't regret it."

"I want you to know I haven't been with anyone for a year and at my last checkup I was clean. I never go commando when it comes to sex and protection of my partner. I don't have any excuse."

"I haven't been with anyone since my husband, and I can't get pregnant, Dex, so it's all right. We don't really need to worry about it or condoms. You're clean. I'm clean, and I can't conceive."

He nodded and let out a breath. "We'd better get going. It wouldn't do for Blessing to find us like this."

"Let me take care of your bandage before we get dressed. Afsana laid out some of Raffi's clothing for you and her son's for me."

"No more burka?"

"No, thank you. I'd rather dress like a man, and the suit I came here in is completely ruined."

"I'm partial to what you're wearing right now, if I'm being honest."

She tipped his chin, bringing his sexy gaze up to hers and his focus off her legs beneath the tunic.

He grinned in a knee-melting, oh-so-sexy male way, his eyes a warm, liquid blue. "Someone is feeling better," she said, removing the bandage and inspecting the cluster of wounds. "They look really good. Barely red at all and healing."

She smoothed antibiotic cream carefully over the injuries, trying to stay detached and focused, but it wasn't easy. "The only easy day was yesterday." Her brother said that enough for her to pick it up.

"Hoo-rah," he murmured as if he was picking up on exactly what she was thinking. "You put a whole new spin on that, lady."

She smiled and rose. "Thanks. I think."

"Oh, it was a compliment," he said, sitting there looking delicious with just the covering across his lap. Now that she knew what he was packing under that wrap, she did wish she was home and in a private, safe place with him.

"Get dressed, Lieutenant."

"Yes, ma'am," he replied in a deep, sexy voice.

She left the room where Dex was recovering and headed to Afsana's room, brought Dex his set of clothes and went back to wash up. Donning the garments on the bed, she made a mental note to figure out how she could repay this family who had risked so much to shelter them and had helped her to save Dex. For that she would be eternally grateful.

As she wrapped the head scarf around her neck, a hand came around her mouth and something hard pressed into her spine. A voice whispered in her ear. "Hello, Senator. You are a resourceful woman."

It was Markam's voice.

Oh, God. She was dead.

Bagram Airfield,
Parwan Province, Afghanistan

Austin was at his computer again, running another search for any information on Lieutenant Kaczewski.

He sent sidelong glances in Derrick's direction. He knew the language. That only added to the mounting evidence in Austin's book that he'd pegged the reserved special agent and colleague correctly. He had been a spook.

CIA.

As in black ops, the deep state, experienced at assassination, blackmail, instigating coups, torture and even brainwashing. Something about Afghanistan was getting under Derrick's skin and it wasn't just the sand. Had something happened to Derrick here, something that had him quitting the company? Sending him to NCIS? Austin was convinced Derrick had been here before. His gut was never wrong.

"You keep looking at me," Derrick said without taking his eyes from his own computer. "You have something on your mind?"

"You know the language."

Derrick sighed. "So? A lot of people know Pashto. What's your point?"

"That's not the only language you've mastered. You know my point. There are other tells, too."

"My sports car with the machine guns in the tailpipes?"

Did that sleek car Derrick drove have...? Damn the man. He sounded completely sincere as usual. "You're always playing your radio at work, and screw it, but you look like the kind of guy who would fit right in."

"You know for a guy who's so good at hacking, I don't see much result, surfer boy," Derrick said.

"Go ahead and try to change the subject by taking potshots at my ego." Austin smiled when Derrick gave him one of his intense looks. But Austin was sure he liked to keep him off balance. It annoyed Derrick that his attempts never seemed to affect Austin. Surfing was all about balance, and Austin paid his dues and then some.

"Why don't you tell me about the marines, especially about that embassy takeover? Weren't you the hero of the day? Saved the ambassador's very pretty wife after three days barricaded with her and fighting for your lives. Didn't they pin a medal on your chest for that?"

"Shut up, Gunn," Austin growled. Damn him. He'd been rummaging around in Austin's record. Maybe he wasn't the only primo hacker here. "How do you know that?"

"You talk in your sleep, Beck."

Austin's phone rang and he answered. "Beck."

"Hey, this is Amber. I've been going through Lieutenant Kaczewski's file and I found a commendation he received for helping out an Afghani man sort out a case of mistaken identity."

"Okay, how is that relevant?"

"He lives in a village about ten miles from Bagram. Safid Darreh. His name is Raffi Jamal."

Austin sat up straighter. "Hey, Gunn, Kaczewski saved some villager by the name of Jamal. He lives about ten klicks from here. Safid Darreh."

"First name?"

"Raffi."

If Austin didn't know Derrick as well as he did, he might have missed the imperceptible tightening of his fellow agent's mouth and the narrowing of his eyes. "Let's check it out." He sounded apprehensive, which was another red flag in Austin's book. Derrick never sounded anxious.

Safid Darreh,
Parwan Province, Afghanistan

Dexter braced himself against the wall, watching as the guy led with the barrel of an M9. As soon as it sufficiently cleared the doorway and was no longer a threat to his body, Dex grabbed it and swung the guy inside. His mind was on subduing this bad guy tango, but he'd compartmentalized the fact that Piper might already be dead.

The tango fought and Dex pushed him against the wall, shoving his arm into the air. A suppressed shot went harmlessly into the ceiling.

The guy struggled, but Dex countered his moves and knocked the weapon out of his grasp, already prepared to use both hands to capture his attacker's hand as he stabbed toward Dex's abdomen with a knife. Deflecting the blade away from his body, he jerked the guy forward and shoved his body into the tango's back, twisting his arm until he heard it snap. The man cried out in agony, then Dex stripped the blade out of his hand and dragged the man's back against his chest, setting the knife against his throat.

Just then Raoul Markam dragged Piper into the doorway across from where Dex restrained the man he'd just fought and now held prisoner with the knife at his throat.

"Kaczewski," Markam said, his voice low and menacing. "Drop the knife and let him go or I'll put a bullet in her head."

"You're going to kill her, anyway, Markam. Believe me, if she dies, I'm going to take you apart and make sure that you die very slowly."

Markam did exactly what Dex hoped he would. Dex watched Markam's eyes and he knew the millisecond he was going to pull the trigger. Dex dropped and with a flick of his wrist released the knife.

The bullet went into the tango's heart, but Dex wasn't watching him as he fell dead in front of him. Markam's head jerked back and he stumbled against the wall, the knife protruding from his eye. He took her with him and, as he slid down the wall, he knocked Piper to her knees. She scrambled away and Dex rushed over.

"Did he hurt you?"

"No." She pushed his arm down and snatched up the gun on the floor at her feet and brought it up, the barrel right along his ear. The gun discharged twice and Dex spun to find another man crumpling to the floor.

Piper sat there for a second, a shocked look on her face, her hand tightening around the weapon. "Not Dex. Not today, buddy," she said fiercely. Then she closed her eyes, snarling through clenched teeth, "I am really getting sick of these guys."

Dex chuckled. "*Hoo-rah*, Senator. Locked and loaded, *ba-by*. I'm going to start calling you Double Tap."

She gave him a grim smile. "Stay here," Dex said. "I guess I don't have to tell you to shoot to kill."

She nodded and Dex moved through the house, the gun at the ready, peeking around doors and into closets. There were no other baddies.

He started back for Piper when the back door squeaked and started to open. Dex waited with his finger on the trigger.

"*Mon Dieu,*" Blessing said, pulling up short and gasping, her hand to her chest. She glanced down the hall where Markam sat. She crossed herself. "Looks like you've had some uninvited guests."

"Piper," he called softly, and she came out from the living area into the kitchen with their backpack. They all headed for the back door.

"My Jeep is parked just outside the gate," Blessing said, hugging them both. "I'd say it's time to leave."

"It damn well is," Dex replied, and preceded both women out the door, checking thoroughly around before he motioned them out. They rushed through the backyard and slipped out the gate. "Sit in the front," he instructed Piper as he climbed into the back.

Blessing jumped into the driver's seat and as soon as she closed the door, she gunned the engine and peeled off.

Piper turned around and wedged herself through the small opening in the seats, then threw herself at Dex. "I don't want to sit in the front. I want to be close to you," she said, her voice firm. She wrapped her arms around his neck and held on as the Jeep wobbled and jostled them against each other until they hit the main paved road.

"There was a man parked at the gate. That's why I went on a circuitous route to get us to the main road. I don't think he saw me."

"Probably another one of Markam's lackeys." He looked behind them and the way was clear. "Looks like we got away clean. Your timing is impeccable, my friend."

"What about the mess we made?" Piper said, looking up at Dex, the gratitude in her eyes shining in their tawny depths.

"Don't worry. Afsana and Raffi will handle it."

"I'm worried about that man. What happens when they get home and he's still there?"

"There's no way to warn them, Piper. We're just going to have to hope for the best."

She looked distressed, her eyes filling. "I don't like this, Dex."

"We can't go back, sweetheart. I know they'll handle it. We have to have faith in them."

She nodded, clearly understanding the need to keep going, but not liking it one bit. Dex didn't blame her.

"We're going to get you home. Pretty soon you'll be back at your mansion with your gardens and your pool."

"I don't use the pool," she said, wiping at her eyes.

"Why not?"

Her head came up as if she'd blurted out something she hadn't meant to say. "I, um, don't like the water."

He narrowed his eyes. "Really? Are you sure that's it or can't you swim?"

"All right. I can't swim. I never learned."

He smiled and brushed at her cheek with his thumb. "Well, if it's one thing I know how to do, it's swim. I'll teach you."

"Good luck with that," she groused. "I do have a brother who's a navy SEAL, and if he couldn't coax me into the water, what makes you think you can?"

"I have my ways. We'll see."

She shook her head and snuggled against him, even though he knew it wasn't a good idea and his chest got tight thinking about them having a future together. There was no damn chance. Which made him realize that he might be looking at a lonely existence for the duration of his military service. Taking a chance again on someone who might not be able to handle his deployments left his gut in a twisted knot of a mess. He despaired of ever finding that unbreakable woman to stand by him. He thought Piper might be made of titanium and the thought of being with her again only added a newer, sizzling dimension. He wanted to tumble her into a real bed and take his time with her. But each time they were together would add one more new layer of need and want spiraling inside him until all his walls would crumble.

Realizing his thoughts were heading into dangerous ground, he closed his eyes and clenched his jaw, not liking the churning in his gut. The old anger was seeping back, and he didn't want it. He didn't want to remember how his relationships in the past had failed.

An hour later, Blessing pulled up to the Kabul Star Hotel. "Here are your key cards, and I took the liberty of buying you toiletries and clothes. Everything is in this bag. You can charter your jet by getting on the hotel wireless. Quickly now. Get out of here as soon as you can."

Piper handed her a check. "Here is reimbursement for you, Blessing, and thank you so much for everything."

"This is too much, Piper." She tried to shove it back, but Piper pushed it back at her.

"Then use it for your clinic." She kissed Blessing on both cheeks and hugged her hard.

Dex then hugged her, too. "Stay safe. I'll see you on the next go-around."

As she drove away, Piper and Dex were heading into the hotel and straight to the business area. Once inside the office, Piper sat down at a computer.

"I think we should just go straight to the airport and charter the flight. Less chance for someone to track us by your credit card."

"I don't need to pay," she said, bringing up the website and making a reservation. "We have a private company on retainer. It's a fractional ownership that my brothers and I enjoy."

"Even better, Moneybags." He smiled.

After they were confirmed to fly out in an hour and a half, they headed for the elevator. Once inside they went to the numbered floor listed on their key cards and were soon in their hotel room.

"We should get cleaned up," he said, and walked to the bathroom.

He would get through his shower fast and maybe eliminate the need that was already climbing up his groin and giving him an aching erection.

He'd like to think he was strong enough. But then she stopped him cold.

"Dex?"

"Piper?" he said, his voice rough now with need, with anticipation, as her eyes darkened with more than fear. She needed comfort and he wanted to give her that, to make her feel safe and secure.

What was left of his flimsy resolve disintegrated. She was still reacting to the events from an hour ago. He would probably never get that image of that gun to her head out of his mind. It almost made him reckless. He wanted her again. Wanted to see that look in her eyes over and over. He wanted to see it when he was inside of her, when he was making her climb the peak, when he was the one who pushed her over. He wanted to be the only one who saw that look ever, and it was that fierce, ridiculous surge of possessiveness that almost gave him back the edge he so desperately needed.

Piper was still shaken. She couldn't seem to get rid of the memory of that gun up against her spine or seeing Dex once more in mortal danger, but with his skill and quickness, he'd saved her again. She didn't want to be alone out here and she felt the need to stick close to him.

When she couldn't seem to get the words out of her mouth, he walked back to her, opened the door, set the Do Not Disturb sign on the handle, then threw the dead bolt.

He took her hand and backed toward the bathroom, stopping briefly to unzip the bag and pull out the toiletries bag. "I need someone to help me wash my hair," he said. "I don't think I can get my hands over my head."

She blinked back the moisture in her eyes. He was able to throw that knife with deadly accuracy, but she was so grateful for his understanding.

He nudged her head to one side, dropped his mouth to the spot below her ear, sending a sparkling shower of electrical shivers down her body, tightening her nipples. His mouth closed around her lobe and sucked and she gasped as he pulled her against him.

Then his mouth found hers and he kissed her, hard, deep and wet.

She set her hands on his bare shoulders. He slid his hand heavily down her spine, cupped her rear and meshed her hips to his, his hard-on caught between them.

She helped him with the tunic and the vest and with trembling fingers untied his pants. When she went to reach for her own clothes, he helped her out of them, his hands lingering as if he wanted to memorize every dip and valley of her body. He was fully aroused. It was a slow, tortuous tease until he reached for the tie to her pants.

"I can't pretend not to want you. My body gives me away," he told her, his eyes hot with passion.

Her response was to kiss his chest and curl her hand around him, stroking him.

She told herself sternly that it was all about comfort. Nothing more.

She couldn't let him be any more.

Chapter 10

Austin stopped the Jeep and parked half a mile away from the good-size village. He could see the sand walls and, as they approached the entrance, there was a man standing by a vehicle. He had a communication device and, even better, Austin recognized him as Outcast's second-in-command, Ted White.

They worked together to subdue him and when he'd been flex cuffed and turned around, Austin said, "So, what are you doing here?"

"Just some Outcast business," he said.

"Does that business include the assassination of a US senator and the murder of a navy SEAL?"

"I don't know what you're talking about."

"Sure, you don't."

They walked him back to their Jeep and shoved him facedown in the backseat. Austin flex cuffed his feet and they closed the door.

"Let's find the Jamals and hopefully they're okay."

Austin nodded. They wrapped their head scarves and entered the village. When they came across an old man, Derrick spoke to him and the man pointed down the street. "He says the house with the red door."

Austin nodded. There were a few people out, but not many. Some used the water pump and a potter fired up his kiln. As soon as they got to the end of the street, Austin and Derrick split up. Austin went to the back and Derrick to the front. In the back of the house, there were numerous goats and a vegetable garden. There was also a gate. Austin positioned himself in front of the back door, taking a quick peek through the kitchen window. From his vantage point he could see a man, woman and two young boys standing in the hall. There was the body of a man with a knife through his eye slumped against the wall. The woman had her two sons' faces pressed into her sides. A man with a suppressed M9 was pointing it at them and he could hear muffled shouting.

"Where are they?"

Austin didn't hesitate. He tried the knob and it turned. He eased the door open just enough so that his body could slide inside.

On cue, Derrick knocked, and the guy glanced over his shoulder toward the closed front door. "Answer that, but if you even look at him sideways, your wife and kids get it." The thug gestured with the gun.

The man, who Austin presumed was Raffi Jamal, went to the door and opened it. Derrick greeted him and started talking to him. Austin entered the room and the woman's head whipped to him. Her eyes widened. Austin put his finger to his lips for her to keep quiet.

"Hey, pal," Austin said, and the guy brought his head around, the gun swinging in their direction. Austin clipped him on the chin and he went down. That's when he saw the two other dead guys. One was face-down on the floor and the other was sprawled in the doorway across the room. *Jesus...* Kaczewski was a juggernaut.

Derrick came through the door, his gun drawn. "Can you believe this? They sent five guys after this SEAL." Austin chuckled. "The guy's a one-man riot."

Derrick didn't answer. His eyes were fixed straight ahead and Austin got a chill down his spine at his colleague's expression, a resigned look and one so full of regret it made Austin's gut clench. Austin was just rising from flex cuffing the unconscious man. He turned to follow Derrick's line of vision. The woman, holding the small boys, had the exact same look in her dark eyes, along with one of abject shock.

She clutched the boys closer and said softly, "Derrick?"

Then it was Austin's turn to be shocked senseless. The older boy turned his head and Austin blinked and blinked again.

He was the spitting image of Derrick right down to his black hair, dark good looks and midnight-blue eyes.

Kabul Star Hotel,
Kabul, Afghanistan

Piper grasped and arched into Dex, the exquisite sensations spearing through her rendering her speechless as well as mindless.

Words like *beautiful* and *sexy*, said in a deep, ragged, melting voice, rasped in the steamy air.

He had her against the tiles, her crossed wrists in his big hand currently at the small of her back, the other roving over her in a possessive slide. She hungered to be taken by him. She wasn't accustomed to a man like Dex—unconventional, raw. Brad was reserved and low-key. Not that he wasn't confident, but he'd never held her like this, ever. They hadn't even had sex in the shower.

"You follow my lead," he said gruffly, not giving her a choice, but she knew she had one. "This is going to get bumpy, Piper. You drive me more than crazy, lady. Mad…completely mad."

She expected that Dex was going to shatter every concept she had of intimacy. He was already so deep inside her head, deep in her trust. "I'd follow you into hell," she whispered. "Mad, bad, reckless, shooting from the hip."

He groaned softly as if he'd lost another layer of himself to her. "I'd die for you, Piper."

"Please," she said softly, "don't. It would kill me." She'd seen him knocked down, his wound broken open by putting himself in harm's way to save her, fighting like a demon to live. She might be reacting to Dex solely from this life-and-death battle, but she didn't think so.

His palm slid across nipples that were achingly tight and sensitive, then he pinched one, cupping her breast. His eyes held hers with an excruciatingly fierce fire and she couldn't look away. A powerful, cherishing gaze, showing not only heat, but the pleasure he took in touching her, the anticipation of all that he planned. There was no doubt he was calculating what he wanted to do to her in the same tactically solid way he did for any kind of combat.

He looked like it might be slowly killing him.

Only this would be sweet. SEALs weren't just intense in combat.

He exerted slight pressure on her wrists, arching her

back. His chest pressed against her breasts, so slick and hot, the skin like satin.

His breath rushed out on a soft exhale, carrying with it a panting male sound that made her hips jerk.

She'd never been so turned on in her life. This slow, excruciating way he was mapping her with his hand was torture. "Are you holding me this way so I can't touch you?"

"Bingo. You touch me and I think it will be over. I've got to...get my bearings."

"Isn't that easy for a SEAL?"

He huffed a laugh, then his mouth settled over hers. His lips were hot and thorough, moving slowly over her, kissing her one second, then the next biting her lip and licking her. He slipped his tongue in her mouth and she sucked on him. He tasted so good.

"The only easy..."

"...day was yesterday," she finished for him. She kissed his mouth, rubbing against his soft facial hair. "Let go," she whispered against his cheek.

He smiled. "Is that an executive order?"

Her eyes flicked up to his. The sparkle in his dark eyes sent her lips tilting, too. He was such a damn tease. "I'm not the president. This would be a congressional order. But I do have something I want to implement, and I believe as a member of the military, you are duty bound to obey."

He grinned now. "Oh, yeah. You have the floor, Senator. Don't ask me to salute." His grin widened. "My hands are much too...occupied."

"Saluting won't be necessary, since you are, ah, quite at *attention*."

He threw back his head and laughed, and she kissed the hollow of his neck.

"Oh, I don't want to propose it. I want to…execute it. It's called *I want to put my hands on you.*"

"I think you're trying to take me out of the action, Senator."

"Oh, no. I'm comfortable with your actions. Carry on, Lieutenant."

"Yes, ma'am," he breathed, and released her. She took her palms on a sensual journey over all that hard-packed muscle, from the astonishing hardness of his rippling abs and up the wide expanse of his solid chest. God, he was so beautiful.

"I want to devour you," Dex whispered.

He moved down her body and she went liquid with anticipation. Not able to take her eyes off him, she trembled hard. The warm water flowed across her naked torso, tapped her aching nipples, slid across her skin. The spray drenching his hair and dripping off his jaw as he continued his intent foray.

His warm breath brushed against her sensitive skin, making her shiver, and he moaned softly as he nudged her thighs apart, just enough to get to the center of her.

She used his shoulder to brace herself, the other hand going into his soaked, silky hair.

Her hips lifted and undulated in rhythm to his tongue and she sank into the deep, aching way he made her feel.

The world disappeared, the danger receded. He—Dex—was here, and he would keep her safe from harm. He trusted in her, too, and she hadn't let him down. She would try to never let this glorious man down.

Then she was just melting like sugar in the rain, her head falling back. Uncontrollable moans spilled while she spiraled up and up, and finally he shoved her over.

Even before she had a chance to absorb all the aching pleasure, he surged up her body and frantically entered her.

And a deep, heavy heat coiled through Piper's body. This is what she'd wanted. Him pushing into her with power and need. The muscles between her thighs were already warm and pulsing, the awareness of him making her groan softly.

His mouth rolled over hers, drawing her into him, and Piper fell back against the tiles as he kissed her. His next thrust came harder, and the one after that faster, each penetration giving her mind-bending pleasure, stealing her breath.

"Dex, please," she pleaded, wanting his heat, his energy, the life of him pulsing through her. She arched into him, urging, her hands sweeping wildly over the contours of his body, her fingertips molding to curved muscle and man.

Then her touch slid lower. His stomach muscles contracted instantly as she neared his groin and his moan of pleasure thrummed through her when she used her nails on his lower abdomen.

"So good," she whispered in his ear, his big hands on her ribs driving anticipation through her.

"Piper," he growled.

He was an experience—something from the tightly guarded places she'd rarely visited. His kiss alone reverberated in every cell of her body; the guttural sound of his need and satiation echoed in her heart. How could she ever let him go, run in the other direction like the smart voice in her mind told her she should do?

She cupped his face, devouring his mouth, and thrust her hips, meeting his hard, fast, deep strokes. He grunted and cursed, then nudged her thighs wide and lifted her against the tiles. She held herself poised, and a million thoughts ran through her mind, nothing sticking long enough to make sense. She felt unbound, her need beyond passion, beyond control.

Piper stared up at him. She never expected to see this man humbled to anything. Yet he was, in his eyes, his expression as if he was questioning everything he knew, and her throat tightened. For the world, the enemy saw strength and deadly skill. Piper saw need and unguarded man. She guided him, loving the exquisite pressure. His gaze became trapped with hers, and they prolonged it, her hips rising to his. He sank into her again, helpless and trembling.

His breath shuddered, almost gasping. "I don't know even where to go with you. So much I want to do."

"I'll take anything you want to give me," she said, brushing her fingers across his hair, caressing down the side of his face. Gently she laid her mouth over his, licking the line of his lips slowly before sliding her tongue between and making them both crazy.

He gripped her hips, his body nail hard and sliding deeply. Her muscles locked and tightened, and yet she smiled, met him and thrust harder. Her whispers mingled with the mist from the shower, their secrets bared and unspoken drifting between them.

He enfolded her breasts, thumbing her nipples, and the sight of him disappearing into her tormented her. She spared him nothing.

Her body rippled like the ocean breaking, battering him in sleek waves of pleasure, and she quickened, thrusting longer and harder.

"Oh, Dex," she said, drawing his name out. She couldn't breathe, her body beyond her control and his. She came, watching as her surrender broke him. He threw back his head and let go, pumping into her as he cried out.

He wrapped his arms around her and held her to him and she clung to him. In a few hours, they were going to be exposed again, go into battle unsure and in the dark. But she had changed here and he had done something she hadn't thought possible. Shown her a different kind of passion, a deeper intimacy. She bit her lip as the guilt consumed her and she fought against it. There wasn't anything to feel guilty about. Despite the short time that had passed, Dex had changed her, changed her so deeply she hadn't even begun to understand that depth. She was a different person. It also frightened her more than going into battle, more than losing her life. It scared her down to her soul, to the core of her heart where she had loved so unconditionally before she hadn't been able to get over it. Now there was another man, a man that meant as much to her. How could she open herself to that again? How could she take it and feel completely safe that she wouldn't go through the same kind of agony again?

She hungered for what she had found with Dex. But his profession… She couldn't stop that fear again. It was raw and real and scored her insides—and broke her heart.

His chest heaving, he held her so tightly as if he thought she might disappear if he let go. After a few moments, they separated, washed up and shampooed their hair. Rinsing off, he took her hand to support her as she stepped out. He turned and shut off the water.

She grabbed a fluffy white towel and started to pat at his stitches until all the moisture was absorbed and they were dry. Then a feeling of acute tenderness washed over her. She leaned down and kissed his injury from the top of the stitches all the way down to his waist. He buried his hand into her wet, short blond hair and kneaded, his touch saying it all. "How is your wound?"

He grinned to alleviate the thickness in the air. "All better now."

"Dex."

"I barely felt it," he said, leaning down and kissing her softly.

Lieutenant Dexter Kaczewski had unraveled for her and she couldn't get enough.

Big, bad navy SEAL. An officer, no less, and that put him a cut above. The elite's leader. That was so sexy; all that brilliance, combat-ready focus and intensity. He was so *hoo-rah* ready, such a tough piece of work, tempered steel. It took a lot to make steel melt. She shivered and he buried his face in her neck.

Slowly their bodies relaxed as they breathed together, still locked in each other's arms, him smelling oh-so-good, all overheated male.

"You okay?" he asked.

"Oh, yeah. You know how to carry out some orders, Lieutenant." She rubbed her face hard against his jaw and he grinned.

"Yeah, I got that overwhelm-and-conquer thing down."

"Hoo-boy, do you ever."

Piper attended to her hair and it felt so good to be squeaky clean, and what a way to take a shower. She highly recommended it. Back in the bedroom, she could see Dex standing before a mirror, already dressed in the black slacks, white shirt and slim black tie that Blessing had purchased. Hot damn, the man was stone-cold gorgeous.

The garment bag was open on the bed and there were delicate, lacy, navy blue undies, an exquisite matching bra, a white and navy striped short-sleeved T-shirt and a pair of navy linen pants. She'd also included a pair of flat red sandals. "Blessing has quite good taste," Piper said as she fingered the material and gave him another appreciating glance.

He sat on the edge of the bed, his eyes trailing over her shoulders and the white terry cloth wrapped around her. He reached out and gave the towel a tug. As it slipped off her, he smiled. "You better get dressed because, from what I remember, you were quite a good taste."

She reached for the panties and slipped them on. "You cheeky devil. Do not distract me."

"Okay, I'll just watch."

She had the bra half on when she felt his warm fingers on her back, then him hooking the clasps. "I thought you said you were only going to watch."

"I couldn't keep my hands to myself," he murmured, sliding his fingers down her back.

She stepped away and finished dressing. Sitting down next to him, she slipped on the sandals.

"Could you tie my shoes?" he asked. "It hurts to bend over."

"You didn't seem to have a problem in the shower."

"I was crouching in the shower. This is a little different…oh," he said when he saw the gleam in her eyes. "You're teasing me."

"A little." She moved off the bed and in front of him. Taking the shiny black oxfords, she slipped the shoe on one foot and tied it, then the other.

He slid his hands under her arms and dragged her up, kissed her and let her go. "One more thing I need help with." He fished the leather gun harness out of the backpack and she took it out of his hands. He spun around and she fitted the straps up his arms and over his broad shoulders. She moved around him and with unsteady fingers fastened the buckle.

"Thank you," he said as she smoothed her hands over his shirt. She moved behind him and picked up the jacket, setting it so he could easily slip his arms into the sleeves and adjust the collar.

He dumped out the contents of the backpack and picked up the wallet, gun, badge and passport, pocketing everything. The last thing he reached for were the dark shades. He put them on.

Her purse was ruined, but Blessing had provided her with a pretty navy clutch.

She walked over to the tumble of clothes on the floor and fished out the head scarf Afsana had given her. The print was beautiful, the cloth finely woven. She smoothed her hand over it.

"Are those my bars?"

"Yes, I kept them safe. Do you want them…?"

"No, Piper, you keep them for now."

She shook the *keffiyeh* out and folded it neatly. This had protected her and saved Dex's life. She wanted it.

She tucked it into the small black suitcase, nestling it along with the gorgeous lacy black nightwear, a change of underwear and a pair of gray cotton men's shorts.

"She really is very thoughtful."

He nodded. "A gem."

He threw the now-empty backpack with the discarded Afghani clothes in the waste bin.

Without looking back, they left the room.

They hailed a cab at the curb and Dex said something in Pashto. The cabbie eyed her in the rearview and she kept her eyes straight ahead, putting on her professional face. Her palms still got moist, but she was probably reacting to the fact that someone wanted her dead.

He put the cab in gear and they navigated the congested streets of Kabul. At the checkpoint, Dex flashed his DS badge and they got through. Dex spoke again, and the cabbie took them to the commercial charter area of the airport. Dex grabbed the bag and they exited the vehicle, paying with money that Blessing had provided.

There was some delay in getting Dex approved because he was carrying a firearm, but once they saw his DS badge and her senatorial identification, they boarded with no issue.

Once inside, they settled in the posh, cream leather seats and buckled up.

They were headed back to DC and Piper was even more nervous. At least here she knew her enemy. But now Hatch and Markam were dead, the other men with him also eliminated by Dex's brute force and the skills her brother taught her.

But at home her enemy was unknown, and the city felt just a tad more dangerous than Afghanistan.

Chapter 11

"Kai Talbot."

"Boss." The supervisory special agent in charge and Austin's superior might be as gorgeous as a runway model, but her no-nonsense tone told Austin that she was one top-notch agent, which he'd seen firsthand. He had great respect for her.

"What have you got for me, Beck?" she said, and it sounded like she was outside.

"Two suspects and news on Lieutenant Kaczewski and Senator Jones." Their coup in Safid Darreh had netted them a wealth of information and one shocker of a secret.

"Excellent. I'm listening." The muffled sound of her car door opening and closing came through the receiver. Then it was much quieter on the other end of the line.

Austin leaned against the wall in the small room. "They're both alive, as far as we can tell. We tracked them to a village about ten miles from Bagram where they were holed up for three days. Kaczewski had his stitches pulled out and got a fever. The senator walked all the way to Charikar dressed as a man to get him antibiotics."

Kai whistled low. "Wow, the senator's got moxie."

Exactly what Austin thought. She was brave as hell.

"We got two live ones at the village. One of them is the co-owner of Outcast, Ted White. They're up to their eyeballs in trouble. The other guy, Aaron Patrick, works for them off the books, if you know what I mean. And so did Martin Carter."

There was silence on the other end of the line. "Martin Carter, the dead merc the SEALs retrieved from Kaczewski's op. Those marines were used to lure the SEALs into an ambush. The director and SECNAV are going to be pissed." The sounds of her getting out of the car and the closing of elevator doors were audible. "Kaczewski was the target?"

Austin shifted. "No. Tyler Keighley."

"The plot thickens."

"It gets more interesting. No wonder Kaczewski is keeping Senator Jones off the radar. He's not sure who he can trust and, Talbot, neither am I. Someone high up had to have worked the deal."

She huffed out a breath. "Do we have any names?"

"Unfortunately, no. White and Kruger don't know, so they say. They are pointing fingers at Markam. But Kaczewski killed him in Safid Darreh." It frustrated Austin to no end, but there was no way to get any information out of a dead guy. "Markam apparently recruited DS Agent Hatch. Markam, who met Kruger when he was working in Kabul during deployment as a marine, was the one who came to Outcast with five mil. And get this, the client apparently changed the deal to include the senator *after* they bungled the mission and Tyler survived. They upped it to another five mil for her death. Two targets with one stone."

Austin rubbed his tired eyes. "I don't like unanswered questions." He couldn't remember the last time he'd slept. He stretched his back, watching Derrick through the interrogation window while he grilled Kruger, who kept shaking his head. They had caught and arrested Kruger as he was fleeing his Kabul office. Jesus, Derrick could look scary, deadly when he wanted to…and relentless. They'd been going at these guys for two days. Finally, the flunky, Patrick, had broken, implicating both White and Kruger. After that, it was just a matter of who could talk the fastest.

"Anything else?" She sounded impatient.

Derrick's a dad. But that wasn't the kind of information you spilled on your fellow agent to your boss. It was personal. Obviously. Austin still was processing this information. Whatever Austin thought he'd known about Derrick "007" Gunn, it was deeper and darker than he could have guessed, a huge secret he was harboring. He'd fathered a child with a beautiful Afghani woman who was, uh, married…oh, about eight years ago, when he couldn't have been very wet behind the ears. But as they loaded up the three dead bodies into the back of the Jeep and shoved the revived Patrick into the backseat with White, Derrick gave Austin the type of look that said: *If you ask, I will kick your ass and you'll be bruised and sore without me telling you a damn thing because it's none of your damn business.*

Austin did not ask.

"I'm getting ready to drive to Charikar and speak to Dr. Blessing Contee. She's the WHO doctor who Afsana Jamal told us stitched up Kaczewski and drove him and the senator to Kabul. Hopefully we can get a location on them."

Kai lowered her voice. "When you do find them, keep that under wraps."

"Yes, ma'am."

"In the meantime, I will start the extradition of Kruger, White and Patrick. Nationalities?"

"Kruger is South African and White is Australian. Patrick is American. I'll send a team over to Outcast and go over their files and computers with a fine-tooth comb and get it all shipped back to San Diego."

"Roger that," she said. "Austin, good job, and watch your back."

"Thank you, and yes, ma'am."

Hours later after he'd spoken to a closedmouthed and apparently clueless Dr. Contee, he called Talbot back.

"She says she doesn't know where they went," he said, hearing his own irritation blowing back at him. "But on the drive back, I figured the senator has some pull. Maybe she chartered a jet. So I drove over to the airport and, sure enough, she has a jet company on retainer. They took off twenty-three hours ago for DC. Looks like she's going home to work out this problem."

"Resourceful. Which means they've already landed in DC."

"Yeah, she's got that SEAL with her." That much Contee would cough up. Her husband, Pierre, a mountain of a man, was quite intimidating. "I called Kaczewski's commanding officer and he's not heard one word, but I didn't give him any information because I'm not sure who we can trust. It's not good if the guys gunning for her hear she's back on home turf." The SEAL had kept her safe this long. Maybe it was better for them to follow up leads and try to find out why Tyler Keighley had been targeted.

"Agreed. Extradition orders came through for Kruger and White. You and Gunn get back here and then you're on the next military transport to DC."

He'd better get his z's on the plane; he sure wasn't going to get an opportunity in the next couple of days for a deep bed rest. Hell, REM sleep was overrated.

Washington, DC

As soon as Piper and Dex breezed through the charter airport security, he changed into jeans and a T-shirt, ditching the suit into the waste bin, while Piper changed into a pair of black capri pants and a multicolored crop top along with a baseball cap and dark glasses. She refused to throw away the gorgeous outfit she was wearing and stuffed everything into the suitcase. She pulled her hair into a short ponytail and it peeked out of the back of the cap. She looked like a teenaged tourist. He bought them two burner phones.

Piper called her car service, relieved to be home, but she still felt like she had a target on her back. Until they discovered who was trying to kill her, she wasn't exactly safe just yet. They waited inside the airport until it pulled up. They got inside and she told the driver to take her home. As soon as they were in the stop-and-go of downtown DC, they slipped out of the car and escaped into the subway, traveling to the Cleveland Park Public Library.

Dex went to the desk and asked to use one of their private reading rooms, and with a smile the woman nodded and directed him down the hall.

They entered the room and closed the door. Dex called his dad and pushed the speakerphone button.

"Admiral Kaczewski."

"Dad."

"Dex!" He pulled in a hard breath and let it out. "Son, it's good to hear your voice. Where are you?"

"In DC." His father's response made his chest a bit tight.

"What?" he said sharply, then lowered his voice. "Where?"

"I can't tell you. It's safer if I keep Piper with me and only I know where she is."

His father sighed. Using his best admiral voice, he said, "I've been getting updates from NCIS. Let them handle this." It was his father's way to mitigate the situation, but turning Piper over to NCIS was like condemning her to death. He wouldn't, not even for his father.

"No, I can't," he said firmly, needing his father to understand how much she meant to him without actually voicing it. Piper was standing there listening to everything he said. "If something happened to her because I walked away, I couldn't live with that. We don't know how far this goes and NCIS isn't immune. Somebody with deep pockets and a lot of pull is trying to kill her." Her face went white and he wasn't sure if it was because his father wanted him to walk away or the fact that she was in so much danger. He didn't care. He wasn't going to turn her over to anyone.

There was silence and then his father's resigned voice. "I see your point."

"You just don't like that I'm in harm's way." Dex tried to lighten the tense situation, but his father would find nothing amusing about Dex with a target on his back.

Surprisingly, his father chuckled as if he knew his

own kid too well. "Son, I know you're always in harm's way, but I understand that you feel responsible for this woman."

Dex clenched his jaw. He felt way more than just responsible for her. Their eyes met and he smiled encouragingly. He knew her, knew she was churning inside, knew her in a way that went beyond carnal knowledge to some other place that defied rational thought or logic. He was utterly himself with her, in a way he'd never been with Melissa or Suzy. No walls, no guarded moments. He was realistic and understood that he would walk away when this was over. But he wasn't sure he could handle losing Piper, having her reject him and what he did for a living. Most women would.

Right now, he simply said what was true. "I'm all she has. All she can trust right now. I can't abandon her." He reached out and brushed his fingers over her downy cheek. "She saved my life," he said simply with heartfelt emotion tingeing his words.

His father's voice was subdued. "All right. Then I'm on board. What are you going to do?"

"Track down possible leads."

"All right, and your wound?"

Dex smiled and said, "I'm okay, Dad."

"If you say so." He sniffed. "What can I do to help?"

"I need a safe place to stay."

"Actually, I've got something for you," his father said eagerly. "Your mother is house-sitting for a very good friend." He rattled off an address. "I'll get the key to you. Anything else?"

"Yeah, I need cash and a weapon. Oh, and, Dad, can you rent a car for me and leave it in the rental lot?"

"Okay. I'll make sure you get all this when you have the keys to the house. How is Senator Jones holding up?"

"She is…" He paused.

"I haven't ever heard you speechless about a woman before. If I remember correctly, she's about your age."

"Yeah, Dad, she's amazing and she shoots like a SEAL." Piper was just…Piper. Strong and brave. He knew that more than anyone.

"Sounds like your mother," his father said with a wry lilt to his voice.

"She's got a lot of Mom's qualities."

"Well, she sounds like a keeper. Give me your number and I'll call you when everything is ready." There was a pause, then his father said, "It's not going to be easy to hide a senator, especially when her face is all over the news. They've kept you out of it."

"I know it won't be easy, but I'll keep her under wraps." He met Piper's gaze for an instant and tried to reassure her with his eyes. There were delicate purple shadows beneath her sepia eyes and a vulnerability around her mouth he was certain she didn't realize was there. He ended the call.

"What now?"

"We just have to lay low until he gets everything situated."

She took a tremulous breath and nodded. "What if he's being watched?"

Dex laughed. "My dad's a navy SEAL. The day he can't outwit a tail is the day he'll be in the ground."

"It must be great to have that kind of faith in someone."

"Don't you have that kind of faith in me?"

She stared at him for a moment and he held his breath. He wanted that, her unconditional trust. "You're right. I do."

"It's your turn. Call Edward, but don't give him

any details and make sure that you don't cave," he said firmly.

"The day that I can't outwit my brother will be the day I am in the ground. If that won't work, I'll bully him. My nickname isn't Bulldozer for nothing."

He laughed again. "Hell, woman, you even have a nickname, or as we call it on the team, a call sign. You are a SEAL in the making."

She dialed and when her brother answered, she said, "Edward."

"Oh, my God, Piper..." Dex could hear the relief and love in Edward's voice over the speaker Piper had set when she'd put the call through. "I should never have let you talk me into you going over there, Bulldozer."

Her voice was strained when she answered. "I'm okay. I had help."

"Well, whoever it was has my undying gratitude. Where are you?"

"I'm safe. How's Tyler?"

"He's stable and in one piece. He's looking at some major recovery time, and I don't know if he'll ever be physically able to continue military service. He's pretty worried about that. I took precautions and got him somewhere safe with medical attention after I got this anonymous tip. I think I owe that to the lieutenant."

The knot of worry eased in his gut, but they weren't out of the woods yet. It hurt Dex to think his big, strong teammate and friend was going to have to go through a lot of rehab, but he never doubted for a moment that Tyler would come out of this stronger. He would be back. He was a SEAL. Broken bones and internal injuries would heal.

"Why did you do that, Edward?" she said.

His voice hardened. "I heard from NCIS. They're actually going to be here tomorrow. Two agents. Derrick Gunn and Austin Beck. They were looking for you in Afghanistan. They said that Tyler's team was intentionally ambushed and he was the target."

"What?" She threw him a shocked glance and rage exploded in Dex. He clenched his hands at his sides at this news. Someone was going to freaking pay for this. "Why?" she asked.

"There's only one thing I can think of that he's doing that may cause someone to worry about anyone digging deeper."

"What?"

"He's never been happy with the result of the police report regarding the accident that killed Brad. He hired a PI to look into it." Dex heard some papers shuffling. "Doug Utley." Edward rattled off a number. "As of right now, Mr. Utley's following some leads. It just worries me that as soon as Tyler starts digging, he gets ambushed. NCIS said that insurgent attack was faked and they were there to finish Tyler off and take you out, too."

"Because of the accident?"

"What else could it be?"

She rubbed at her forehead, her voice angry. "I don't know, but we have to figure it out. Until we do, I'm not safe."

"Who are you with? That navy SEAL, Tyler's friend and leader?"

"Yes, his name is Dex."

"Thank you, Dex. I'm sure you're listening. I owe you, man, for saving my sister. Now it's best for you to come home. I took leave and I'm at the mansion. We'll get you protection."

Dex grabbed the phone. "That would be a bonehead move."

"You do realize, Lieutenant, I'm a trained government bodyguard. I can take care of my sister."

"I don't give a damn. Piper is safer with me. It's too risky because of the DS connection," Dex said flatly.

She took the phone back with a glare. "Edward, Dex is right. I'd be safer off the grid. I can't really trust anyone right now."

"Not even me?" He sounded hurt, but Dex didn't care. This was about a lot more than a trust between brother and sister. He couldn't protect her like Dex could.

Dex said, "No," and she shushed him.

"Yes, of course, I trust you, but they'll be watching everyone I'm close to. Here's my number."

"Got it. And maybe you're right, but, sis, I was out of my mind with worry when you disappeared five days ago, so forgive me for being overprotective." He sounded frustrated and Dex didn't doubt he loved Piper, but she was sticking close to him.

"I forgive you," she said, her voice softening.

"Keep me in the loop and updated. I'd like to know my baby sister is alive and well. Let me know if I can help."

"I will. Bye, Edward. I love you." She ended the call.

"So this is about that car accident." There had to be something there. Something someone was trying to cover up or… He didn't want to mention to Piper at this time that her husband could have been involved in something shady, too. This was Washington, DC, and there was plenty of money and power to be had here. Maybe Brad Jones had wanted more and it had gotten him killed. "What do you remember about it?"

"Not much. I've tried to block it out, Dex," she said as he pulled her out of the small room and back outside. He clasped her hand and crossed the street. "I've had dreams about it." She blushed and he knew she was remembering the first time they made love right after he'd woken her up when she was having a nightmare. She had been reliving the accident. "But I can't be sure what I'm dreaming is real or an illusion."

His cell phone rang and he fished it out of his back jeans pocket. His father said, "Son, I've got everything delivered to the safe house. It's in the mailbox. It's gated, but you shouldn't have any problems. The key code to the gate is in there, too."

"Thanks, Dad. Stay alert and keep me posted." Dex ended the call. "Let's get to the safe house, get something to eat and some rest. We'll need to break all this down, get in touch with your brother's PI and put the pieces together."

She nodded.

Whoever was after Piper was going to rue the day they attacked her. He was beyond livid that someone had gotten their secret op info, kidnapped marines and killed and wounded his men, not to mention maybe ruining Tyler's promising SEAL career. Those people were going to pay, and he wouldn't rest until he unearthed each and every one of them and neutralized this threat to Piper, regardless of the means. Even if it was the deadly force of one pissed-off SEAL.

Stephen J. Montgomery's Office, The Montgomery Group, New Jersey Avenue, NW, Washington, DC

Stephen Montgomery sat looking out the penthouse office straight down New Jersey Avenue to the sight of the Capitol Building, nestled among the height of the summer greenery. He'd just gotten off the phone with Edward Keighley.

He'd filled him in that Piper was alive and right here in DC.

Stephen had been one of Edward's father's closest friends, his confidant and golf partner. He'd had his fingers in the political pie for some time with the innovations and government contracts he'd procured through his "contacts." He'd watched Edward, Piper and Tyler grow from small children to adolescents with their braces, get involved in soccer games and Scouts and through their teen years and college years. He attended Brad and Piper's wedding, had been there when Edward's wife had died of cancer and when Tyler had chucked the whole political thing and gone into the navy. He'd been there when both of their parents died.

There had been plenty of times when Piper's father, Randolph, had given him inside information, stating that *Business was business*. Sometimes it was ugly, sometimes it was messy and sometimes it was downright…deadly. He'd used whatever means he had at his disposal to leverage the Montgomery Group into the billion-dollar company it now was. He intended to keep it right where it was.

His phone buzzed and he answered. "Yes."

"There's a Senator Robert Mullins here to see you, Mr. Montgomery. Should I show him in?"

"Yes, Ms. Collins," he said, totally curious as to why he was being graced with the presence of the top candidate for the next presidency of the United States. "I'll see him."

"Yes, sir," she said.

Not more than thirty seconds later, his assistant ushered the powerful Mullins through the sleek, glass-block door.

"Will there be anything else, sir?" She stood there

waiting for his orders, her dark hair in a neat black bob, her suit even at the end of the day looking as impeccable as it had at six this morning.

"No, thank you. Ms. Collins, you are free to go." He smiled at her and she nodded.

She closed the double doors on the way out as Robert Mullins took Stephen's hand in a strong clasp for a brief shake.

"Senator, have a seat." Mullins was tall and imposing, and had the looks and the athletic body of a man half his age. His hair was just the right amount of salt and pepper to instill wisdom and youth, as if he walked that fine line, keeping the balance like a pro. The American public loved him.

The man unbuttoned his lightweight suit jacket and settled in one of the leather chairs in front of the big, imposing mahogany desk.

"What can I do for you?"

"I think it might be what I can do for you."

Stephen felt a little tingle of wariness at the base of his neck. This would be a formidable opponent, but a powerful ally. He knew it instinctively, one predator to another, could feel the power of his personality in his gaze, even while he could read nothing of his thoughts.

"Oh. What is that?"

"I have feelers everywhere, Stephen. I know you were involved in Brad Jones's death."

"I don't know where you're getting your—"

"Does it matter?" Stephen's lips pinched together over what he was going to say. "I thought not. I don't really care why you had him killed, but it served my purposes well. Brad was getting tiresome. I am impressed. You know that family. You're their mentor. Hell, man,

you attended their wedding. I have to admire someone
who will go to any lengths for power."

Stephen's smile was thin. "What do you want?"

Mullins smiled his J. R. Ewing smile. "I have a cash
flow need. I want the Oval Office and you want that bill
dead. The whole fiasco with Outcast has really blown
up in your face." Shock coursed through Stephen. He
thought he was being so damned discreet. But it seemed
that Mullins wasn't being modest. He really did have
what it took to be president and Stephen liked to back
winners. "That could be really embarrassing and will
likely destroy you and your company if it got out to the
press that you hired them to murder navy SEALs and
a US senator."

Apparently a little blackmail wasn't off the playing
table. "I'm listening."

"I'm former CIA. I have the contacts to make this
go away, if you make my cash flow problem go away."

Stephen stood and the senator rose with him. He
reached out his hand. "Done."

Robert Mullins smiled. "Consider this handled."

He turned and walked out of the office and Stephen
looked back out the window. This bill was damaging
in several ways. No one in the business world wanted
to lose corporate freedom. The cost of reorganizing
his company and making it more socially sound was
a big cost factor. He tried to talk sense into both Brad
and Piper on each occasion. But Brad wouldn't listen
and Piper had dedicated herself to carrying out her late
husband's wishes.

He had done his best to talk Piper out of taking her
late husband's seat for grief purposes, tried to steer her
away from the corporate law change, and he'd hated
like hell to order her elimination. But Tyler was smart,

and when he started looking into the car accident, he couldn't let either of them live. Tyler was supposed to die a hero on the battlefield and Piper had been slated for an overdose. The poor dear couldn't ever get over her husband's and daughter's deaths, but when she impetuously ran off to Afghanistan when Tyler was wounded, he saw a chance to take them both out without anything blowing back at him.

He wasn't going to let anyone tell him what he could and couldn't do. He was the ruler of his empire, had slaved for years to make it a powerhouse in the tech world. He didn't want anyone to diminish his control.

Washington was a cutthroat place to do business and politics were part of a means to an end.

Business was—after all—business. Sometimes it was ugly, sometimes it was messy and sometimes it was downright deadly.

Chapter 12

Robert Mullins settled into the Lincoln town car. His assistant sat back in the shadows. "Did he go for it?"

"Hook, line and sinker."

"As you predicted, the tail lost Kaczewski and Jones downtown."

"I am surrounded by incompetence." He ran his hand through his hair. Everything did not go to plan for the first time in his life. He had had a backup, but Hatch bungled it, got himself killed. Who the hell was this navy SEAL? A frigging fly in the ointment. But no one was going to stand between him and his Oval Office chair. No one.

Brad Jones had been a more devious and skilled player than Robert had expected. Encouraging and pretending to support Jones's corporate bill to incite Stephen Montgomery was a calculated risk, but it got Jones out of the picture and Montgomery in his pocket. He didn't really give a damn about the bill, but Montgomery did. Mullins knew Montgomery was a proud man who wouldn't like anyone taking away his power. That would make him do something drastic and then Mullins would get his big payday by blackmailing Montgomery to give him consistent and large donations to his campaign fund—all above board.

A lot of Mullins's constituents wanted that bill dead now. He wanted to keep his backers happy, so he'd put his might behind defeating it. Now that he had Montgomery on the line, it was time to put this bill to bed.

He hadn't anticipated his widow would take up Brad's seat and try to pass it herself. Still, Robert needed to find that evidence Brad had on him, but after eighteen months of searching, he had come up short. Maybe with some prodding, Piper would lead him to it? Hmm. That was a thought. "Give me your cell." The man handed it over and Robert pressed in a number, then he tapped in the code when prompted.

Five minutes later, as the town car turned onto Constitution Avenue, the cell rang. "Nyx." A name that was whispered in underworld circles.

"What do you have for me?" The soft voice rasped in Robert's ear.

"You will be sent four pictures in the next fifteen minutes. For the first two pictures, Dexter Kaczewski and Piper Jones, I want them found, terrorized, but don't kill them until I give you the word."

"Deep-sixing on your command."

"I want all this done quietly. It would be even better if their bodies were never found.

For the third picture, Jones's brother, Keighley. Make it look like a medication overdose. His whereabouts will be at the bottom of his picture, but take care of the two in DC first."

"And the fourth picture?"

"A PI. DC is full of violence. Poor Mr. Utley. Just another unsolved street crime."

"It will be done," came the chilling response.

Suburbs of Washington, DC

The air-conditioning kicked on and the blinds in the window of the dim room fluttered, the sound intruding on Piper's dream. She came awake and popped up in bed. A bed? For a moment, she was disoriented. Where was she?

It wasn't the DC hospital. Her hand went to her abdomen and she gasped on a soft breath. Her heart pounded in her ears and her breathing was labored. She felt as if she'd been running. She closed her eyes and then opened them, blinked. An unfamiliar but well-appointed room. Cathedral ceiling with an inordinately beautiful disk in the center, a decorative accent. The bed was comfortable, the headboard a cream tufted leather. Antique end tables with Tiffany lamps.

The safe house. The one Dex had gotten access to from his father. Her head whipped around, but the place beside her was empty.

She pushed the covers off her, realized she was naked and a full blush enveloped her. That black wispy thing hadn't stayed on her long after they had gotten into bed.

Dex…damn. He was so freaking good in bed. She was actually a little sore. The man was rough and she discovered that she liked it very much.

She went to the window and looked out. The pool was right off the bedroom. A small sun room opened out to the pool deck. Dex was in the crystal-blue water, streaking across her sight as he swam laps.

She pressed her hot face to the cool glass. Usually she spent her time after one of those nightmares trying to block out the memories, but now, she wanted to remember what had happened.

Had her husband been murdered? Had someone so callously deliberately run them off the road?

She closed her eyes, her stomach churning. She'd woken to pitch-black, except for the one street lamp that had illuminated her husband's face. His open eyes. The blood running from his nose and ears.

A sudden sweep of dread made her whole body tense and she closed her eyes, feeling sick and shaky.

She'd screamed then, the sound reverberating in her ears. She pressed harder against the glass, trying to remember how the car had been hit. What had happened?

It was no use. It was just a bunch of jumbled memories. Trapped in the car for hours, someone finally coming, firefighters prying open the doors, being barely conscious, the only sensation was blood and fluid sliding down her leg. During the ride in the ambulance, her questions about Brad went unanswered, then at the hospital, the loss of her child confirmed, the news about her husband.

Her throat tight, tears slipped down her cheeks, but she brushed them away and took a deep breath. She went to the closet and found a silk turquoise robe. Shrugging into it, she opened the bedroom door and stepped into the heat and humidity of a Washington, DC, summer.

She stood there for a minute, soaking up the warmth as she felt clammy and cold. She hadn't thought that was possible after the heat, sand and sweat of Afghanistan.

He barely made a ripple; he was all tanned, sleek skin and muscles slicing through the water.

He stopped when he hit the end of the pool and flashed her a grin. She walked to the lip. Looking up at her, he said, "You wanna learn how to swim, cutie?"

She shook her head.

"Ah, come on. The water is really refreshing." He reached up and tugged on the end of the robe.

She arched a brow and gave him a dry look. "So is coffee."

He chuckled. "I'll teach you how to blow bubbles and dog paddle."

He clasped her around the ankle, and even with all the weight of her past and the danger of her present, she huffed out a laugh and said firmly, "Don't you dare. Remember, I know how to handle a weapon."

His voice dropped an octave and he said, "Yeah, I've experienced that firsthand."

The man was definitely a sexy tease.

She crouched down, placing her hand on his forehead, and shoved him back into the water. "Go soak your head."

"You want to be specific about that?" He treaded water like a dolphin. Or was that more like a killer whale?

"You're a very bad man." She leaned over and used the heel of her palm to splash water at him. He dove like a fish and came up laughing. Then he turned his powerful body and cut through the water again. He sure had been right. The man knew how to swim.

Leaving him to his exercise, she headed to the sliding glass door and the kitchen. Still feeling strung out, she started the coffee. She didn't even want to know what she looked like. She had to pull herself together and talk about the past. It was now overshadowing her future, one she wouldn't have if she didn't figure out who wanted her dead.

That car accident was the key.

Forcing herself to take a calming breath, she went to the fridge and was delighted to see that Dex had been shopping. She reached for a grapefruit and sliced it in half.

The door opened and Dex came in, the stitches still dark and running down his left side. He was dry, except for his hair, which he was rubbing with a towel around his shoulders. From the delicious scent of him, he'd obviously showered and changed into the gray shorts.

He glanced at her, his expression going still. Without saying anything more, he studied her a moment longer, his gaze narrowing, but if he read something in her face, he left it alone. His tone was noncommittal. "Good morning, babe."

She gave him a warm smile. The soft way he said *babe* curling into a glow in her stomach. She could so get used to domestic life with this man. But this would only be fleeting and in between deployments. She was kidding herself if she thought she could handle that.

"You're up early."

"I couldn't sleep."

"You had another nightmare?" he said as he came to her and wrapped her in his arms. He smelled heavenly, citrus and cinnamon. This was what she needed. She leaned into his warmth. She had to get a grip or she'd never make it through the day.

He let her go and she grabbed her half of a grapefruit and coffee and settled at the island. Dex poured himself some coffee, then leaned back against the counter to drink it.

"Do you want to talk about it?"

"Yes and no," she admitted, and he came over to the counter. He reached over and tucked her hair behind her ear.

She would have thought she'd be over how he affected her. But her heart skipped a beat, her pulse ramping up. She suddenly felt as if she had too much blood in her body. Too much heat. Too heavy a response. She worked at bringing her body under control. Dex had ramped her up from a low-keyed woman to this responsive fireball, all in six days. This had all started out as a simple mission—Dex rescuing her—but all of a sudden it had gone way beyond that.

"I don't remember much."

"Why don't you tell me what you remember?" He caressed her forearm. Dex was mixing it up and it was hard to deny he had a steadying, calming influence on her now.

He was always so in control, so certain of himself and his abilities. It wasn't arrogance so much as assuredness, and that was powerful stuff for her at the moment. It was hard not to be tempted to lean some more on him. Just a tiny moment more. He was sturdy and strong.

She'd better get the stars out of her eyes and keep her two feet planted squarely on Planet Earth.

She told him the bits and pieces she remembered.

"The police investigated the accident, correct?"

"Yes, and came to the conclusion that Brad just lost control. I checked with them several times."

"I know that you weren't thinking this back then, but now that you've had some distance and the fact that Tyler was targeted after he hired the PI to look into the accident, do you think someone could have wanted Brad out of the picture enough to kill him?"

That had her looking up. "I—I don't know. I can't think of anything that would be damaging enough to want him dead. He was a senator, for God's sake, not a SEAL."

"People kill for a variety of reasons, Piper."

She shivered. In all the times she'd relived that night, over and over again, awake and in endless nightmares, she'd never once contemplated that possibility.

"Honestly, no. I didn't think he was murdered. If I had, I would have pushed much harder to find the person. But now I believe you're right. It can't be a coincidence that both Tyler and I were marked for death right after he started snooping around. When they find us, they're going to kill us."

He reached out and put his hand on her arm. "Not while I'm still breathing. I'm not going to let anything happen to you."

She held his gaze a bit longer, then finally sighed. "I'm lucky you were there."

"I don't know, Bulldozer. You handled that pretty well. Fought like a wildcat and put a slug into him. That's pretty badass."

She rolled her eyes. "That would turn you on." She huddled in her seat. "Okay. What's our next step?" She wasn't used to this, used to someone else having any say in how things were going to be handled. She ran almost everything for Brad and handled all the details. His campaign, his office, his life.

"Come here," he said, reaching over and tugging on her arm.

"What?"

"You're too far away. This can't be easy for you," he

said, pulling her off the stool and into his arms, so her back rested against his chest. "Much better." He leaned down and pressed a kiss to her temple. "I know this is scary and we don't know who's trying to kill you, but we're going to get out of this."

Brad was a good husband and they had a good life, but he'd never been this in tune with her needs. She wasn't used to a man recognizing how she was feeling and putting it out there. Being in a political family came with certain requirements. Never do anything you wouldn't want posted on the internet, never show the public any negative emotions and always be professional.

This was so new to her—unburdening herself, trying to reconcile having someone else in the loop instead of being this self-contained, have-it-together senator's wife, and now a senator herself. This overload of sensations with him holding her, caring about her... "I could get used to this," she murmured, leaning against him.

"Me, too," he said, tipping her head back so their gazes could meet. "Let's get breakfast and get ourselves something to wear, then we'll contact this PI, Doug Utley, and see where he's at. Sound good?"

She trembled a little, wanted to be strong enough to step away from him and handle letting Brad go on her own. You know...because she'd been doing such a good job up to now. She'd never really dealt with moving on and it was not surprising that she had been marking time for eighteen months. What had she been waiting for? What? For it to get better, for the pain to recede, to finish out Brad's wishes? Dex was opening her eyes to the fact that having someone to lean on didn't just mean physical support, but it meant emotional support, too. She turned in his arms and looped hers around his shoulders. "It does sound good and I *am* eating breakfast."

He frowned and glanced at the grapefruit on her plate. He shook his head. "That's not breakfast," he scoffed. "That's juice. Let me show you what a real breakfast is."

"Mmm-hmm. I'm sure this is going to add weight to my already generous hips, thighs and butt."

"That's easy to fix," he said, slapping her butt as she turned.

She gave him a narrowed-eyed look. "I know you're not saying I'm fat."

He held up his hands and stepped back. "Do I look like I have a death wish?"

"You have a point, Lieutenant?"

"Yeah, Senator. You know what's good for burning calories?"

"Swimming?" she said acerbically.

He laughed and headed for the fridge and started to pull out bacon, eggs and butter. He gave her a very wicked grin. "Oh, that would have been my second choice."

"You are a bad man."

Marriott Hotel, Pentagon City,
Arlington, Virginia

"I freaking hate DC," Austin said as he slammed the car door in the parking deck of the Marriott. "We got nothing out of nobody. Admiral Kaczewski stonewalled us. I think he knows where his son is. And Piper's brother, more of the same."

"Man, you need some sleep. I've never seen you so cranky."

"I need some exercise," Austin snapped. "I'm used to surfing every day."

"Yeah, apparently you need that Zen bullshit to calm the hell down."

"You might have ice water in your veins, Derrick, but I don't."

"What is that supposed to mean?" Derrick growled. He hadn't gotten any more sleep than Austin and apparently his fuse was also a bit short.

"Are we going to talk about what happened in Afghanistan?"

"Nothing happened in Afghanistan."

"Derrick…"

The man exploded into action, slamming Austin back against their vehicle, his forearm across Austin's throat. "I'm going to cut you some slack because we've been grinding this case for six days straight, but don't ask me about Afghanistan, ever," he said through clenched teeth. His dark eyes narrowed dangerously, so intense Austin broke the chokehold and pushed Derrick back.

Derrick looked at him and shook his head. "You've got some moves."

"I was a *marine*, Gunn. I know how to handle myself. You might not have any respect for me, but I served, college on the GI Bill, computer counterintelligence at the Pentagon, graduate study at Cornell."

Derrick looked away. "I never said I didn't have respect for you, Austin."

"All right, fine. I'll mind my own business. But you need to get that shit out of your head and reconcile with it before it eats you alive."

"Okay, buddy. I'll do that if you tell me about that picture of the ambassador's wife to Ja'arbah, a small country in the Middle East, you have tucked away in your desk drawer. Why don't you tell me about the three days you two spent together in a life and death struggle? Why your engagement ended?"

That's what happened when you poked a rattlesnake. You got bit and bit good. Austin shifted and took a breath.

"Yeah. Right. When I want life advice, I'll ask my guru. Now instead of talking about crap neither one of us really wants to talk about, why don't you haul your ass into some running gear and we'll blow off steam, run the Mount Vernon Trail? Then the both of us are going to get some sleep. When we wake up and after we get coffee and a doughnut, you can put your freaking Cornell degree to work tracking down something we can use."

Derrick walked away and Austin allowed himself to think of Jessica Webb for one hot second. As a marine he was duty bound to protect the ambassador and his family. His memory of those days should make him break out in a cold sweat. But instead, it wasn't the danger and the combat or the struggle he remembered. It was soft skin and warm blue eyes, tousled short black hair and a voice like an angel that haunted his dreams.

He pushed off the car, compartmentalizing the memory back into a lockbox he kept closed. Derrick was right. Austin's curiosity had gotten the best of him. Derrick's personal life was none of his business.

They had a job to do and Austin's gut told him Kaczewski and Jones were in way, way over their heads. There was something going on with this case and he was going to push until he found out who had orchestrated an attack on their marines and their navy SEALs. Who was gunning for Piper Jones and her brother?

The perpetrator didn't need to watch his back, because Austin was coming right at him, a full-force frontal attack.

Suburbs of Washington, DC

"All this stuff is so not my style," Piper said as she set the bags on the bed. "I'm used to suits and dresses and high heels, not cute tops, leggings, jeans, shorts and capris."

"I think you look beautiful in anything and—" his voice dropped to a heated tone "—nothing. Clothes don't define you, Piper. Wasn't it you who wore a burka, then dressed as a man and slipped into Charikar right under their noses? Clothes are just covering for one awesome woman. So, we need to fly under the radar, and you need to change how you dress."

"You look pretty comfortable in anything."

He flashed her a grin. "And you can pass for a college kid."

They had tried to reach Doug Utley several times, but he hadn't answered. Night was falling and Piper wanted to take the next step. Feeling jittery, she knew she was safe here. Dex had taken every precaution, but it still felt like someone was breathing down her neck.

"Let's give Mr. Utley another call," she suggested as she dumped everything onto the bed. She had a great wardrobe in her Georgetown town house not far from here.

Dex pulled out the phone and dialed. "Mr. Utley," he said. "We need to talk to you about the investigation you're conducting for Tyler Keighley." He listened for a few moments. "I'm working for his sister." He listened and his eyes flicked to her. "We'd be interested in what you found. Petty Officer Keighley is…" He trailed off. "I see. Yes, we could be there in half an hour. See you then."

He ended the call. "He heard about you in the news and he said he wanted to talk to you. He's been trying to reach Ty, but of course the ambush information has been kept out of the media. He says he found something and can meet us at a coffee shop across from the Pentagon."

They exited the subway at Pentagon City, Dex suggesting that they could duck into any of the many stations nearby. They were to meet up at the Lincoln Memorial if they got separated.

"I guess you know this city."

"Born and raised, and my family *loved* Washington. It is our lifeblood. So yes, I know this city like the back of my hand."

Dex was subtle about it, but she noticed how he kept his surroundings under constant scrutiny and monitored everyone around them.

"We can go scope out the street and coffee shop before we commit ourselves to anything that looks sketchy."

"Good thinking."

Piper settled the ball cap on her head, pulling her hair through. She was dressed in jeans, sneakers and a cute gray T-shirt with black lettering that said, "Wake Up. Kick Ass. Repeat."

The street was crowded with people going in and out of the busy mall. Everything was lit up.

"I'm embarrassed to admit that I don't know this city that well, except for areas around the Pentagon and Arlington Cemetery. Too much of Arlington Cemetery," he said with a sad cast to his voice. "And I've been to the White House a couple of times."

"You toss that out like it's an everyday occurrence to meet the president, when I know it's not. Medals, right?"

He turned to look at her as they approached the coffee shop.

"Yeah...medals." He changed the subject. "If I were ever to be a politician, I don't know how I'd like living here."

"You could never be a politician," she said. "You can't twist the truth to save your life."

He chuckled as they hit the plaza. "He did say Coffee Now," she murmured.

Dex took her hand and smiled. They were just a couple enjoying a walk from their hotel to take in the sights of Pentagon City.

A shot rang out just as they got to the front doors of the café and Dex pulled her back against the building. A man, dressed in black and a hoodie obscuring his face, emerged from a parked car. When he saw them, he raised the gun he was holding and suddenly she and Dex were in the assassin's sights.

Chapter 13

Dex started moving. The guy in the hoodie moved along with them, cutting off their access to the subway. Reaching to the small of his back and grabbing the grip of the handgun, Dex pulled it free and thumbed the safety. People ran and the bastard ducked into the crowd, effectively blocking any attempt he had of taking the guy out. With every fiber of his being, he wanted to run him down, but he couldn't leave Piper. Dex pulled her across the street. He raced through the parking lot. The Pentagon was straight ahead, the illumination of the 9/11 Memorial flickering as they ran.

"This way," Piper said, and they veered off, crossing over the GW Parkway, and didn't slow down. Skirting Arlington Cemetery, they curved around, heading for the Memorial Bridge. Dex looked behind him and a bullet pinged off metal. They hit the edge of the span, sprinting straight out. Piper was visibly laboring, but Dex was barely feeling the burn. When they reached the other side, huge bronze sculptures of two knights on horseback flanked either side of the bridge and she looked fearfully over her shoulder as they passed. Dex pulled her to the side and the dark figure chasing them slowed to a walk. The man who had been chasing them raised his arm, bringing the gun up and he pulled the trigger. Piper gasped in Dex's ear.

"Let's hot foot it to the Foggy Bottom subway stop," he growled. She nodded.

There was a shout from behind the assassin and two running figures started after them.

They took off as the assassin's gun discharged again, using the cover of the bridge until they were farther down the trail. Dex turned to shoot at the running men, joggers from the look of them. Then the assassin headed after them.

Dex lost sight of all three of their pursuers as they looped around and came up behind the glowing Lincoln Memorial, with the past president forever cast in marble sitting on that huge chair. He grabbed her hand as they cut across the memorial, but the assassin materialized and cut them off from Foggy Bottom. Changing direction, they raced down the side of the reflecting pool toward the Washington Monument.

Dex got off two shots, but the guy was constantly moving and it was hard to get a bead on him. They sprinted across Constitution Avenue with horns blaring, the hooded figure keeping pace.

Sirens sounded in the distance and he increased his stride, pelting down Seventeenth straight for the Farragut West Metro Station. When Dex looked back, he was no longer behind them, and Dex stopped and pressed up against the building. The two joggers materialized at the head of the street.

His chest heaving, he took her by the shoulders and said, "I want you to make for McPherson Square," he said, panting.

"Dex, no. Lafayette is right across the street."

"Go, Piper. Don't argue with me."

Her face contorted and she left him. Dex ducked down E Street and took a right on Eighteenth, slowing. He checked every alley and possible hiding spot, but it looked like the bastard was gone.

He loped to the Farragut West Metro, approaching with caution. He heard a shout for him to stop, but he got on the escalator and jumped down, two stairs at a time, until he reached the underground tunnel leading to the turnstiles. He stuck the handgun into the small of his back, keeping his eyes peeled for the assassin, but moving fast. He slipped his pass through and got onto the platform, looking around as the two men had to stop and get tickets before they could get on the metro. But instead they jumped the turnstiles, causing the metro cop to come barreling out of his booth. No sign of the shooter.

Luckily a train was pulling up as the two guys argued with the metro cop. Dexter got on board and pulled out his burner, dialing Piper. When she answered, his breath rushed out in relief.

"Are you okay?" she said in a rush.

"Yes, I'm on the train and there's no sign of him. Where are you?"

"The train's here. I've got to go."

"Meet me at Metro Center."

The phone went dead and he wasn't sure if she heard him.

It was a tense ride all the way to the Metro Center. He got off and he saw her standing in the shadows by the stairs. When she saw him, she rushed out and he ushered her up the escalator and out of the station.

They made their way two blocks over, then hailed a

cab, got out about a mile from the safe house and hoofed it the rest of the way.

Once they were inside, Dex locked the door and set the alarm, then he pulled Piper against him. He was trembling, not from reaction or adrenaline, but abject fear for Piper. They held each other for a long time and Dex was quite aware that he was harboring more than just simple feelings for her. He was getting deeply attached.

She pressed her face against his and he captured her chin and tilted her head up.

He kissed her then, sliding his fingers into her hair, displacing the cap, stripping off the elastic band.

"Dex…"

"Let me," he murmured, splaying his hand against her face, tilting with his thumb beneath her chin, placing kisses along her jaw to the downy hair at her temple. She sighed and tipped her head back, and he was torn between tenderness and desire.

He slid his hands to the nape of her neck, sent his fingers into her hair and tipped her mouth up to his again.

Finally, he was able to let her go. He clasped her hand and went and turned on the news.

There was an aerial view of Pentagon City with tons of flashing police cars.

A woman anchor came on and said, "Police are combing the streets looking for a shooter, a man in a black hoodie and dark pants. It's believed that he shot and killed Douglas Utley while he sat in his car outside this Coffee Now. Mr. Utley was a private investigator by trade and at this time the police believe it was a simple carjacking. This is Wanda Donovan reporting from Pentagon City, back to—"

He shut off the TV and knew what he had to do. "It's

clear this whole conspiracy goes deep and is connected to your car accident. I've got to get to that PI's office before the police."

"Okay," Piper said.

"No, Piper. Alone. I want you to stay here. We have no idea if that guy followed Mr. Utley and we were the targets all along. I want you safe."

"Hell, no! I have to go. If this is about my accident and someone murdered Brad, they also are the murderer of my child! Whoever killed him robbed me. I can't have any more children. I want justice. I want someone to pay for this! They took my life. My future."

He wrapped his arms around her and held her tight as she sobbed against him. "I know. I know. I'm so sorry. He could be waiting for us there."

"We have to risk it. If we don't find something... Dex..."

"All right. But do exactly what I say, and if I tell you to run, you run."

She looked mutinous.

"Piper..."

"All right, but I want a weapon."

He walked out of the room and into the bedroom they were sharing. He pulled out the suitcase and retrieved the handgun he'd brought back with him from Afghanistan, then checked the safety. Back out in the living room, she was standing there, looking like her world had caved in.

He took her wrist and set the weapon in her hand. "You comfortable with this?"

She looked down at the gun, then up at him. "Yes," she said. "Let's go."

Doug Utley's office was located on a residential street in a nondescript neighborhood. They once again used the metro, with so many escape possibilities. It was better than a car that could be traced right back to his father. They approached down the dark street and luckily there were no cop cars.

Dex led Piper to the back of the house. A dog barked in the distance and Dex opened the screen to the back door and tried the knob. It was open. He looked over his shoulder and whispered, "Be careful and stay close."

They entered, the door squeaking. Whoever was here had to have heard that, but they needed whatever information Utley had. Now that he was dead, there was only his office and hopefully his computer to help them figure out the mystery and free Piper from a death threat.

Every sense in his body was heightened as he made his way slowly through the kitchen. They entered a short hall with closed doors. Checking everywhere before he moved, he went to the first door. Opening it, he found it was the powder room. The next room was a closet. He crossed by the open living room area, scanning for any movement, but there was nothing. No sound except the barking dog. Piper's hand was clenched into his T-shirt.

Together they crept down to the end of the hall and Dex turned the knob. Standing to the side, he pushed the door open.

Dismay rushed through him. Utley's office was a mess. He ducked inside and brought Piper in with him before he closed the door. There was no one there, but the person who had chased them at Pentagon City had done what he needed to do.

Dex found Utley's laptop under the desk, smashed beyond repair. The back was pried off, the hard drive of the machine gone.

He swore soft and low.

He heard a footfall on the front porch, then knocking. He moved the curtain and saw one of the joggers who had chased him into the metro.

"Who is it?" she whispered, and Dex put his mouth to her ear, letting her know and telling her to stay quiet. Who the hell were these guys? The man reached back and pulled out a weapon, and from the way he held it, Dex could tell he was either law enforcement or military.

"Cops, I think. We've got to get out of here," he whispered. He pulled open the door and he and Piper moved as fast as they could toward the back door.

In true cop fashion, one of them had been sent to the back. Dex stood to the side, dragging Piper after him.

The guy came through the door, leading with his gun. Dex handed his to Piper. No way was he killing a cop. Silently Dex slipped behind him. He got him into a headlock and the guy elbowed Dex in the ribs, right into his wound. He cried out, but didn't let go, just tightened his arm around the guy's neck, but the other man broke free and threw a punch, knocking Dex into the sink. Glassware, silverware and plates tumbled off the counter, hitting the floor with a terrible crash.

His partner shouted something from the front and Dex heard him ram the door, trying to get in. Dex wrestled with the second guy until he heard the metallic hum and a thud.

The guy dropped and Piper stood there with a frying pan in her hand. He grabbed her by the arm and they burst out of the back door as the sound of splintering wood came from the front of the house.

They ran down the driveway and didn't stop running until they hit the metro.

Doug Utley's Home,
Washington, DC

"Are you all right?" Austin asked as he extended his hand to help Derrick stand. He wobbled a bit and Austin steadied him.

"Damn," Derrick said with a low growl, rubbing the back of his head. "Kaczewski is one strong son of a bitch."

"Did you get clocked by a frying pan?" Austin tried to keep the humor out of his voice.

He obviously failed because Derrick gave him a narrowed look. "Yeah, the senator wields a mean one."

"Are you sure it was them?" Austin bent down and retrieved Derrick's gun and handed it to him.

"Yeah, it was dim, but I recognized him and he had a blonde with him."

"That was a good call, thinking they would come here."

"Where the hell does this dead PI fit in?"

"I don't know, but this has been one of the most interesting, confusing cases I've ever been on. We better check in and I think we ought to just go to bed and get some sleep. You need a doctor?"

"No, I've got a hard head."

"Freeze. Don't move a muscle."

Austin and Derrick raised their hands. "Great," Austin grumbled as the cop took their weapons and cuffed them.

"We're NCIS," he said as they hauled them out of the house.

"We'll get this straightened out downtown, gentlemen."

Kai wasn't going to be happy.

And she wasn't, but she talked to the DC brass and after an hour they released Derrick and Austin with a request if they had any information regarding Doug Utley's death they would share.

When they got back to the hotel room and got ready for bed, surprisingly Austin couldn't sleep. It was pretty clear that Kaczewski and Jones were holed up somewhere in DC that had good access to downtown, and they were in the process of figuring out who was trying to kill her. In their shoes, he'd do the same.

He pushed back the covers and grabbed his laptop. On a hunch, he started searching social media. When he saw that Dexter's mother had an account, he started hacking.

Suburbs of Washington, DC

"I can't believe this," she raged as she and Dex entered the house and he set the alarm. He gently caught her shoulders.

"We're going to figure this out."

"How? Our best lead is dead, his office trashed and his computer smashed."

He caught her against him.

"We're going to figure this out," he said again, his voice a little fiercer, his hands squeezing her shoulders.

She nodded, not trusting herself to say anything for fear she would break down completely. She didn't want to feel hopeless, but nothing, not one tiny thing, had gone their way tonight. The night had been a complete bust.

Dex wrapped his arms around her and held her for a moment, hugging her, but when her arms snaked around his waist, he made a soft, pained sound.

"Oh, Dex. I'm sorry."

"I'm okay," he said, but she wasn't convinced. The man had taken enough blows to his wound to last her a lifetime. She peeled up his shirt and took a quick breath. No blood and the stitches were still intact. "Looks like you're going to bruise." She pressed gingerly around the area and he grunted.

"Who do you think those guys were?" she asked, taking his hand and dragging him into the kitchen. She opened the fridge, pulled out one of the soft ice packs in there, wrapped it in a kitchen towel and pressed it to his side.

He shrugged. "They looked like cops to me."

"They were the joggers who were chasing after us in the mall."

"Could still be cops. Maybe detectives. Wouldn't be a surprise if they were. DC would have dispatched homicide detectives over to Utley's place. Now they know it wasn't some carjacking."

"Maybe. This is just one jumbled-up mess. Sit down," she said, and he went to one of the stools and slid onto the seat.

"Let's get something to eat," he suggested, "and talk about this a bit."

"I'll cook. It'll keep my hands and mind busy. I don't know what there is to talk about."

"Piper, I don't want to cause you any more worry and pain than you're already experiencing, but you're right. I can't twist the truth to save my life or help the fact that I think through every scenario."

"What do you mean?"

"It occured to me that DC is a place where there is a tremendous amount of temptation to stray, to go down the wrong path for whatever purpose, be it money, power, recognition."

She frowned, not quite sure where he was going with this. "Yes, there is a lot of corruption and greed. What is your point?"

Piper stared at him, her heart suddenly hammering, a sense of foreboding settling heavily in her. And she knew—just knew by the tightness in his voice, by the rigidity of his body—that what he had to say was going to change her world, rob whatever peace she might have eked out in the last eighteen months. She wasn't sure she wanted to hear it. She wrapped her arms around herself, her voice wobbling. "What is it?"

He straightened and his eyes reached out to her. Unnerved by the silence, she pressed her back into the counter, instinctively feeling the need for support, suddenly cold.

Bracing his hand on the countertop, he leaned forward and Piper experienced a disquieting chill. "Maybe Brad was dirty," he said quietly.

His words seemed to echo in her head for a moment. Then they cut through her with slicing strokes of pain. It was as if someone threw ice-cold water in her face. She was speechless, iced to the bone. She had never for one second thought that Brad was the corrupt one. Dear God. If he had done something illegal and then it had caught up to him, he was responsible for his own death and the death of their child. She clutched her middle and doubled over.

Dex was there, but she could only feel a horrifying agony as if her insides had been ripped out of her, feeling so empty.

He made a helpless gesture with his hand, and for

the first time it looked like he didn't know what to do. "Jesus. I'm sorry, Piper. I shouldn't have said anything."

She couldn't draw breath to even speak. The man she had loved, had given her heart to, had supported and protected and cherished, had conceived a child with... no, it was too much.

When she didn't say anything, he scooped her up in his arms and carried her to the sofa. She shivered and shook and clutched at him as if he was the only solid, sure thing she had in her life.

He watched her as if she had gone somewhere he couldn't follow, unease and apology in his eyes.

His warm voice caressed her and she remembered that he had been the man to stand by her. The heaviness in Piper's chest increased as dread settled in and she felt as if she was at the edge of a dark, deep hole.

"Talk to me, babe," he said, his voice strained with guilt.

She tucked her arms closer around her waist. What if Brad was dirty? She didn't want to even contemplate that, but now that he'd said it, she couldn't seem to dismiss it. Her gut said no. Every fiber of her being said no.

"I could be wrong. It was just a thought. A possibility."

She made a soft sound.

"I'm an idiot. I'm going to stop talking now." He groaned.

She really hadn't known him that long. They'd been going on fast-forward since he put his life on the line for her, leaving her little time to think things through. She was overwhelmed by him on a sensual level that was off the charts. Had she been a complete fool? Anger blasted through her at him. "You didn't know him. How do I know I can trust anyone? Even myself."

"You can trust me, Piper. I won't let you down. It's just nothing makes sense, except that Brad was involved somehow. This all revolves around the accident and he was the target, the catalyst."

She dropped her face into her hand and took a breath. She thought about that, the scope and depth of what he had already done for her, their bond. This was a man she could trust. She should be thanking her lucky stars he'd come into her life, not doubting him.

"You're right. I know you are. You shouldn't spare my feelings. If it's the truth, then it needs to be... acknowledged and accepted."

He sent his hand through his hair, his face contorted with remorse. "I'm so sorry about all this."

"So am I. This is all my fault. I should go to my brother, get you out of this."

He dragged her against him, held on to her, not letting her go, turning her face to his. "No, I'm not going anywhere."

"Dex..."

"Hell, no."

"But..."

"Piper," he said, the gentle tone of his voice at complete odds with the riveting intensity of his eyes. "We're in this together. We're going to figure it out. Whatever it takes. I'm not abandoning you, so you can get that notion out of your head, right now."

"I couldn't bear it if something happened to you."

"No, not part of my game plan. I have the skills for this, to protect you and figure this out." He cupped her chin, capturing her gaze.

"Dex..."

He cut her off. "What kind of SEAL...what kind of

man would I be if I left you?" His voice ragged, he said, "You matter to me."

She couldn't look away from the fire in his eyes. He was a man of honor, the kind of man who put his life on the line for strangers, to keep Americans safe, to protect and serve his country.

"I'm sorry I insulted you. You matter to me, too."

He took her mouth then, silencing the rest of her protests with a kiss that left her breathless.

She was so scared to death something might happen to him she could barely think straight. Something shifted inside her as she ravaged his mouth. It was no surprise she reacted to him on such an intense physical level, but what terrified her and made her want to run in the other direction was the understanding of the depth of the connection she was forming with him. He was like that with everything, so focused and intent, whether it be her body or just what they were discussing. He was alert, always, to every nuance, every word, every sound, breath, scent and texture of the world around him. No wonder he scared the living hell out of her. It was intimidating to be on the receiving end of all that power.

She was in jeopardy, all right, but it had nothing to do with this dangerous situation and everything to do with Dex.

He lifted his head, but before he could move away, on instinct she framed his face in her hands, needing to feel him, needing to look into his eyes, needing to tell him what was going through her mind. "You matter. It scares me how much. I'm going to trust you... I do trust you. But if I'm going to care, then you can't let anything happen to you. Ever."

He smiled. "Ever, huh? That's a tall order. I'll do my

damnedest. I have a vested interest in keeping us both safe and sound."

He gathered her into his arms.

"Dex, your wound."

"We're going to get something in our systems, then we need some sleep. We'll tackle this again tomorrow."

He tucked her into the curve of his strong, warm body, and with each second she was near him she started to relax.

But her mind wouldn't shut down.

"Dex…"

He tightened his hold on her. "In the morning, babe. Shut down that beautiful mind and just let it go until you've gotten some rest. You know, I could be wrong. Totally off base."

She nodded, but as she let herself drift, she thought, *What if he wasn't? What if Brad betrayed me and everything he said had been a lie?*

Chapter 14

Since the accident happened, Piper had usually woken up out of a nightmare, but this morning it was different. She woke to the heated strength of Dex's body and the knowledge that she might never get enough of him.

Something had shifted in her. Something had changed. Dex had shattered that glass wall she had between the Brad she had immortalized and the real Brad, making her examine not only her perceptions and beliefs of and about her deceased husband, but making her take stock of who she was now.

She realized that she had made herself an extension of him, thanks to pressures from her family; the mingling of two powerful families into one had put enormous pressure on Piper back then. She'd given up everything to be his political spouse, dedicated to making him the best senator possible, to forge their own political empire. Even now, today, she was still an extension of him. Still carrying out his wishes.

She hadn't even considered what she would do when

his term was up and she didn't have all the responsibility of his political legacy to uphold any longer. Brad was gone and so were her parents, and Piper realized all of a sudden she had no goals beyond Brad's term.

Dex shifted in his sleep, and the darkness in the room told her it was the middle of the night. The warmth of him felt so right against her, even in this bed that wasn't hers and wasn't his. In this safe place he had provided for them in his quick-thinking and competent manner.

Dex made her feel safe in a way no man ever had. Even Brad. With him, she had the constant fear she would let him down in some fundamental way. But with Dex, truly she could be herself. She wasn't the woman who had married Brad any longer. She was Piper—not Brad Jones's wife, his office manager or his sounding board. A woman who was competent in her own right, not just a Keighley, which made her realize that she was also not just an extension of her powerful political family name.

You look good in everything and nothing.

He was right. She was the one who defined herself. It made her sad that she had diminished herself. It wasn't really Brad's fault. He had been happy to accept her sacrifice because he'd wanted to build a legacy, as well. Had he wanted that so badly he'd compromised his principles?

She reached out and smoothed her hand down Dex's side, her fingers catching on the stitches, and her heart turned over. Her battered, bruised and battle-hardened navy SEAL. He was inseparable from his profession, a career man. She knew it and it both made her want him and scared all at the same time. Jumbled-up emotions— moving on, falling in love again, letting go, guilt and hunger. All of those needed to be sorted out before she could come to any conclusions.

She hiked herself closer to him, her world filled with the scent of citrus, cinnamon and sleepy, sexy man.

She sank her fingers into his hair, threading the silky strands through a couple of times before finding his mouth, loving the way his lips went pliant beneath hers, were so soft against hers as she took him slowly, sweetly.

He moaned softly. "Piper."

"You were expecting someone else?" she whispered against his lips. Her fingers tightened in his hair, keeping his mouth warm and wet where she wanted it.

He chuckled, the amused sound a soft rumble in his chest. She pressed her body against his side, her leg going over his, the inside of her knee rubbing over his hard-on.

"You prepared for an early-morning assault, Lieutenant?"

"Babe, I'm always ready, anytime, anywhere." Her hand replaced her knee as she stroked the length of him and he gasped. "The enemy never looked or felt this freaking…ahh…good."

"Locked, loaded and *cocked*," she murmured, and he lifted her and pulled her across his body with one powerful move.

She straddled his hips and he groaned again, the heat and length of him nestled between her legs. It seemed like a lifetime ago that she'd first met him, wrung out, losing it over the loss of his men. Then the first time he'd touched her with intent when he'd been out of his mind with fever, but even then he knew what he wanted. Her.

Her thoughts drifted there and clung to those moments like a lifeline, helping her to block out the present reality and spend some time in this sensual place. A reprieve. As he'd said, she'd leave it for the morning.

Right now she had a bare chest to explore. To do with what she wanted.

And beyond the bone-deep fatigue, beyond the sheer terror and almost debilitating fear…there was a wealth of longing.

Her entire world narrowed down to the smooth expanse of his honeyed skin wrapped oh-so-tautly across his chest. She dipped her head and drew her tongue slowly from his collarbone down to the valley between his pecs, and then teased her way over to his nipple.

He drew in a sharp breath when she flicked her tongue across the sensitive tip. His hands came up to her hair.

"Babe," he said, his voice barely more than a rough whisper.

"Dex," she said, making his name a vow.

He cupped her head and slowly drew her mouth down to his, his eyes on hers as their lips met.

She took his kiss, letting her eyes drift shut as waves of sensation poured through her. He was heat and muscle and smooth skin. She opened her eyes and he gave her that slow, sensual smile that turned her insides to honey, an unmistakable gleam in his blue eyes.

She loved his smile and at that thought her breath caught in her throat. No, she couldn't go there and let herself get carried away by his hands sliding up her back and down again.

A violent shudder coursed through him, his breathing harsh and labored in the silent room. "You feel good all over me, Piper," he said, his hand moving up her stomach, over her breasts, until his hand wrapped around her neck.

That move made her feel claimed, his, and she couldn't stop the thrill that gave her. She slid on him; his breath caught and she moved again so she could hear the sound again. Then she took him inside her, thrust down on him, teasing him, holding herself so still, second after endless second, until even the slightest movement made him groan.

"Piper...please."

She pulled out and pushed back on him so slowly she thought she might lose her mind.

His hands went to her hips. She clasped his wrists and pulled his arms over his head, then smoothed her palms over him, then back up, holding him loosely. His eyes were closed, his head thrown back. She leaned into him, pressing her breasts against his chest. He was lost in the pleasure and she watched his face, his open mouth, the way a man looked when he was aroused. Beautiful. She licked his neck, her tongue gliding over his stubble, rasping against her tongue. Then she licked his upper lip, then bit his lower.

He arched his back and with a cascade of groans pushed up inside her as she let go of his wrists. He reared up, bracing his arm across the small of her back. Panting, he dragged them both backward until his back was against the headboard.

He held her and thrust harder, then even faster. She clung to him, riding his hips, the pleasure immeasurable. He dragged her higher, crushing her against him, and Piper sobbed out his name; he was so hard, so full. Dex shuddered, his arms convulsing around her. Roughly angling her hips, he took her on another wild ride. She clasped the back of his neck and sealed her mouth over his, surrendering everything to his hot, searching lips.

Stroking her tongue against his, she moved against

him, desperate for the feel of him, silently begging for more, and it was too much as sensation after sensation pulled into one hot, pulsating rush of pleasure that burst inside her.

Before the next contraction started, he clutched at her, a low, tormented groan ripping from him as he jerked against her.

Even as fierce pleasure scored her, she clung to him, incoherent and shredded. She wrapped her arms around his neck, tears mingling in with the sweat and the pleasure as she lost it. This moment, this golden moment, was what she'd been searching for, for a long, long time, but had completely eluded her.

Dex was a sanctuary, so much more than her protector and so much more than her rescuer. He was safe, a place where she could rest.

And it wasn't that she hadn't loved Brad, because she had. So, so much. But she hadn't known this…oh, God…this was possible.

With her breath slowing, reality punched a hole in her heart. He was a warrior and what he did for a living was make war. He was damn good at it.

She wasn't sure she could live with that, survive losing a man like him, waiting and watching every day, so many days of being without him like this. The magical as well as the mundane.

Even as he uplifted her, her heart lay heavy, feeling the thudding of his.

"Babe. Freaking hell, babe," he whispered, holding her so that she wouldn't leave him just yet, rubbing his face against her. Without being able to let her go, he slid down the mattress. "Just give me a minute," he rasped.

He rolled her, his arms still around her, his breathing still fast, then he kissed her, slanting his mouth over hers and sliding his tongue in deep.

It was a real kiss—the kind a man gave a woman he really cared about—deep, warm, communicating what he either couldn't or wouldn't say in words. The kind of kiss that was an exploration, a take-your-time kiss. Kind of perfect because she kissed him back the same way, not just learning all about him, but the taste of him, the feel of his stubbled jaw beneath her fingers, the contours of his hot, muscled body, his weight and height.

God help her…she couldn't stop the flood of sensation, the overwhelming crashing of her emotions.

She was falling for Lieutenant Dexter Kaczewski not because of what he'd done, but because of who he was and who she was with him. If the danger had a hand in throwing them together, it wasn't what had sealed her fate here. That might have been the catalyst, but she felt him in the fiber of her soul.

He was her man, her warrior. She was so his.

She was desperate to have this situation solved, desperate for him to go back to his life and for her to take up her own again.

Except… God help her, she wasn't going back to the Hill the same person. He had changed her, profoundly, and she was grateful, so grateful, for that.

The only thing that hadn't changed was her fear. That remained like barbed wire around her heart, but even as it kept him out, it also made her bleed.

Marriott Hotel, Pentagon City,
Arlington, Virginia

Austin swore for the five millionth time. Okay, he wasn't sure how many times he'd sworn, but his gut was shrieking at him that this was it. Getting into Thelma Kaczewski's social media account was going to net him something big.

Derrick was still asleep, but Austin couldn't stop. He'd gotten through all of the levels of security except for the very last one.

Frustrated he leaned back against the headboard, his eyes gritty, his back sore. Then his cell buzzed and he leaped for it. He said hello as he grabbed his key card and slipped out of the room. He headed downstairs to the bar.

"Hello, is this Austin Beck?"

"Yes, how can I help you?" He lifted one finger, then the bartender poured a beer from the tap and set it down in front of him.

"This is Russell Kaczewski. I'm Dexter's brother and my dad told me you were on the case. I want to know what is going on with my brother."

"We're following—"

"Don't give me that following leads line. I was a RECON marine. I know the score, so give it to me straight."

Austin took a cold sip and sighed, but couldn't help a small smile. This was a fellow marine, his brother in arms.

"Okay, he's here in DC and it looks like he's fine."

There was a release of a deep breath on the other end of the line. "To tell you the truth, I thought you were going to stonewall me."

"You mean like your dad did to us?"

"My dad knows Dex is in DC?"

"He's a wily one, your dad."

"He plays his cards close to the vest and always on a need-to-know basis. I guess I can't fault him for that."

Austin heard sounds of traffic, then a loudspeaker in the background. "Ah, man, don't come here. There's nothing you can do."

"It's my brother and he's wounded and people are trying to kill him. What would you do?" Damn military types. "I'll be staying with my dad. Could you keep me posted?"

"I can't promise…"

"Beck, c'mon."

"I'll see what we can do," Austin said, polishing off his beer. He disconnected the call as he headed back to the room. He was cracking that damn security wall tonight. Inside the room, Derrick turned in his sleep, mumbled something unintelligible. Ha. And he said Austin talked in his sleep, which, of course, he didn't.

He pulled the laptop back onto his lap and typed and swore some more, tried something else and then *bam*, he was in!

"Yes," he hissed into the darkened room. He ran a search and, bingo, her information popped up and he started to scroll through her posts. About halfway down the page, he struck pay dirt. Gotta love social media. She had posted about house-sitting for some friends. The Kramers in the 'burbs. He chuckled, looking through her friends list until he found Kevin and Mary Kramer. Getting their address was going to be a piece of cake. Once Lara got into the office in four hours, he and Derrick would be heading over there.

His gut was never wrong.

Suburbs of Washington, DC

The world smelled faintly of sex…and sugar. Dex stirred and the silky sheets slid across his skin, nearly as soft and fine as the woman wrapped in his arms. He wasn't sure he was still flesh and blood; surely this girl grenade had blown him to smithereens last night. He got hard just thinking about her moving over him, the sensual tease of her hips and her deliberate movements to drive him insane.

She made him feel like he was drowning and for a SEAL that was kind of scary. In fact, if he was being truthful with himself, and he always tried to be, he knew she would take him under and hold him there, struggling for air. Except it would be a sweet struggle with her melting all over him, ready to take him inside her, and he didn't mean his erection. The most beautiful woman he'd ever seen with hands he wanted on him, and he knew deep in his heart just how good it would be between them.

The problem was he was liking her way too much. Tyler's sister. Even as he heeded Rock's warning and got more guilt dumped on him by the bro code, he'd long ago crossed the line. He didn't want to lose Tyler's friendship over this, but he also realized that he was going to hurt her. Because even though she was the most amazing woman and he was amazing with her, and they were amazing together, he still wanted to be a SEAL. Every day in her presence made him think more and more that she was his other unbreakable half. He hadn't known there was a vulnerability in his armor until he'd met her.

He thought he'd fallen before… Jesus…not even close.

Protecting his heart wasn't even an option now.

The woman had done him inside out.

The problem here was that he wanted every moment he could get with her. It was a flat-out admission and his cue to back off. Maybe take stock of the situation, reclaim a little pride, but he didn't take his hands off her. He didn't lean back and give her room, and he didn't lift his head from the curve of her neck.

Screw it—he opened his mouth on the soft, sweet skin beneath her ear. He tasted her with his tongue. He slid one hand up her body and moved her hair away from her neck, letting the silky strands drift through his fingers.

It was just one big forbidden mistake after another and he used his other hand to slide down over her bottom and press her into his hips, grazing her throat with his teeth, letting her scent seduce him.

His match...and he sensed that he was going to lose her, even as he entered her from behind and she gasped and arched her back, even as he thrust and thrust, took her body, took her heart, greedy and insatiable for every sound she made, every gasp, every indrawn breath.

He rolled her over onto her stomach, his shaft so hard and aching as he lost his control and drove into her.

He was lost, caught between what he wanted and what he couldn't live without. There was only one answer, one way he could go.

His job wasn't just what he did for a living; it fulfilled him at a level that nothing else could. He needed both to survive and be whole, but he would have to give up one.

"Dex," she whispered in a pleasure-soaked voice, and she rippled around him. He spasmed and came, his body jerking and emptying.

She was still in love with her husband, not over him. He had hurt her last night and with that memory came true, aching regret.

He was so damned selfish. He wanted all of her heart.

He collapsed over her, wincing as he slid to his side.

One thing was for sure, he was getting plenty of blood pumping into his wound. He cuddled her against him.

"Dex?" she said into the brightening room.

"Yeah," he replied, his arm wrapped around her waist, her sated body languid against his.

"I've been thinking. I want to get help."

He stiffened, his whole body going on alert.

"This isn't the same crap you were trying to feed me last night, Piper. Because you can forget it."

"No," she said, sending her hand over the back of his, caressing him.

"What, then?" he said cautiously.

"I want to contact Stephen Montgomery. He's very well-placed, has a lot of contacts, is discreet and he cares about me."

"I don't know, Piper." Dex didn't care if the guy was a priest and was personal friends with the freaking Pope. Someone wanted her dead and he wasn't taking any chances.

"Maybe he can make some headway. We can at least talk to him. We don't have to reveal our whereabouts. Just get him working for us."

He sighed. "You trust him?"

"Yes. I do. Not as much as I trust you, but yes."

That warmed him up inside like a sappy idiot. "All right, but no particulars."

After they showered and played some more—damn, she was a tease and made him forget everything—they settled on stools in the kitchen and ate breakfast.

"You sure about this Montgomery guy?"

"Yes. I'm sure." She bit into her toast and chewed, giving him a reassuring look. Her beauty struck him hard, like a metal pipe to the head—a brutal beauty that twisted a guy the hell up.

He just wanted to say, "Yes. Anything you want," but Dex was a navy SEAL and he was made of tougher stuff. *O-kay*, he might be 5 percent cream puff around her, but mostly sterner stuff. He had a gut feeling and he was going to follow through with it. She wasn't going to like it, but he figured he'd feed reality to her a little bit at a time. He didn't have anything more at stake here than his own life and Piper's. Those were pretty big to him and he wasn't going to go soft now, not when she needed him armed and dangerous.

"Call him," Dex said, "but be vague about exactly where you are. You don't even have to tell him you're in DC." He still didn't like this idea, but they were pretty much at a standstill. He had a hunch he wanted to execute, but he was sure it was going to put Piper in a tailspin. Couldn't be helped. He needed to find answers and he didn't like having to rely on people he didn't trust to deliver.

Piper was right. He was rich and he was a wild card. Dex liked a sure bet. And unless Montgomery was a navy SEAL, he couldn't extend his trust that far.

"Yes, sir," she said, saluting, and it was downright cute as hell.

He chuckled. "There's no saluting unless there's a cover on."

"A cover?"

"Hat," he said.

"You can't make an exception in my case, Lieutenant?" Her lower lip protruded in a pout.

He felt like a sappy idiot again. *Cream puff.* "Well, maybe." He tapped her phone. "Go. Dial. Put it on speaker."

She reached for her phone as Dex sipped his coffee. She punched in the number and it rang.

"Hello."

"Monty?"

"Oh, my God! Pippy!" Dex mouthed, *Pippy*, and arched his brows, a smile forming on his face, and she hit him on the arm. "Honey, it's so good to hear your voice. Edward was pretty closed lipped about you and I was going out of my mind with worry. Where are you?"

Dex shook his head and Piper nodded and said, "I'm safe, but I could use your help."

"Anything. Name it."

"I don't know if you're aware, but Ty wasn't all that convinced my car wreck and Brad's death were accidents."

"That's very troubling. Go on."

"The police were sparse on the information. I don't even know what they had found out, if anything. They kept telling me it was an accident. Brad had been drinking that night, but he wasn't drunk. I'm sure of that. They think he just lost control of the car, but I'm not sure that was the case. It's jumbled up in my head and I'm not sure myself."

"Let me get this straight. You think Brad was murdered and the police covered it up?"

"I don't know, but someone tried to kill Tyler by luring him and his SEAL team into an ambush and someone compromised my protection detail. Both of my DS agents tried to kill me. The only connection between Ty and me is that accident."

"This is very upsetting," he said, his voice choked. He paused and went on, "Brad was like a son to me. What do you want me to do?"

"I figured anyone who could make those things happen could easily pay off the police. I was wondering if it would be possible for you to use your influence to find out more information from the police. You know the commissioner. Surely, he would be helpful."

"I will call him now and get back to you with anything I find out. Where can I reach you?"

Dex covered the receiver. "Tell him you'll call him," he whispered.

Old Monty didn't like that; Dex could hear the disgruntlement in his voice. Before he could badger Piper, Dex hit the end button.

"That was rude, Dex. I didn't even get a chance to say goodbye."

"Well, when all this is over, *Pippy*, I'll personally apologize to him."

She huffed a laugh. "Don't you dare call me that. That's his childhood name for me. I bet you have one, and if you're not careful I'll find out what it is."

"I only have one nickname and it's a SEAL handle."

"Oh, and what's that?"

"Machine."

"Machine? As in robot with metal parts?"

"Machine. As in terminator. I don't stop coming."

"Oh," she said a little breathless. "That's sure a fitting nickname. I'd prefer you call me Piper, but I do like 'babe.'" Her voice softened.

"Not Bulldozer?" he said with a wicked grin. "As in you bulldozed me right into calling Montgomery." He shook his head. One of the richest men on the planet and she was on a nickname basis with him. "Yeesh, I can't believe you call him Monty."

She laughed and nudged his arm. "Bulldozer is better than Pippy."

"I don't know. I like Pippy."

"Stop it, Dex. I swear…"

His hair stood up on the back of his neck and shortly

after that he heard a furtive footfall. He cut her off by grabbing Piper by the arm and hustling her out of the kitchen, pulling her with him against the wall. She didn't say a word, her eyes wide and so golden. He put his finger to his lips and pulled his weapon out of the small of his back.

He indicated that she should head to the bedroom. "Get your weapon. Come around the back," he whispered. She nodded.

He checked his magazine, drove it home and chambered a round, thumbing off the safety, then he set his finger over the trigger, cupped his left hand under his right and took a breath.

He heard the sliding glass door open.

Whoever came through that door was a dead man.

Chapter 15

Austin moved into the sunny kitchen, his eyes roaming over the counter, immediately noticing the breakfast dishes and the coffee cups. He moved soundlessly up to the mug and pressed his fingers against it. Still warm.

He was just about to announce himself when a steely voice said, "Freeze." He was partly shielded by the wall leading out of the kitchen. Austin raised his hands.

He wasn't going to take any chances and piss off an armed navy SEAL. But the guy stiffened and he heard Derrick order Dexter Kaczewski to raise his hands and step into the kitchen.

Derrick and Dexter were about halfway to Austin when Derrick said, "Where's Senator Jones?"

"Right behind you, and I'm feeling a bit wobbly after being chased and almost killed several times, so I would suggest that you get that gun out of Dex's back and drop it."

"Piper," Dex warned, but it was too late. Derrick spun and disarmed her, but it was enough for Dex to get his gun up and pointed at Austin.

"Let her go," Kaczewski said in a voice that said Austin only had a few minutes to live.

"Wait!" Austin yelled. "I'm going to reach for my badge."

Dexter Kaczewski had some deep, penetrating intimidation going on there in his eyes. A cool, I-mean-business blue.

"Easy," Dex said as Austin reached into his back pocket and pulled out the badge. "NCIS Special Agent Austin Beck, and that's Special Agent Derrick Gunn."

"NCIS?"

"We've been chasing you two around the globe. Just missed you in Afghanistan."

"Is that so?" Dex said in an I-don't-give-two-flying-hells tone. "Well, aren't you the resourceful Boy Scouts? How did you find us?"

"We're here to help," Derrick said, letting Piper go and putting his gun away. "The boy genius hacker over there tapped your mother's social media accounts and had this hunch you were here." But Kaczewski didn't move a muscle.

"Thing is. Her detail tried to kill her, so I'm not inclined to trust any alphabetfreakingsoup agency, no matter who they are."

"I get that, Lieutenant. But you see, I can't be bought. All I care about is surfing and, well, that whole karma thing always comes back to bite you in the ass. And Derrick, well, he's already rich. I'm working on him to come around to the karma-is-a-bitch thing. He's a work in progress."

The lieutenant looked at Derrick and he shrugged. Piper reached out and clasped her hand around his forearm. "Dex…"

He lowered the weapon and Austin took a deep breath. *Hoo-boy*, nothing like having a gun pointed at you by a guy who's a sniper and a SEAL. Who had the ability to throw a knife across the room with precision accuracy and kill a guy in one fell swoop.

Yeah, he was holding on to that karma thing.

Piper offered them coffee, but Dex didn't relax. He watched them, his gun on the counter within easy reach.

"Thank you, Senator," the smart-mouthed one said— the one who did look like a California surfer dude with his messy shaggy light brown hair and blond highlights. The other one looked like an assassin. Dark, cold blue eyes, and he'd disarmed Piper like he was taking candy from a baby.

He got a good vibe off them, though, and he was inclined to believe them. Actually, it was good they were here. He had something he wanted them to do. Piper came over to him.

"Stop glowering at them, Dex. They're here to help." Piper studied Derrick when he wasn't looking and Dex got immediately jealous. The way she was looking at him got his hackles up.

He went to the coffeemaker and poured himself a fresh cup. He leaned back against the counter and met her gaze.

"You trust these guys? 'Cause it's our lives on the line."

"I do."

They had already filled Dex in on the dead PI and the fact the police had no leads on who murdered him. No forensic evidence whatsoever. That meant a hired gun, black ops, probably former CIA.

When Piper went to take a shower, Dex went into the living room. "I have a job for you guys." He held out a set of keys.

"What are these for?"

"Piper's house. I want you to box up everything in her husband's office, including his computer, and bring it here."

"What do you think you're going to find?"

"I don't know. Since his death was deemed an accident, they didn't disturb any of his stuff, but Piper did say she had a break-in the day after Brad's death. I think someone was looking for something."

The surfer dude nodded. "I'd be happy to go over the computer."

"He went to Cornell," Derrick said dryly.

"And you went to the School of Hard Knocks," Dex said, but Gunn just shrugged again.

When Piper emerged from the shower, she looked around and set her hands on her hips. "What did you do with the nice federal agents, Dex?"

"Sent them on an errand." He came up to her and brushed at the hair on her forehead. "Why don't you call Monty back and see if he's uncovered anything?"

"What are you up to and what errand?"

"Hopefully something that will shed some light on this whole situation."

Piper wasn't going to like that he'd violated her husband's office and her privacy. She'd told him she hadn't been in there since he died. Everything was exactly where he'd left it. What if there was something in his papers or files that indicated whether he was dirty or vindicated him? Something on his computer. He wasn't sure Piper wanted to know, but he was going to press the issue. Maybe he was digging up dirt on one of his fellow senators. Robert Mullins came to mind, the senator that was giving Piper a hard time about this corporate change bill. As far as Dex was concerned, he was at the top of his list of people who might want Piper dead.

His search for any information on the guy was limited by his abilities and his access.

Piper narrowed her eyes at him, but even though her stare was right up there with one of his Basic Underwater Demolition/SEAL—or BUD/S for short—trainers, he didn't budge. She would find out soon enough.

She walked over to the counter and dialed, then put it on speaker.

"Hello? Pippy?"

"Hi, Monty. Did you find out anything?"

"Yes." His voice was subdued. "After some digging, I found that the lead cop was paid off. Don't ask me how."

"I want to talk to him. What is his name?"

"It won't do you any good. He was killed in the line of duty. The incident report he filed said your crash was an accident."

"Killed?" She threw Dex a look that said the conspiracy was covering their tracks. "When?"

"A week after the accident. I can try to follow the money trail for you and see where that leads."

"That would be great. Thank you, Monty."

As she hung up, Austin and Derrick came in through the garage carrying boxes. They set them down and went out for more. Finally, they ended up with ten stacked in the hall. Austin handed Dex back the keys.

Piper's mouth thinned and she eyed the boxes. "What are these?"

Dex didn't answer and Austin and Derrick exchanged glances. She marched up to one of the boxes and pulled off the lid. Her breath caught and her eyes went moist and Dex felt like the biggest asshole on the planet.

"These are my husband's…things. You went to my house and packed up his office. You think he's dirty."

"Piper," Dex said, drawing her to the side. "I don't know. I know this is hard, but we can't find out any information if we leave everything where it was when he died. This will give you a chance to move on. Put this behind you. Maybe get answers."

"I can't see him doing anything illegal to get ahead. I've thought about it since last night, and I swear I'm being as objective as I can be. He wouldn't, Dex. Not this. Not to me, not to his constituents, his backers. He just… It's not who he was any more than it's who I am. For any price."

"Don't take this the wrong way, but what if he wanted the White House? You said he was ambitious. What if he was willing to do anything to get there?"

"He would have told me he was going to run for president. I would be affected by that."

"Would he, Piper?"

"You didn't know him."

"No, but you did. You told me you did everything for him. Maybe he just expected you would be on board for the presidency. Political royalty, politician's wife, just a couple of steps to First Lady. I'm not saying he's dirty, but we have to keep all options open."

She looked into his eyes for the longest time, then gathered herself and said, "I know. I understand. But you've talked a lot about gut instincts. That's why I told you about Brad. It's why I've kept nothing back, ever. I knew I trusted you instinctively. I won't believe it's true until I see some proof." Her eyes looked bruised. "I can't believe you did this." She turned and left the room.

Austin and Derrick looked at him. "Let's get this stuff into the dining room," Dex said, watching Piper walk away. He'd give her some time. He was sympathetic to her feelings, but he cared more about getting to the bottom of this and making sure the threat to her was neutralized. He wanted her safe, no matter what it cost him. Even if it cost him her. "There's a big table in there we can use."

They started hauling. After about ten minutes, Derrick sat up straighter.

"What is it?" Dex asked.

"Maybe nothing, but there are several articles from the Net that Jones printed out."

"Investment?"

"Maybe. Worth noting." Derrick picked up his cell and punched in a number. "Hey, Amber, I need you to do a search for me. Omni Corp, Sundown, Leeson-Group and JackTrades. All you can find. Also, do me a profile of Senator Robert Mullins." He listened for a minute. "Yup, that would be the guy." He smiled a rare smile. "Yeah, yesterday."

"Amber? Amber Dalton? You work with her?"

"Yeah, we know she's marrying your brother's best friend. We're keeping her in the dark. Personal connection and all."

Dex nodded. "She's good people." He relaxed a bit. If these guys worked with Amber, they had to be on the up-and-up. She was a really good judge of character, as evidenced by her falling for Rock's best friend.

Dex went to the bedroom to try to talk to Piper one more time. He felt like hell that he had to force this issue, but she would have pushed back on this. As he approached, he stopped dead. Muffled sobs drifted to him as he stood outside the door. His gut clenched and he put his hand on the jamb to steady himself.

And he knew there was no protecting himself from this. Or from her.

Hours passed and midnight came and went, with disheartening results. The computer was wiped, completely and unrecoverably wiped. Austin couldn't restore anything. Of course, they weren't sure who had wiped the system, but it couldn't have been Brad because it had occurred after he was dead. On the night of the break-in. Not a coincidence.

Derrick's cell rang and he tapped the speaker. Amber's voice said, "Hey, guys. I got that information you needed on Omni Corps, Sundown, LeesonGroup and JackTrades, which are all Fortune 500 companies trading on the stock exchange. They are also heavy supporters of Robert Mullins, according to what I could find. No red flags there, but I did find that Mullins was connected to a CEO of—" she ruffled some papers "—Markset Limited, who was found dead in his penthouse apartment in New York just before Brad Jones died. It might not be anything."

"How did he die?"

"Alcohol poisoning. Ruled an accident."

"Did he drink?"

"It seemed moderately. I couldn't find much about him drinking in excess, but people in the limelight don't broadcast that. Also, there was a PI killed in New York that same week. Sam George. I thought it was interesting because he worked out of Brad Jones's office."

"It seems a lot of people surrounding Mullins end up dead."

"Seems so."

"You got a profile on him?"

"Yes. Robert Michael Mullins. He's fifty-seven years old, a former New York governor who is well-known for revitalizing the FDNY. He also served as New York's attorney general, intelligence briefer for President Sharons, CIA station chief in Riyadh, Saudi Arabia, and before that he was an analyst for the CIA. Education, BA Princeton University, JD Harvard Law School. Married to Crickett Ames of the Texas oil baron Ameses with two college-age daughters. He's pugnacious and unapologetic and brings a brash style to everything he does. He was known for being a hard-charger when he was attorney general. He's often accused of embracing an ego-driven and needlessly abrasive style. Otherwise, guys, Mullins profile reads like he deserves to be the next president of the United States. The guy's Mr. Clean."

"Thanks, Amber."

"Anything else you need researched, let me know. Bye, Derrick."

"Bye, Amber."

An hour later, Austin jerked in his seat at the halfway point with five boxes down. He rubbed his eyes. Dex was losing steam, too. "Good job, Hang Ten."

Austin grinned and held up his fist for a bump. "You gave me a call name, so maybe you're warming up to me?"

Dex sighed and fist bumped him. "We'll see."

Austin looked at Dex and nudged him. "What call name would you give Derrick?"

Dex never hesitated. "Assassin."

"Yeah, I see that. He's got that dark and deadly thing going on there."

Derrick just rolled his eyes and set down the file he had been riffling through.

"Let's call it a night, guys. There are three other bedrooms in this place. Choose whichever ones you want. I will see you in the morning and we'll go through the rest of this stuff."

Austin groaned when he stood and stretched. "Don't worry, man. She'll come around. It is better to know."

Dex nodded. He took a step forward and his foot kicked a box, tumbling it to the side. He bent down to scoop the spilled contents inside and saw a manila envelope. He picked it up.

"What's that?" Austin asked, looking over his shoulder.

The corner was stamped with the name of Washington Hospital Center MedStar Unit. He broke the seal and dumped the contents out. There was a wallet, keys, tickets to a cancer fund-raiser, small pink booties, some change and a cell phone.

"Jones's personal effects," Austin said, picking up the phone. "It's dead, but we can charge it overnight and see if there's anything useful on it."

Dex nodded, his eyes riveted to the booties, wondering why Brad had them on him when he'd died. Had he been planning to give them to Piper? His heart twisted for her. He walked toward the master bedroom. He slipped inside and stripped down, sliding into the warm bed. Piper was sleeping as far away from the middle as she could get without falling off the edge of the bed, telling him that she was still mad at him.

He closed his eyes, drifting, aching to pull her into his arms. They felt empty without her snuggled up against him, but maybe this was for the better. He clenched his jaw. Better for whom? Certainly not him.

When this was finally over, what kind of future did the two of them have? She lived in DC. He was based out of Coronado. He was a SEAL. She was a politician.

He squeezed his eyes closed and his heart beat painfully.

Dex was in love with her.

She was still in love with her husband.

And he was jealous of a dead man.

"Oh, Brad, the baby is kicking."

They were leaving the very long, very boring fundraiser and Piper was ready to get into something more comfortable, although Brad had said she was a glowing stunner in her little black dress.

She'd snorted then because there was nothing little about her dress or her. Her stomach was full of their baby daughter—Sophie. Brad, looking good in his tux, slipped his hand over her stomach as they stopped walking to the car. For a moment, they waited.

"There it is," he murmured, and sure enough the fluttery kick turned into several really strong ones. "I can feel her foot," he said as Piper's stomach bulged.

"She is an active one," Piper agreed, and Brad slipped his arm around her, pulling her to him.

"I have an appointment tomorrow."

"What kind of an appointment?"

"It's nothing. Just some financial matters with our lawyers. I shouldn't be more than two hours."

She nodded. "Sounds good. I can hold down the fort."

"You really should start staying home and resting."

"I can work and I love to support you. I'll be home after Sophie's born."

He held the door for her and closed it after she was inside. Walking around, he got in and loosened his tie.

"You okay to drive?" she asked. Brad looked preoccupied. In fact, he'd been subdued for the last three weeks. Maybe he was getting nervous about the baby's birth.

She covered his hand and smiled. "Everything is going to be fine," she said.

He started and his head whipped around to hers. He looked surprised and spooked. "What?"

"With the birth. You'll make a great dad."

She squeezed his hand and he laced his fingers with hers for a moment. "I know. I love you, Piper."

"I love you, too."

He started the car and they pulled out of the parking spot as he navigated to the GW Parkway.

Piper leaned her head back as Brad accelerated and lights reflected in her rearview side mirror. She squinted as they got closer and closer until they moved to pass. It was a dark car with tinted windows. Suddenly, the driver swerved and Brad swore.

Piper sat up, gripping the side of the door. The vehicle threatened them again and, in response, Brad swerved. As they approached the exit for Route 123, the pursuing car crowded them to the shoulder. Brad wrestled with the wheel, but the shoulder was soft and he lost control. Their car broke through the stone retaining wall. Piper screamed as the car tilted, then went into a dizzy whirl as it rolled over and over, glass breaking, the sound of wood splintering and metal grinding until it came to an abrupt stop and Piper blacked out.

When she opened her eyes, she saw Brad, his body draped over the deflated air bag, his eyes open and staring, blood running from his nose and ears.

"Brad?" she screamed. But he didn't stir, didn't look at her. She closed her eyes tight. He wasn't breathing. "Brad! No!"

Then she felt it—the slide of blood and fluid—and her throat closed up. Sophie. Oh, God. Her baby.

"Brad!"

She sat up in bed and Dex was there, slipping his arm around her, and she turned to him, seeking his warmth. The nightmare had been so vivid, as if it wasn't something she'd conjured in her own mind, but actual events. She remembered the first part vividly, but the details of the accident had been fuzzy. She'd been told at the hospital that she might not even remember it at all. Was her mind trying to fill in the blanks? Had the danger and adrenaline skewed her thinking? But then it all felt right and in a flash, she knew that she had relived the accident.

Tears streaming down her face, she cried, "I remember. I remember everything. We were driven off the road. Oh, God." She clutched at Dex. "Brad was murdered. They killed my baby." She cried harder. All the pain came rushing back at her. "They took everything."

He rocked her, murmuring to her, his jaw tightening. But she was lost in her grief.

She felt so cold and physically disconnected. Feeling raw and exposed, she looked up at Dex, every nerve in her body stretched to the limit.

He brushed her cheek with his thumb. "It's going to be okay, babe," he murmured, looping a strand of hair over her ear.

His words warmed her, his encouragement and support wrapping around her like a cozy blanket. The throbbing thickness in her throat eased, the tears slowed. Murmuring her name, he tightened his embrace.

Rattled by the feelings swamping her, it was a long time before she stirred.

She became aware of him stroking her back and her face was buried in his neck. Inhaling unevenly, Dex pulled them back, braced himself against the head-board, drawing her deeper into his embrace; his touch was meant to comfort her as he massaged the base of her spine.

"If you're right, Dex, about Brad, his actions could have caused the death of our child."

Dex raised his head and looked at her, his gaze solemn. "I know, but you're strong enough for that truth, Piper."

Was she? She had gone through so much.

"I can get through this. I have to. And you're right. I do need to know the truth. I need desperately to know the truth now."

"Then we'll get the truth for you, Piper. Somewhere, somehow, we'll find the answers." He loosened his hold so he could look into her face.

"I have to go to the police and get the accident re-opened now that I remember. A car drove us off the road. There had to have been evidence of that."

"We can't go to the police yet."

"Why not?"

"Piper, you're still in danger. We can't trust anyone at this point. We're going to dig some more tomorrow. Hopefully we find something."

She nodded, understanding, but her heart ached that she couldn't go right away. Get them working on who had done this.

She couldn't help remembering Robert Mullins's change of heart about the bill. He had at first supported

Brad, then changed his mind and gone in a different direction after Brad had been killed.

He was more interested, he said, in getting a proper bill written and put through the process. The way the bill was now, he worried that it might not pass. Then, when she'd refused to drop the legislation, he'd gotten more agitated, then he started to threaten her.

"Dex. We should check Brad's congressional email. Maybe Mullins sent messages to Brad through that channel."

"That's a good idea, now that his computer was wiped and everything lost. Can you access the email?"

"Yes, I have his password. I have just avoided everything to do with Brad. I was the one who handled most of his correspondence and he trusted me with all his codes. But he really handled that email account himself. I usually didn't go in there."

"All right. We'll check it out. Do you have his cell phone password?"

"Yes," she said, and rattled it off.

"I think Robert Mullins murdered your husband to keep that bill from passing. I think he hired someone to do it. Maybe even the same someone who attacked us at Coffee Now in Pentagon City."

"It makes sense," she said, snuggling up against him as he pulled her down into the bed and his embrace.

He kissed her temple. "Now that you've remembered what happened, hopefully you won't have any more nightmares."

Her voice was unsteady when she answered. "I hope so. I've relived that particular one more than enough."

"You have. Try to relax now and go back to sleep. I'm here, Piper."

"I'm sorry about how I acted. You were only trying to help."

"I get it. It's your life and you're still trying to make sense out of it. But you do what you have to do. I admire that."

She cuddled closer to him and kissed his chest and breathed him in, and after a moment she confessed, "I want answers. I want the truth. Really, whatever that is. Do what you have to do and I'll help as much as I can. Whoever did this stole my future and needs to answer for it. Brad and Sophie need justice."

"Aww, Piper...Sophie?"

Tears gathered and slid down her cheeks and he just held her.

She smoothed her palm over the broad curve of his shoulder and continued upward, tunneling her fingers into his hair. And she kissed him, one long moment after another, luxuriating in the sensuality of having him naked and close, and in the comfort she felt—even the way he smelled made her feel safe.

Chapter 16

Austin was already up and on the phone, his hair more tousled than normal, when Dex came out of the bedroom. Was that just the way he wore it? He heard the shower going in the bathroom down the hall, evidence the dark assassin was up, too.

Piper was still sleeping, but she had given him the password for Brad's email account. He made coffee. Ripping a piece of paper off the tablet in the kitchen, Dex wrote the cell phone code down. He set it on the charging device and headed to the pool. This inactivity was grating on him. He was used to action and plenty of conflict to keep his mind sharp.

Diving in, he started to swim laps, slow and steady to warm up, letting his body take over, releasing his mind and his thoughts and feelings for Piper.

He'd done what he hadn't intended to do. Got so entangled with her, a woman who was emotionally unavailable to him.

She was his match, the kind of woman who would be able to stand by him every day in what he wanted to do with his life. The kind of woman who could handle two hundred and twenty days out of three hundred and sixty-five without him. To be a SEAL's wife—oh, yeah, right, he was going there. He wanted her...in his life. That was certain. She was the very definition of strength and grace. Piper had already proven that she could embrace her husband's goals and take that stand along with him.

But in her case, she never held any resentment about it toward him. She was a woman to stand alone when he was deployed and stand with him when he was home and needed her. What had destroyed his other relationships was that he'd chosen the wrong women to stand by him. In the end, they resented him. He'd just realized that this minute because of Piper.

She had been more interested in making a strong family for her man, supporting his political goals. His only regret was that she hadn't pursued her own dreams. He would be all for that.

She cared about him. That was evident, but maybe it was more because of the constant danger and the fact that he'd saved her life. She needed his protection.

This had started out as a rescue, then had changed and snowballed until his throat ached with how he felt about Piper. He loved Ty as a brother and that got all knotted up in him, too. Rock had been right—it was best to steer clear of your best friend's sister.

But regardless of how Piper felt about him, he was going to see this through to the end. No matter the cost.

On his thirtieth lap, Dex was just getting warmed up when someone called from the pool deck. "Hey, Flipper! I've got something you need to see."

Dex leveraged himself right out of the pool by his arms. Austin threw him a towel. "The phone's charged and I found a video on it. Brad made it the day he died."

Dex dried off his upper body as he followed Austin back into the house. "I copied it to my laptop," he said.

"I'll go get Piper."

He entered the bedroom and she stirred. He crouched down, kissed her soft lips. "Piper?"

She opened her eyes and smiled. "Good morning."

"Morning, babe. We charged your husband's phone last night. There's a video on it that he made the day he died."

She released a shaky sigh and sat up, sliding her feet around to the floor as he rose. She reached for her robe at the end of the bed and stood, slipping it on.

He cupped her face, then smoothed down her hair. "I'll be there every step of the way."

"Let's see what he had to say." Her voice was uneven.

She reached for his hand and he threaded their fingers together. Back in the living room, Derrick was seated on the sofa and Austin had set the laptop on the coffee table. He was perched on the arm of the sofa.

"Morning, gentlemen."

"Senator."

"Please, call me Piper," she said with a small smile, and sat, Dex folding down right next to her, his hand still around hers.

"Are you ready, Sena—Piper?"

"Yes." She went a bit white, her hand going to the locket around her throat as she cupped it.

Austin reached forward and clicked Play.

Brad's face was conciliatory. It looked like he was in his parked car. "Piper, I want to tell you how much I love you. How much your support, energy, enthusiasm and willingness to take our dream as far as it could go has meant to me." He smiled and Piper's eyes welled.

"I also want to apologize for what I'm about to tell

you and feel like crap that I haven't confided in you all along, but I was selfish. I didn't want you in harm's way. I've been investigating Robert Mullins." His voice was subdued, but Dex could hear the underlining strain and fear.

"He's tried to bully me out of the corporate change bill. But I had no idea what heinous acts he would commit in his bid for the White House." Anger tinged his words and his face hardened. "I've gathered a lot of evidence against him, thanks to a man who was killed last week in a hit-and-run car accident in New York City. My PI, Sam George. His death was no accident. It just adds to the long list of people Mullins got out of his way. He's got special interests in corporations that are paying into his campaign funds through blackmail and conspiracy. Mr. George has given me evidence that an assassin was involved in murdering the CEO of Markset Limited. Mr. George was a brave and loyal man and I'll miss him. I'm pretty sure that Mullins is aware of what I've uncovered, as Mr. George's office was ransacked and all his computer files taken." He took a deep breath.

"I'm going to Edward with all this evidence I've gathered. I'm sorry I lied to you. If you're watching this video, I'm probably dead." He brought the booties out of his jacket pocket and Piper made a soft sound. Dex slipped his arms around her shoulders as tears spilled over and tracked silently down her cheeks. "I carry these around with me to remind me that making a better world for our daughter is more important than being safe and sound. I pledged my service to the people of California. I care what happens to the US and embrace what our forefathers in their brilliant way set up to govern our great nation." Brad choked up and he took several deep breaths to get control. "Men like Mullins don't deserve to even step foot into the Oval Office, let alone run this country."

He leaned his head against the backrest, squeezing his eyes closed. "If I don't…make it, tell our daughter, our Sophie, how much I love her. I'm sure she's beautiful." He rubbed at his eyes, his voice husky. "Don't let her forget about me. Tuck her in each night knowing that I tried to make a difference. Everything I gathered is on my laptop, but in case that's destroyed, you have what you need close to your heart to take to Edward." He impatiently brushed tears away. "Stay safe, Piper, and please don't mourn me too long. Life is too short for you not to be happy. Find love again. Hold on to it hard and live. Don't let my sacrifice be in vain, sweetheart."

The video ended and Piper covered her face and wept. It was the only sound in the room. Austin went to the window and looked out. Derrick's eyes were filled with compassion.

A low sound of agony broke the silence of the room as Dex, unable to stand her pain, gathered her close. Austin motioned to Derrick and they left through the front door. It closed softly behind them. He rocked Piper. Catching him by the back of the head, Piper hung on to him.

"It's okay, babe," he choked out. "It's okay."

Piper tightened her hold and Dex dragged his hand up and down her back, molding them together finally in a crushing hold comforting her through this terrible revelation, this horrible news, driven by a need that burned through to his very soul.

"I've got you, babe," he said, trying to swallow the knot in his throat.

She raised her head and met his eyes, hers swimming

in tears, visibly moved beyond words by his gruff admission showing in those moist depths.

Neither of them spoke for a long time. Finally, she raised her head. He wiped away the moisture with his thumb. She faced him, her gaze frank and steady. "What do you think he meant about me having the means to take down Mullins close to my heart?"

"I don't know. It was cryptic, but was probably meant to be. If someone got ahold of Brad's phone and saw the video, they would know you had the evidence. But where could he have put it?"

Dex rose and went to the front door. Opening it, he motioned for Austin and Derrick to come back inside. They had to figure this out.

Dex paced and Piper watched his powerful body move. "We thought your attack was about a bill," Dex said, "but it had to be about this. About what dirt Brad dug up to nail Mullins to the wall."

Piper fingered her locket, her heart still breaking over Brad's video and the fact that she had never got to see her baby. Sophie had never been born. She felt so empty, yet so filled with rage.

Dex stopped pacing and stood still, staring at her. Piper felt his gaze and she raised her head. His eyes were watching her fingers caress the locket.

"Piper. You said Brad gave you the locket. When?"

"Just out of the blue, about two weeks before he died. I never take it off except to shower."

He came closer, his eyes alight. "Does it open?"

"No, it's old. Brad said it was…fused shut." Her heart skipped a beat. "What? You think there's something inside?"

"'You have what you need close to your heart to take

to Edward,'" Dex said, and reached out his hand. "That locket is close to your heart, Piper. May I? I'll try to be careful with it."

She reached back and unclasped the locket and set it into the palm of his hand. Austin and Derrick followed him over to the dining-room table. He set the locket down, pulled out a wicked-looking knife and slipped the point into the seam in the locket and pried. He worked at it for several seconds, then the two halves separated.

Piper held her breath until she saw it, a dime-size metal square with a black head.

"It's a flash drive," Austin said. "Son of a bitch. She's been wearing it around her neck all this time. Well played, Brad Jones. Well played."

"If I hadn't ignored everything after Brad's death, people wouldn't have died. Those marines, those SEALs, Mr. Utley." She gripped the counter, guilt making her gut churn. She ran from the room and just made it to the bathroom before she lost everything in her stomach.

Her brother Ty…he could have died.

Dex was there, pulling her hair back as she was sick again. She closed her eyes, but this time there would be no tears. There would be action and justice.

After she rose and he handed her a washcloth, he said, "I know what you're thinking."

"It's all my fault. I didn't want to face any of it. When I lost them…"

"Goddammit, Piper. Listen, and listen good! This isn't your *fault*." His voice shook with his barely contained anger, his jaw so tight. "I told you that in Afghanistan and I'm telling you now. You didn't do any of this. Mullins did. He's the one who's got blood all over his hands." His voice was husky and filled with steel. "Not you, babe," he said viciously, dragging her against him.

She wrapped her arms around his neck and held on to him as fiercely as he was holding on to her.

When they left the bathroom, Derrick and Austin looked concerned and fired up. "We can contact…"

"No."

Derrick went toe-to-toe with Dex and Piper's stomach jumped, the queasiness not going away. "Look, Kaczewski, we have a job to do. Find out who masterminded an attack on a contingent of US Navy SEALs, lured them into an ambush. Attacked a wounded SEAL. You! That's what we were tasked with."

Austin's eyes narrowed and the surfer boy suddenly looked much more menacing. "Your men, Lieutenant."

"I'm well aware of who died in my unit—good men— but I'm not turning this over to NCIS or anyone. I don't give a damn what your chain of command is. This information stays locked down so no one else dies. This is Piper's show. Her husband was murdered for this information and she lost her child over this. We're giving it to someone she can trust. Her brother Edward."

"But SECNAV…"

"SECNAV can bust me out of the navy, but I'm not budging. I don't trust anyone. We're taking this to Edward Keighley, Piper's brother, and we're keeping this under wraps until all the arrests are made."

Piper curled her hand around Agent Gunn's forearm. "Please," she said softly. "Trust Dex. He's kept me safe all this time."

Derrick turned to look at her and quite plainly wasn't happy, but as she held his gaze, he huffed out a breath and looked away. "All right. You've gotten us this far," Derrick said, covering her hand and squeezing. "Beck?"

Austin agreed. "Kai is going to chew our asses, but we'll take this to her brother."

Piper called and set up a time to meet her brother at his house that night. She told him that what she was bringing to him was huge and that it was Brad who had died for the evidence to put away Robert Mullins.

"I've got to call Monty," she said as Dex and the two NCIS agents were busy strategizing. She picked up her cell and went into the kitchen. She dialed his number and as soon as he answered, she said, "Monty."

"I've got evidence for you, Piper. We should meet."

"Yes, that's a good idea. We're planning on giving evidence we've uncovered to my brother Edward at his home tonight at seven." Piper was so numb, moving on autopilot, trying to sort through everything she'd experienced since she got the call that Tyler had been wounded. She wanted to shut down, but she couldn't. She had to see this through. "Could you be there and bring what you have?"

"Gladly."

As they drove over to Edward's house, Piper asked again, "Where are Austin and Derrick?"

"They decided to go back to San Diego. There wasn't anything else they could do here. This situation is solved and you're in good hands with me."

It was over. She was going to be safe after she gave Edward the evidence that Brad had gotten with his life. She would be free to continue with her own.

Dex would slip out of her life and suddenly she felt so bereft that she wouldn't see him every day, go to sleep with him, wake up to him, make love to him.

Her emotions had been so tested this week, along with plenty of danger and shocks that had been hard to take. How could she even begin to sort it all out?

When he was in DC, Edward lived in Bethesda, where

their family estate was located. He'd taken over the mansion and the upkeep. It was a lot of responsibility, but Edward was so darned responsible.

They pulled through the gate once Piper gave Dex the code and it closed behind them.

"Just park out front," she said. They got out of the car and went up the walk.

Dex's brows rose as she used her key to get inside. "You really are filthy rich."

They entered the grand foyer, a beautiful chandelier illuminating the white marble floors.

"Go ahead. I know you want to say something about the pillars."

"No. Just that you have them in your foyer."

She walked through the house and Dex followed her, looking around. "I can give you the grand tour. Sounds like Edward's on the phone, anyway."

She took him into the formal dining room, the more casual living room and then into the gourmet kitchen. "My mom loved to cook."

"Is your Georgetown home this large?"

"No, but I do have a six-bedroom home."

"Wow, that's a lot of space."

She bit her lip. "I was hoping to fill it with children. The beginning of our political legacy."

Dex squeezed her shoulder. "I'm sorry, Piper."

"Thank you," she said.

"Hey, now look here. There's a pool. Why didn't you learn how to swim?"

"I don't know. I was too busy doing things and the shallow end of the pool was fine."

The doorbell rang and Piper headed back toward the front of the house. "I've got it, Edward."

He came out of a wood-paneled room and covered the receiver. "I'll be a few more minutes."

She pulled open the door to Monty, who had a man with him dressed in a suit. "Pippy," he said as he wrapped his arms around her and held her tight for a minute. "I'm so sorry about all this terrible news and all that you've been through."

"Come in." Monty entered the foyer and eyed Dex. "This is Lieutenant Dexter Kaczewski."

The man behind him lifted his arm, and before she could even shriek, he shot Dex in the chest. The bullet pushed him back and he hit the floor hard.

Piper's scream echoed off the walls as the man grabbed her by the hair and dragged her down the hall, past Dex's prone body.

Sobbing, he took her into the library where Edward backed up and the man shot him, too. By this time, Piper was in so much shock and pain she could barely think straight. The man shoved her onto the small sofa in the mahogany-paneled room.

This was the man who had chased them and tried to kill them in DC. She was sure of it, and he was with Monty.

It was almost more than she could process. "I trusted you."

"This isn't personal, Pippy. It's business. Now turn over the evidence to me and this will be very painless for you."

"No," she bit out.

"Pippy," he said softly, like he was still in her good graces and she was little again. "Don't make this hard on both of us. Nyx isn't a patient killer."

"No, he isn't," Robert Mullins said as he strode into

the room. "Senator Jones, I warned you about going against me."

"You're in on this together."

"No," Monty said. "He's blackmailing me."

"Monty had your husband killed because of the bill, but I made sure to let Monty know how damaging it could be to his company. When your brother started digging, Monty got nervous. He used my contacts to get the information about the SEALs, and when you went running off to him, it was the perfect scenario. I made sure to include one of my men to make sure the job got done right, but then your navy SEAL stepped in and all bets were off. The two of you were very good at hiding, but now it's over."

"Nyx," Robert said, and he raised the gun.

Piper closed her eyes. They were going to kill her whether she gave them the flash drive or not. She wasn't going to give in. The assassin turned slightly and pulled the trigger. Suddenly, Monty staggered back, his face going white as he clutched at his chest. "You…bastard."

He careened into the bookcases and fell to the floor.

"Poor Monty," Mullins said. "He thought he was going to get the information and turn the tables on me. But I always have a backup plan. Now, Senator, give me what your very resourceful and goodie-two-shoes husband collected on me."

Piper glared at him. "You're not going to get away with this."

"You mean those two NCIS agents." He shook his head. "That's the trouble with law enforcement. There's always a chance of dying in the line of duty."

"You're a monster."

He advanced on her, grabbed her by the shirt and hauled her up. "I will be sitting in the White House and you will be nothing but a memory. They're never going to find your body. Oh, and Nyx will take care of Tyler. Just so you know." He backhanded her across the face and shoved her back on the sofa. "Kill her, search her and make sure her and the SEAL are never found. Leave Montgomery and Edward here and clear out the place of anything valuable. Ditch that rental of theirs. You can keep any of the profits you make."

The man turned to her with a cold smile on his face and her insides iced over. He raised his gun. "Goodbye, Senator Jones. You'll get to see your SEAL and your brothers soon." Mullins said with a smirk.

The shot exploded with a violent crack.

Chapter 17

Dex watched the assassin drop and he set his sights on Senator Mullins. "Sooner than she thought," he growled. Recognizing the sharp edge in his voice and the almost uncontrollable urge to double tap the bastard, he made his muscles relax. Locking his jaw against the rolling sensation in his belly, he clenched and unclenched his teeth, trying to bring the rage under control. The hot, violent surge of adrenaline finally abated.

"Dex!" Piper cried. She tipped her head back and closed her eyes, and he could tell that she was so relieved. He hated the subterfuge, but he was only doing what he promised to do. Protect her. He and Edward had worn vests in the event that Montgomery was the one who had betrayed Piper and Ty. Derrick and Austin hadn't really gone back to San Diego. He'd just let Piper think that. They were on hand to handle an arrest if needed.

"Move a muscle. Please, just give me a reason," Dex said.

Mullins held his hands up. "I didn't have anything to do with those SEALs."

"Maybe not, but you are part of the conspiracy and are just as guilty as Montgomery."

Austin and Derrick came into the room and Austin roughly cuffed him while Derrick went over to Edward and gave him a hand up.

Confusion darkening her eyes even more, she made a helpless gesture with her hand. "You're wearing vests. Oh, thank God," Piper said, jumping off the sofa and running to her brother, hugging him tight.

"Bulldozer. It's so good to see you." He looked over at Dex. "You the SEAL?"

Dex walked into the room and took the hand that Edward offered. "Thank you so much for saving my sister and for uncovering my brother-in-law's murder. We owe you so much."

Dex nodded as the sound of sirens in the distance got closer.

"Did you get everything?"

Edward walked to his desk and picked up the camera and pushed a few buttons. "Yup, got it all. Mullins isn't going to be able to either buy his way or talk his way out of this. He confessed to everything. Unfortunately, Montgomery isn't going to stand for his crimes, but he got what was coming to him."

EMTs came into the room, but the billionaire and the assassin were both dead.

Edward removed the digital card and put it in its case, handing the evidence to Derrick.

"The NCIS agents didn't go back to San Diego. They came here and you set all this up. Gave you two vests and planned the video." Piper looked at Derrick. "Why did you leave me out of this?" she demanded.

Derrick looked at Dex. "This one is all yours, boss,"

he said, and left the room, Edward following him. They were alone.

"Why?"

"You already had enough heartache and I didn't see the need to add to it. If Montgomery was on the up-and-up, we wouldn't need the vests and the camera, but if he wasn't, we were covered. Well, Mullins wasn't the only one with a backup plan. I sent NCIS here and you know the rest. I knew you would trust me to keep you safe. I wished he hadn't been involved. A betrayal by a friend is so much harder to deal with."

She nodded and went into his arms. Now she knew how she would react to losing Dex, and the thought of him in the kind of danger a SEAL lived every day was too much for her.

"Piper, I've got some military stuff to deal with. I've got to call my CO and let him know what happened and they're probably going to make me go to Walter Reed, but I want to talk to you about us."

She closed her eyes and slipped out of his embrace. Leaning against the desk, she folded her arms and she looked at him. "I can't," she whispered, her voice breaking. "I want to be strong enough to be the woman you need, but I can't take the risk of losing you to…"

"Combat."

She huddled in her arms, a terrible anguish lining her face. "I see what you deal with in a war zone. I'll know you're in jeopardy every day and I can't ask you not to do something you're so passionate about and so good at. I would never do that, never let you down."

He swallowed hard, knowing with all his heart this was the woman for him. The problem was, she didn't know how strong she was. She didn't think she could stand by him, but he knew differently. She was scared and she had been through a lot the last week. He would let this be for now. But he realized he had to let her go. It had to be her choice to want to be with him. She would have to come to him.

There wasn't anything more to talk about. She cried silently as Dex turned and left, stopping briefly to tell Edward that Piper needed him.

He walked out of her house and got into the rental and sat there for a moment as if that assassin's bullet had pierced his chest and opened a gaping hole.

He called his father and brother and let them know it was over and he was done.

When he called into base command at Coronado, California, and asked for his commander, he was sitting on the bed he'd shared with Piper; the suitcase from Afghanistan was stuffed with the meager clothes he had.

When the call went through and Dex explained where he'd been for six days, his commander ripped him a new one for a full fifteen minutes and ordered him to Walter Reed. His mother was already taking care of the house, and the files and computer had been confiscated by NCIS.

Austin and Derrick had already gone back to San Diego, and Mullins was being processed, charged with so many crimes, least of all treason. Stephen Montgomery was lucky he was dead.

Experiencing another jolt of fury, he stripped down and donned swim trunks and hit the pool, swimming lap after lap until his lungs shut down and his legs gave out. That's where Rock found him.

His brother hadn't said a word, just hauled his ass out of the pool and into the house. He forced him into the shower, his mouth tightening when he saw the wound on his side.

"Jesus. Why aren't you in the hospital, for God's sake, Dexter?"

"I got my ass chewed and I'm supposed to get some goddamned R and R before my CO wants to see my ugly mug in Coronado. I've been ordered to Walter Reed."

"Well, let's get you over there."

He just gave Rock a hard, flat look and Rock backed out of the bathroom. Dex stood there and then, dizzy and feeling sick, he leaned against the counter.

The face reflected back at him showed a haggard, hunched man with thick scruff and shaggy, dripping hair. He'd chased his brother out of the room. He didn't want him to see him come apart at the seams. He stared at his reflection in the mirror, struggling with the tightness in his throat.

Piper was finally safe. He could finally let go.

"I'm coming back in there if I don't hear that shower come on…like…now."

He stood there for a moment and thought about Spaceman, Slim and DJ. He gave them some head and heart time, pissed that they had died for nothing.

The room started to spin and he held on tighter to the counter.

"Rock…" he breathed, his knees buckling. He was heading to the floor, but as he started to fall, his brother was there, catching him.

"I got you."

Dex came to lying on the bed and Rock was on the phone. As soon as he got off, he helped Dex to his feet.

"That was Walter Reed. They're expecting you," Rock

said as he set his broad shoulder under his brother's armpit and half carried him out of the house.

Dex rose, catching the lingering scent of Piper as he exited the room. He didn't know why, but he was suddenly angry with her. Maybe it was because anger was safe and it shut down everything else he was feeling. And when he was around Piper Jones, he needed to be shut down.

Maybe, he thought grimly, that was how he would survive losing her.

His diagnosis was exhaustion, mental fatigue and incomplete rest and healing of his wound. He slept for eighteen hours straight, then found out he was stuck at Walter Reed for a week. He would then be discharged and he would fly back to Coronado and stay with Rock until he was fully well and was cleared by the doctors there. Rock was in and out and his parents came to visit him.

On the third day, there was a light knock on his door and he looked up into the soft eyes of Piper.

"Is this a good time?" Her voice was so soft, so unsteady, he could barely hear her. "I can come back," she said, taking another uneven breath when he didn't answer.

"No," he blurted out. "Now is fine."

As if bracing herself, her voice stronger, she said, "I wanted to thank you." Her voice caught. "I was pretty much wrung out when we last talked…and you left before…before…" She paused, and Dex knew she'd been crying. He felt torn up inside. "I wanted to tell you how sorry I am that you got dragged into my mess."

Her voice was doing painful damage to his heart. Clenching and unclenching his jaw, he reached down deep for an easiness he did not feel. "Hey, Senator," he said gruffly. "All in a SEAL's day."

"It meant something," she said, the same heart-wrenching catch to her voice. "You were always there when I needed you."

She walked to the open closet door where his two uniforms were hanging. Rock had gotten him his military gear to fly home. She stared at them, then reached out and ran her hand over the fabric, clutching it. He looked away.

A funny, uncomfortable sensation coursed through him. He blinked a couple of times and stared at the ceiling, his insides going dead still. Another woman was leaving him. But this one, this woman, mattered the most. His other relationships paled in comparison and it hurt so damn bad.

She approached the bed and he wasn't sure how much longer he could hang on to the pressure in his chest.

"I'm glad I was there for you, Piper. I'm glad that you're safe. No thanks are necessary. I would have done it for anyone. Protect the weak. Defend the innocent."

She smiled then and his heart rolled over. "Goodbye, Dexter," she said, bending down and kissing him on the side of his face. *"Sois prudent, mon amour,"* she whispered, then rushed out of the room.

Feeling as if he'd just taken a blow to the heart, Dex dragged his hand down his unshaven face, his throat cramped up, his eyes smarting.

Ask more of yourself than others. Even when it was hard to bear.

Piper resumed her activities, well aware of the day Dex was leaving, and when the time of his flight came and went, she locked herself in her office and cried like a baby. After that, it got easier. She took the next three weeks hour by hour, but the funny thing was, the ache for Dex never went away. It only got worse. The mornings were the most terrible because she remembered how wonderful it was to wake up in his arms.

That night she curled up into a ball and cried some more. Her nightmares had disappeared and with them her holding on to the memories of Brad. He was gone and she had to let him go. Let him have peace, so that she could find her own, but it eluded her.

She had word about Tyler weekly. He was improving and that was a boon to her heart. Soon he would be home.

As the days passed, she felt more fatigued than normal, falling asleep at her desk when she'd been able to work with no problem in the past. The simplest thing would set her off, but she chalked it up to getting less sleep and missing Dex.

The Mullins scandal and the whole horrible story got released to the press and Piper spent almost as much time dodging the media as she did working.

A month after Dex left, Brad's bill went to the floor and it passed. The last thing she needed to do for him was done. It was only a formality now and the president would sign it into law. That's when she went into his congressional email and saw evidence that Brad had planned to run for president. Something he'd just assumed she would go along with. Without even consulting her. It made her so sad that she had been so complacent. Lost her identity along the way.

With the overwhelming evidence, Mullins went to prison and Piper was free to move on with her life.

The problem was, she had no idea what she wanted to do with it.

She told Brock she was leaving early, and she stopped at a florist, then drove to the cemetery. She parked her car in the lot and started walking. Early September in DC was still steamy and she was hot and sweaty when she reached the grave site.

She stared down at Brad's large stone, brushing off grass, leaves and twigs. Then she knelt down and did the same for the tiny little headstone beside his. She set eleven roses on Brad's grave and one lone rose on Sophie's. Then she sat back on her heels and felt the sun on her face and the wind against her moist skin, giving her a temporary reprieve from the humidity.

She had six weeks left in Brad's term, mostly a formality. After she got home from the graveyard, she put her Georgetown town house on the market and it sold within a week. Since it was a cash offer, she was able to finalize the deal. She donated and sold off all of her furniture and household goods, and as each possession disappeared, she felt lighter and lighter.

In the back of her mind, she thought about the beautiful California house on the ocean. It called to her.

She moved back to the Bethesda mansion with Edward.

The first morning she was home, something sharp and staccato intruded on the heaviness of sleep, pushing back the gray trailers of a dream. Piper sighed and stirred, annoyed that the dream had evaporated. It was lovely and it featured Dex, naked in a pool, trying to coax her into the water.

She got up and looked outside to see that the grounds keepers had started on the hedge trimming. She went downstairs and found Edward at the table watching the morning news.

"Hey, you. Sleep well?"

"Moderately."

"There's eggs and bacon." She went to the pan and dished herself up a helping.

Settling at the table, she said, "Edward, why are you keeping this monstrosity of a house?"

"It's our home, Piper. Do you want to sell it?"

"I don't know. I'm restless and…"

He gave her a sympathetic look. "Unhappy."

She sighed. "Edward."

He set down the paper and sat forward. "What's wrong? You sold your house, your term is ending. Seems like you're letting go and moving on."

"Brad told me to."

"Doesn't make it easy," he said.

"No. I'm just thankful that I wasn't wrong about him, Edward."

He reached out and squeezed her hand. "I saw the video, Piper. You weren't wrong. He was a brave and loyal man. He didn't deserve to die like that." He was silent for a minute. "Piper, do you want to talk about the SEAL?"

"No." Her throat got thick and tears flooded her eyes. She brushed them away.

"It was obvious to me that he was head over heels for you. Had it bad."

"We bonded." That was such a paltry answer to what she and Dex had together.

"No kidding. Look, it's easy for me to tell you what to do. But guys like him don't come along every day."

"It's his profession."

"Really, he's serving his country, Piper."

"I don't think I could take another loss."

"Seems to me, sis, that you *are* experiencing another loss. You're afraid of taking a risk again, and even though he's in a dangerous profession, isn't it better to have him every day than live without him forever?"

That hit her hard.

"Ty's coming home next week. He'll need some care, PT. I'm hiring a nurse to take care of him."

"If she's pretty, he's going to charm the heck out of her."

Edward took a bite of his toast. "Ha, maybe I'll hire a pretty one. Might motivate him."

Piper smiled. Then her stomach protested and she raced for the bathroom. She was sick.

She cried after she threw up, not able to get Edward's words out of her head. She wished she could stop feeling so bad.

Edward was waiting for her when she came out. "Are you okay?"

"I am. Must have been something bad I ate." He turned to leave. "Edward?"

"Yes?" He turned back.

"Would you teach me how to swim?"

He grabbed her behind her neck and pulled her against him. "Of course I'll teach you."

"You're so totally going to dunk me, aren't you?"

He got her in a headlock and laughed. "So totally."

True to his word, Edward taught her, and every day she got better and better until she was streaking across the pool.

"Damn, you're a fast learner. You've excelled at swimming in just three weeks."

They got out of the pool and headed for the house. The doorbell rang as Piper was going to go upstairs. She walked to the door and opened it. "Tyler!" she screamed, and threw her arms around him.

An hour later, he was settled on the couch, his leg

still in a cast and his arm now in a sling. She set a tray on his lap. "Do you need help eating?"

"Naw, I learned to eat with my left." He eyed her. "How are you doing? You look like hell."

"Dex and I were…intimate. We had a fling," she blurted out, and Tyler stared at her, then blushed.

"Did you freaking break his heart?"

She dropped her head into her hands. "Yes, I think I did."

"Well, that's great. He'll be court-martialed and heartbroken." He dug into his meal.

"What did you say? They are not going to court-martial him!"

"Yeah, our CO was livid. Dex's got a meeting with him tomorrow. They'll strip him of his rank, bust him down to seaman and then throw his ass into jail with a dishonorable discharge."

"Over my dead body," she sputtered. She ran for the stairs and pressed her assistant's number. "Get me the next flight out of DC to San Diego." Then she was too busy packing and heading for the airport to think straight and question what it was she was doing. She must be out of her mind.

Was this what it was to feel completely alive? Had she just been marking time or had she been ignorant? She'd pushed away the guilt, Brad was gone and he was never coming back. Had she died a little each day to keep his memory alive? Paying homage to a man who could never be here and present for her ever again? No matter how much grief or agony she'd gone through, *she* hadn't died that day.

She *hadn't* died. *Oh, God.* She'd been living like she had. Until Dex. Until he'd come blazing into her life and showed her what heat was, what need was, what it was like to be a part of something…explosive and substantive.

Her hand went to the locket and with a deliberate move she unclasped it and set it on her dresser, then she pulled off her wedding band. The locket had given her what she needed to get her husband justice and the ring was part of Brad. She was ready to put that vow to rest and pledge herself to another man. What was now hidden in her heart was revealed.

There was no going back.

And she knew in her heart that even when Dex was deployed, he would be with her every day.

Naval Base Coronado,
Coronado, California

Dex slammed the door to his car as he made his way to his meeting with his commanding officer.

He had just spent the last four weeks recuperating and getting back into shape. Doing a lot of swimming, running and lifting. He felt he was ready for active duty.

His heart was still raw over Piper and he thought about her, dreamed about her.

Before he left DC, he went to Arlington Cemetery and visited each grave of the fine men he'd lost.

Then he'd left DC with Rock, who had supported him every step of the way. He went first to Philly to pay his condolences to Peter "Slim Jim" Camden's widow and their newborn son. Then to Cleveland, Ohio, to Jerry "DJ" Sanders's family and his beautiful, heartbroken widow. Then lastly to Albuquerque, New Mexico, where he visited Mike "Spaceman" Carver's widow and his two adult sons and three grandchildren. He broke down. He'd never forget how Mike's widow was the one to comfort him.

He reached into his front breast pocket to take out his ID and stopped dead in his tracks when he felt something soft against his fingers. He frowned and clipped the ID to his uniform. Then he reached in and pulled out a pair of pink baby booties.

His heart stalled and his throat closed up. Piper must have put them in his pocket when she'd visited him in the hospital. He closed his eyes, overcome with his love for Piper. He wished things could have been different.

Tucking the booties back in his pocket, he gouged at his eyes. He would carry them with him always to remind him what he was fighting for.

He reported to the commander's assistant, who told him to go in.

Entering the office, he walked to the desk and stood at attention.

"At ease," Commander Hodges said.

Dex went into parade rest and waited.

"What you did in Afghanistan was above and beyond the call of duty. SECNAV called me personally and sang your praises. Not only did you protect a US senator from harm, but you solved several crimes along with vindicating those six men who died. Thank you for your exemplary service."

"Sir, are you giving me…?"

"Another medal? I'm afraid so."

"Is it necessary?"

"Also, I'm afraid so."

Suddenly there were loud voices outside the door. A woman's voice was raised in argument. Then the door flew open and Piper marched through with the commander's assistant protesting all the way.

"You can't court-martial him! I won't stand for it. I'll get the best lawyer on the planet to defend him." Her eyes were blazing and she was so angry her fists clenched at her sides. She looked delectable, mussed and elegant at the same time, her mascara smudged. She was dressed in a cute navy dress with epaulets. He figured she was subtly showing her support and solidarity with the navy.

"But…" Commander Hodges said.

She talked right over him. "If it wasn't for him, I would be dead. He saved my life so many times. Figured out this whole conspiracy and put some very bad people behind bars. That has to count for something." She leaned on the desk and got right in Commander Hodges's face.

He reared back and his mouth twitched. He looked at Dex, then back at Piper. "It does. We're not court-martialing him. We're giving him another medal."

It was her turn to sputter.

She reached out her hand. "Senator Piper Jones, with my big foot in my big mouth." Dex couldn't hold back the snicker and she gave him a wry look.

Commander Hodges chuckled. "I'll give you some privacy." He stepped out of his office and closed the door.

"What are you doing here, Bulldozer?"

She smiled and stepped closer to him. "Making a fool of myself because Ty told me they were court-martialing you. I had to come."

"Why?"

Her eyes welled. "Because I love you, Lieutenant Dexter Kaczewski. You came into my life to save it. And you did. You made me see that I'm so alive and I have so much to give. I am the woman you need, the woman who will stand by you no matter what. Be a SEAL. Be whatever you want and I will be with you, because I can't be without you."

"What do you want to do with your life besides be with me?"

Her eyes glowed. "It's important to you?" She reached up and held his face, and the look in her eyes almost undid him.

"Hell, yes. I want you to find what you want to do that will fulfill you."

"I don't know what that is right now, but thank you for saying that. It means everything."

"I want to be with you, but Piper, you understand I'm gone two hundred and twenty days out of the year. I've got a dangerous job and I don't want you to just *say* you can be with me, but be with me, stand by me. I'm putting my heart on the line for you. I love you beyond measure."

She wrapped her arms around his neck and pressed her face into his chest, breathing him in. "I'm not scared anymore."

He wrapped his arms around her. "I know. You are so damned brave, babe, so brave." She let go of him and he cupped her face, kissing her mouth so softly. "This... *this* is my unbreakable woman."

She smiled into his eyes. "We're unbreakable together."

Epilogue

The dust kicked up by the six goats traveling the road into the entrance to Safid Darreh blew into the face of the man dressed in traditional desert garb who herded them. He kept them moving as they bleated, catching the attention of several of the villagers. Several small children ran along with them as the man traveled to the end of the street and stopped at the red door of the last house.

He knocked and Afsana Jamal answered the door, her face frowning at the unfamiliar visitor.

"These goats are for you." His voice was deep and he spoke the language like a native, but there was something about this man.

She petted one as it curiously snuffled her skirt. "Oh, my, they are beautiful. But why are you giving me goats?"

The man pulled the *keffiyeh* away from his face and Afsana smiled broadly.

"Dexter."

He returned her smile. "Well, Piper wanted you to have these as a way of saying thank you. They're excellent milk producers. Also, I was instructed to get your recipes for these dishes." He dipped under the tunic into his camo pocket, his hand brushing against the soft yarn of the pink booties for the piece of paper. He handed her a list. He wouldn't dare go back to California after this mission without them. He couldn't believe how lucky he was to have Piper.

He'd been deployed only two weeks after she'd moved to California. This current two-week mission was complete, but he'd taken a short leave to make this delivery to Raffi and Afsana. He would be heading back to Coronado tomorrow. He couldn't wait to see Piper.

"You came all this way to give us goats?"

"Yeah." He winked as she invited him inside. "Seems FedEx doesn't deliver."

She laughed as the door closed behind him.

Ocean Beach, California

Piper was all finished making this beach house she was going to share with Dex as much a part of him as it was of her. She'd moved all his stuff in and replaced all the furniture. She'd loved his Moroccan headboard and a lot of his possessions that he'd picked up during his travels.

She didn't know where he was or when he was coming home, but he was right here with her. She could feel him and she knew he could feel her, the bond traveling across distance and time. She bolstered him every day with her thoughts, knowing that the soft pink talisman he carried protected him.

Her term had expired a month ago and she should

have been feeling elated, but she was having a hard time keeping things down and she'd wake up in the morning all queasy. She hoped she wasn't getting the flu. She'd been feeling run-down for days, and achy.

She was due to start her new job as a fund-raiser for the International Humanity Foundation, an organization that worked to educate and feed children in Africa and Asia. Dex had suggested she try something like this with her background in raising money for Brad's campaign, and it had all just clicked together with very little effort. She was so excited to use her skills to help people.

She picked up the head scarf that she'd had framed and hung it over the bed, Dex's bars still pinned to the cloth. As soon as she stepped away, her stomach twisted and she ran for the bathroom.

She used the toilet, giving a sigh of resignation when she saw the dime-size stain in her panties. No wonder she was feeling so moody. She didn't have anything here and decided she'd have to run to the store. While she was walking to the register, she passed the pregnancy tests and felt wistful for a second, then she went stock-still, a fizzling sensation coursing through her. She counted back in her head, then closed her eyes, the fizzling sensation turning into a cold rush. Tired. Tears.

She couldn't be.

It was impossible. The scarring.

The complications.

She numbly stood in the aisle, suddenly so shaky she wasn't sure her legs were going to hold her.

She grabbed two pregnancy tests, eager to get home, trying not to get her hopes up too high.

As soon as she got in the door, she was back in the

bathroom and it was an excruciating five minutes until the test showed her the double pink lines.

She was pregnant. Suddenly too shaky to stand, she sat down on the edge of the tub, trying to remain rational. She hadn't bothered with birth control because her doctor had told her she couldn't get pregnant.

But by some miracle she was going to have Lieutenant Dexter Kaczewski's baby. Elation washed through her in one fantastic rush, and she started to cry and tremble all over. Sliding to the floor, she drew up her knees and rested her forehead against them, so weak from shock that she felt light-headed. A baby. She couldn't be more thrilled—or more scared.

So many emotions were cartwheeling through her she couldn't tell one from the other.

"Babe," he said softly, and she opened her eyes to find Dex bending over her with an anxious expression on his oh-so-handsome face. A perfect time for him to return from deployment. "I hope these are tears of joy and not oh-crap-I-made-a-mistake tears."

"They are. Tears of joy."

"Good, that's all I need to know." He hauled her up against him, making a choking sound and crushing her roughly against him, holding on to her as if she were his next breath. God, she loved him so much. He'd given her life, a future.

His chest heaved, and he clutched her tighter, his voice raw and shaking. "Ah, God, Piper," he whispered raggedly. "I love you, babe."

"Welcome home, Dex."

Night sounds filtered in through the open windows, and the clock on the bedside table said it was late. Piper shifted her head on Dex's shoulder, then slowly smoothed her hand up the thick wall of his chest. He trapped her wandering hand beneath his, and she smiled, finding it incongruous that someone as big and as male as Dex should be ticklish. He caressed her hand, then raised it to his mouth and kissed her fingertips. "What are you smiling about?"

Rising up on one elbow, she looked down at him, glad that she could see his face in the muted illumination from the streetlights. "I'm smiling because I'm happy, and I'm smiling because I'm so glad to be here with you. And I'm smiling because I'm done with politics." She leaned down and kissed him on the mouth, running her free hand back up his rib cage. "And I'm smiling because you are so darn cute," she whispered against his mouth.

He gave a huff of laughter and caught her hand again, holding it secure against his chest. "Stop it, or I'll throw you in the pool."

Shaking back her hair, she grinned down at him.

"You're on," she said, and then she leaned over and kissed him, settling her mouth on his while he wrapped his arm around her waist, pulling her close—and Piper was in heaven.

She never would have guessed life could get as perfect as it had been since the night she'd first cradled a mourning SEAL in her arms. The missions he went on with his team were full of risks. The SEALs operated on the cutting edge of special ops. She knew that, but she wouldn't have him be anything other than what he was: a soldier, a warrior and hers.

The kiss was sweetly luxurious and led to the inevitable need they had for each other, for the intimacy they created and shared. His body was so hard to the touch, so strong.

She loved being with him, making love with him, being his woman—and she was all his. He slid down more fully beside her, and she intertwined her legs with his, feeling the heat rise between them. Dexter Kaczewski, the most dangerous man she'd ever met, made her feel safer than she'd ever been. She snuggled in as close as she could get, loving the smell of him and the way he felt, like a slab of granite, except warm and vital. His hair was longer now, dark and starting to curl around the back of his neck. She loved the curve of his muscles and the strength in his arms and the stubble along his jaw. After endless minutes of tasting his mouth and holding him close, she broke off the kiss and met his gaze.

"Afsana loved the goats."

"I'm so glad. Thank you for doing that."

"I wouldn't want to be a goat herder, but it was a thoughtful gift, Piper."

"She saved us. There is no price on that. The goats will help her family to prosper." She bit her lip. "Did you see her oldest son?"

"Yeah," Dex said. "If NCIS agent Derrick Gunn isn't that kid's father, I'm no SEAL."

"Exactly."

"I have something for you. It's not a goat…"

"I'm so disappointed. I had 'Nanny' picked out as the name."

He laughed, and it sounded…a little nervous.

"What's going on there, sailor?"

He turned away and rummaged around on the floor, then he came back to her. He extended his hand and in the palm was a velvet ring box.

Her breath caught. "Dex."

He opened it. "Piper Jones, my unbreakable, tough little angel. Will you marry me? I love you and I can't imagine my life without you. I've never been willing to fight for the relationship I wanted, but now I've found a woman that I would die for. So, being a SEAL is my passion, but you are my life."

Tears welled in her eyes and she reached out her hand as Dex pulled the beautiful diamond out. "Yes, you gorgeous man." He slipped the ring on her finger. They kissed and that led to more, until they had made love three times in three hours.

"How do you feel about being a father, Dex?" she asked quietly.

He smoothed back her hair, then met her gaze, his expression interested and open. "I think it's one of the most important things I could ever do in my life. I would tackle it like a SEAL. Why?"

"Well, you might be tackling it, oh, say, around six months from now."

He didn't move a muscle. He stared up at her, and when she smiled, he closed his eyes and hugged her fiercely against him. She felt his chest expand, and he tightened his arms even more. "Are you sure? How is that possible?"

She chuckled. "Dead sure. I've been having three months of morning sickness and the absence of my period."

He didn't say anything; he just held her like that and Piper could feel his heart hammering beneath her hand. She knew he needed time to assimilate the news, to digest it. She gave him a few moments, then she kissed the curve of his neck, and Dex inhaled deeply. Catching her under the chin, he lifted her head and stared into her eyes. "Babe, I can't believe it. How do you feel?"

She smiled, running her thumb over his mouth. "Blessed. So, so blessed."

He closed his eyes and drew her head back down against his shoulder, his fingers tangled in her hair. She felt him swallow, then he pressed a kiss against her forehead. "So do I," he whispered huskily. "God, so do I." His chest expanded again, and he tightened his hold on her. He held her for a long, long time—just holding her, as if he couldn't let go, as if he needed to hold her more than he needed anything.

Finally, he eased away and raised her face, giving her a soft, searching kiss. Releasing a breath in a long sigh, he looked up at her, the expression in his eyes making her heart roll over.

"I love you, Piper," he whispered, his voice uneven.

Piper held his beautiful blue gaze for a moment, her heart so full that it was almost too much to contain, the last knot of uncertainty unfolding in her in a joyous rush. Closing her eyes against the sudden swell of emotion, she hugged him hard, her happiness absolute and complete. Swallowing against the ache in her throat, she cradled his head tightly against her.

"God, but I love you, Dexter. So much."

He hugged her back, his hand buried deep in the tangle of her hair. He didn't say anything for the longest time; then he raised his head and looked at her, his eyes dark with emotion. "We're going to have a blast, babe," he said, his voice uneven. "And you know SEALs never go back on their word."

* * * * *

REQUEST YOUR FREE BOOKS!
2 FREE NOVELS PLUS 2 FREE GIFTS!

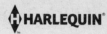

ROMANTIC suspense

Sparked by danger, fueled by passion

YES! Please send me 2 FREE Harlequin® Romantic Suspense novels and my 2 FREE gifts (gifts are worth about $10). After receiving them, if I don't wish to receive any more books, I can return the shipping statement marked "cancel." If I don't cancel, I will receive 4 brand-new novels every month and be billed just $4.74 per book in the U.S. or $5.49 per book in Canada. That's a savings of at least 12% off the cover price! It's quite a bargain! Shipping and handling is just 50¢ per book in the U.S. and 75¢ per book in Canada.* I understand that accepting the 2 free books and gifts places me under no obligation to buy anything. I can always return a shipment and cancel at any time. Even if I never buy another book, the two free books and gifts are mine to keep forever.

240/340 HDN GH3P

Name	(PLEASE PRINT)	
Address		Apt. #
City	State/Prov.	Zip/Postal Code

Signature (if under 18, a parent or guardian must sign)

Mail to the **Reader Service:**
IN U.S.A.: P.O. Box 1867, Buffalo, NY 14240-1867
IN CANADA: P.O. Box 609, Fort Erie, Ontario L2A 5X3

Want to try two free books from another line?
Call 1-800-873-8635 or visit www.ReaderService.com.

---

* Terms and prices subject to change without notice. Prices do not include applicable taxes. Sales tax applicable in N.Y. Canadian residents will be charged applicable taxes. Offer not valid in Quebec. This offer is limited to one order per household. Not valid for current subscribers to Harlequin Romantic Suspense books. All orders subject to credit approval. Credit or debit balances in a customer's account(s) may be offset by any other outstanding balance owed by or to the customer. Please allow 4 to 6 weeks for delivery. Offer available while quantities last.

Your Privacy—The Reader Service is committed to protecting your privacy. Our Privacy Policy is available online at www.ReaderService.com or upon request from the Reader Service.

We make a portion of our mailing list available to reputable third parties that offer products we believe may interest you. If you prefer that we not exchange your name with third parties, or if you wish to clarify or modify your communication preferences, please visit us at www.ReaderService.com/consumerschoice or write to us at Reader Service Preference Service, P.O. Box 9062, Buffalo, NY 14240-9062. Include your complete name and address.

HRS15

Tension wafted from Josie. "It's just like my father described—the tree, the carvings and the creek."

"Did he tell you what the carvings meant?"

She shook her head. "No, I'm not even sure he's the one who made them."

"Then, let's see if we can dig up an old watch," he replied.

They hadn't quite reached the front of the tree when a man stepped out from behind it, a gun in his hand.

Josie released a sharp yelp of surprise and Tanner tightened his grip on the shovel. What in the hell was going on? Did this man have something to do with whatever had happened to Eldridge?

"Josie Colton," he said, his thin lips twisting into a sneer. "I knew if I tailed you long enough you'd lead me to the watch. I've been watching you for days."

"Who are you?" Josie asked.

"That's for me to know and you not to find out," he replied. "Now, about that watch…"

"What watch?" she replied. "I—I don't know what you're talking about." Her voice held a tremor that belied her calm demeanor.

Tanner didn't move a muscle although his brain fired off in a dozen different directions. The man had called her by name, so this obviously had nothing to do with Eldridge.

Why would a man with a gun know about a watch wanted for sentimental reasons? What hadn't Josie told him? Was it possible to disarm the man without anyone getting hurt?

"Don't play dumb with me, girlie." The man raised a hand to sweep a hank of oily dark hair out of his eyes. "Your daddy spent years in prison bragging about how he was going to be buried with that cheap watch and then nobody would ever find the map to all the money from those old bank heists." He took a step toward them. "Now tell me where that watch is. I want that map."

Adrenaline pumped through Tanner. He certainly didn't know anything about old bank robberies, but a sick danger snapped in the air.

A look of deadly menace radiated outward from the gunman's dark, beady eyes. The gun was steady in his hands, and Tanner's chest constricted.

He tightened his grip on the shovel, calculated the distance between himself and the gunman's arm and then he swung. The end of the shovel connected. The gun fell from the man's grasp, but not before he fired off a shot.

The woods exploded with sound—the boom of the gun, a flutter of birds' wings overhead as they flew out of the treetops and Josie's scream of unmistakable pain.

Don't miss
COLTON COWBOY HIDEOUT by New York Times
bestselling author Carla Cassidy,
available July 2016 wherever
Harlequin® Romantic Suspense
books and ebooks are sold.

www.Harlequin.com

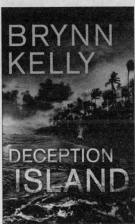

EXCLUSIVE
Limited time offer!

$2.00 OFF

BRYNN KELLY

A stolen boy
A haunted soldier
A cornered con woman...

DECEPTION ISLAND

Available May 31, 2016.
Pick up your copy today!

HQN™

$26.99 U.S./$29.99 CAN.

$2.00 OFF the purchase price of
DECEPTION ISLAND by Brynn Kelly.

Offer valid May 31, 2016, to June 30, 2016. Redeemable at participating retail outlets.
Not redeemable at Barnes & Noble. Limit one coupon per purchase.
Valid in the U.S.A. and Canada only.

52613467

5 65373 00082 3   (8100)0 12139

® and TM are trademarks owned and used by the trademark owner and/or its licensee.

© 2016 Harlequin Enterprises Limited

PHBK0616COUP